I saw his attention wander as he shoved his legs under the table. He leaned over and moved the tablecloth so it didn't drape over his sandaled feet. He jerked back and for a minute I thought he'd been stung by an insect. Color drained out of his face, leaving two dark splotches of red on his cheekbones, where his beard didn't reach.

After a brief hesitation, he shifted his chair and turned so most of his body faced away from the audience. He put his microphone on the floor and leaned over slightly as though to touch his sandal.

"Look under the table," he muttered.

I stumbled over whatever word was in my mouth and opened my eyes wide. I didn't dare say anything because my microphone was still in my hot little hand and I was facing the audience, who stared expectantly at me as I gaped at him.

Lonigan picked up his microphone and fiddled with the index cards in his hand, slipping one out of the stack. "Whoops." He dropped the cards and the mike, the small squares sliding across the rug to my feet. "Sorry," he said loudly to the audience, his voice unamplified but carrying in the quiet room. "Thank goodness that was the last question I had."

As we both leaned over to pick up the cards, he whispered, "Check under the table."

I stretched forward and flicked aside the tablecloth draped down to the floor over the table. For a second I didn't see anything then my eyes adjusted to the darker space.

Patrice Samuels was sprawled under the table, lying on her back. She wore a golden-brown pantsuit and her signature turquoise necklace, this one shaped like a dolphin, was resting on one ample breast.

The chain of the necklace was tangled in the knife stuck in her heart

Review for *Candy, Corpses and Classified Ads*

This is a wonderful story full of quirky characters, a fine mystery, and a great love story between two people who are old enough to know what they want.

~Maura Frankman, The Romance Studio

Review for *If Not For You*

This is a first I have read from JL Wilson and won't be the last. It was interesting to see a woman who is not your average age in heroine but one who has been married and given up on love. For Layla it comes so hard to believe that love is a possibility in her life once again. I so loved Max, for even though he is an older man he still has insecurities about getting old. One big one is the attraction he feels for Layla and the feeling of love for the first time is scaring him. It was hilarious in a way to see what he would do in finding love for the first time especially a woman his age. "Great book" to the author and can't wait for more of her books.

~Melinda, Night Owl Romances

Review for *Your Saving Grace*

Adorable cats, police corruption, and Spongebob Squarepants play roles in the novel of grown-up romance and suspense. Wilson's characters are realistic and likable. She knows that grown-ups can be just as insecure as teenagers and she knows how to plot the twists and turns of a fine mystery. The climax is filled with danger and action, and the loose ends are tied up nicely.

~Lynn Bushey, The Romance Studio

Sun, Surf, And Sandy Strangulation

by

JL Wilson

Sun, Surf, And Sandy Strangulation

Cover Art by *Kim Mendoza*

The Wild Rose Press
PO Box 708
Adams Basin, NY 14410-0706
Visit us at www.thewildrosepress.com

Publishing History
First Crimson Rose Edition, 2008
Print ISBN 1-60154-359-X

Published in the United States of America

Dedication

To the hundreds of volunteers who make writing conferences work. They are the unsung heroes of the trenches and helped this author attain published status. Thanks.

Chapter 1

"It was about time someone bumped her off the best seller lists, although I have to admit, murder is a bit extreme."

My ears pricked up at this intriguing comment. Of course, I was at ClueCon, a mystery conference, so murder would be a topic, but still...

"Wouldn't you know it? I missed that writer's conference last year and Jan Pritchard was murdered. I heard that our keynote speaker was there. She was implicated in the murder."

I sank down lower on the hotel lobby couch and leaned my head back, the better to eavesdrop through a potted plant on the two women sitting behind me and to my left, on a similar couch. If I could have, I would have swiveled to see who was talking, but that would be obvious. The last of the setting sun angled through the windows, casting me in shadow, adding to my stealth-mode.

"B.R. Emerson? She was implicated? How?"

"The police investigated her. She was poisoned or something before they found out she wasn't really involved."

I stiffened in outrage. The woman made it sound

like being poisoned was a trivial event. Believe me, it wasn't. My stomach still hurt when I remembered all the barfing I'd done because of that poisoning.

"I heard she got the guy, too." This was said in a sly, knowing tone of voice.

Disappointment washed through me. No, I didn't get the guy. In the six months since October, when Lucas Remarchik and I had briefly reunited, we'd had a half-dozen weekends together. Now I wasn't sure when—or if—I'd see him again.

"Did they get married?"

"I don't know. I heard that..." The voices drifted away.

No, they didn't, I thought, glaring at the two women who passed me. *No, we haven't lived happily ever after.* I was traveling to promote my latest book and L.J. Remarchik—the aforesaid 'guy'—was coping with retirement from the Abilene Police Department. Since I lived in Minnesota (when I was home) and he lived in Texas, we spent a lot of time talking on the phone and exchanging email. Marriage hadn't even been discussed in the rare times we were together.

"I hate to bother you, but ..." A young man, mid-twenties, stood in front of me holding out my novel. He was chubby and nerdy looking, with glasses, a prominent nose, and long hair unattractively cut.

I recognized the look in his shy but intent eyes. "No problem." I took the proffered pen and signed the inside front cover, smiling and nodding as he explained how much he loved the book and how I had such an intuitive grasp of the problems facing people who were trying to start their lives over. When he left, I slouched lower and examined the tips of my red Keds. Of course I had an intuitive grasp—I was living the story, wasn't I?

Life as a best-selling author wasn't working out the way I thought. I normally wrote mysteries starring a fictional hero, Cal Delvecchio, but my last book had been a romance based on an event that happened when I attended a writing convention in Abilene—the convention that almost ended my life and that introduced me to Lucas J. Remarchik. He was supposed to meet me here in Florida at ClueCon (the one for mystery writers, not the one for telephony developers), but so far he was AWOL.

I was also working on a paranormal political thriller, but I'd had to put that aside when my romance novel hit the best-seller lists and my publisher wanted me to go on tour. I was hoping to return to writing and L.J. as soon as possible.

"Hey, Ralph!"

I jerked upright. Clair Johnson waved to me from across the crowded lobby. Heads turned to see the object of his enthusiasm. Clair and George Delacroix, his writing and life partner, moseyed through the lobby toward me, pausing along the way to chat with people. As always, Clair and George had been at the conference for mere hours but had already made dozens of friends. I envied their schmooze power.

"You're as sartorially elegant as always," George said, flopping next to me on the couch. George is a solid, muscular individual who looks remarkably like an over-sized Danny DeVito. I sagged toward him on the lumpy sofa.

I looked down at my Happy Bunny '*Not Listening*' T-shirt. "I bought new jeans for the occasion." I held up one denim-capried leg.

George rolled his eyes. "Doesn't count, Beatrice Raphaela."

"Hush." I looked around. "You know I don't share my name with everyone."

"Your secret is safe with us, B.R.," Clair said, dropping next to me on the other side. Clair was as tall and skinny as George was short and solid.

"Speaking of initial people, where is the lovely L. J. Remarchik?"

I shrugged with what I hope appeared to be nonchalance. I suspect it really looked like bewilderment. "He's meeting me but I'm not sure when he's showing up." I made a big mistake and looked into Clair's sympathetic basset-brown eyes. "I mean, he called but..."

Clair put an arm around my shoulders and squeezed. "Problems in Love Land?"

I nodded miserably. It had been a few months since I'd seen Clair and George and a lot—and not much—had happened. "I'm not sure what's going on. The last time we planned to get together, Lucas canceled and I've just had emails from him since. That was a month ago."

"Maybe Margaret is keeping him busy," George said.

"Margaret Troolin? My ex-lawyer in Abilene?" I wiped away a tear that threatened to dribble down my face.

George nodded. "He's doing some investigative work for her."

"Really? He never told me about it."

"You've been busy," Clair pointed out. "Traveling, schmoozing, and promoting a book in which he figures prominently as a hunky, sexy star."

My face turned hot with embarrassment. I was still flustered by the attention my book had generated. "How long has he been working for her?"

"Two months. I talked to her a week ago. She and Dan are still going hot and heavy."

I stifled the resentment I felt at the mention of two people in a happy relationship.

George shrewdly read my emotion. "It's easier for them. They live in the same city."

"I suppose." I twisted my light brown braid, a common reaction to nervous stress.

4

"Although I could have sworn that you and Remarchik would overcome any obstacle after what you went through together. The man shot someone to save your life, not to mention braving a blizzard to sweep you off your feet. And —"

"Isn't that Richard Gere over there?" I pointed across the lobby.

My diversionary tactic worked. Clair stood up so fast he almost toppled. "I saw someone who looked like Richard Gere earlier, but I figured I was wrong. Where?"

To my amazement, the man was making a beeline straight for us. Maybe I was still bemused by my transition from Minnesota's still-frosty April weather to Florida's hot climes, but it seemed to me the guy had mischief in his startling gray eyes as he gazed at me.

"Do you know him?" George whispered, watching with me as the drop-dead gorgeous guy cut a swath through the crowded lobby like Charlton Heston parting the Red Sea.

"I don't think so," I whispered in return.

"I think you'd remember if you did," Clair said, smiling and holding out his hand to the tall, dimpled stranger who had stopped in front of me.

"You're B.R. Emerson, aren't you?" he asked, ignoring Clair.

I gaped up at him and nodded like a doll on a string. He was coolly elegant in his leather loafers, faded and so-fitted denims, and white linen shirt open at the collar. His hair, like Richard Gere's, was mainly white with a bit of steel gray thrown in. Up close I could see he wasn't Gere but he was a damn close approximation.

"I want to be your hero." He pulled me to my feet, wrapped his arms around me, and stared down into my eyes. "Your Cal." Then he lowered his face and kissed me.

I was so surprised I barely moved. My first thought was *This guy is meatier than Lucas,* who was lean and wiry in my arms. My second thought was *He's not a very good kisser*, which surprised me since he was so gorgeous. My third thought was *Why the hell is he kissing me?* I struggled feebly in his grip and he immediately released me.

He tugged playfully at my waist-long braid. "My name is John Brody and I want to be the hero in your next book." Something in his eyes told me he wouldn't mind being my hero in the next few hours, too.

"Man, you're taking your life in your hands. Her boyfriend packs a gun." George peered around the lobby. "Where is L.J. when we need him?"

"He doesn't pack a gun anymore. He's retired." I turned my attention to Brody, who was watching us with a bemused expression, dimples flashing at the corners of his mouth. His face was so smoothly shaven it looked waxed and his tan was perfect, right down to the little lines around his light gray eyes.

"L.J.'s a Texan and an ex-cop," Clair said, inching closer to me—and to Brody. "He's still packing heat."

"No, he doesn't. I'm sure of it." I peered up at Brody. "Who are you?"

"Oh, look!" Clair waved. "There he is. We can ask him." He waved again. "Hey, L.J.! Are you packing heat?"

George laughed. "That's why they call it a concealed weapon, dummy."

I turned slowly. Dear God, Clair was right. Lucas was staring at me from near the lobby's registration desk, his brown eyes cold and accusing.

"Trouble?" Brody asked, his breath warm on my ear.

"Oh, shit." I swayed and Brody put an arm

around my shoulder. I jerked as though scalded. Not a bad analogy since it felt like my face was on fire.

"Yep." George nodded. "Trouble. We'll handle L.J. You handle Richard Gere."

"I want to handle Richard Gere," Clair protested as George strode across the crowded lobby. He cast me an imploring look but followed his partner to corner Lucas near the front desk.

"Did I cause problems?" Brody asked, looking from me to my lover.

I jerked my gaze from Lucas' accusing brown eyes and confronted Brody, hands on my hips. "Yeah," I snapped. "Why did you do that?"

He reached into a shirt pocket and withdrew a small set of cards, held together by a brad in one corner. When he fanned the cards out I saw his picture in various poses and stages of dress, from swimsuit to tuxedo. "I'm a finalist in the Mr. Boddy contest."

"The what?" I automatically took the card set, peering past him at Lucas, listening politely to Clair, who was gesturing wildly. Lucas' eyes kept darting from Clair and George to my unknown male companion.

"The Mr. Boddy contest. It's a chance for one of the male models here to win a cover contract. Didn't your publisher tell you?" He smiled at someone behind me and started to move away. "Your books are part of the contest."

"What contest?" I turned as he joined another man, equally handsome in a rugged Harrison Ford way, who was chatting with a near-swooning group of women.

"Check with your publicist," he said, giving me one last devastating smile. "I'd like to be your Cal. I think we'd make a great team." He gave my arm one final squeeze. "Don't forget to vote for John Brody for Mr. Boddy."

I tried to hand back the set of cards but he was gone, listening attentively to an older woman with upswept ginger hair wearing an elaborate turquoise necklace. He glanced back once at me and smiled then turned his full attention to the woman, whom I belatedly recognized as the head publisher for Red Nail Press, a small publisher that specialized in erotic mysteries.

"So glad I could join you." Lucas' slow Texas drawl didn't fool me. He was pissed.

I turned slowly, my eyes traveling up from his hand-tooled lizard boots, his black denims, the gray sports coat and the black shirt, to finally land on his craggy face topped by his white hair, the usual tangled toss of cropped curls. I tried to see humor or love in his dark brown eyes, but all I saw was polite curiosity. "Damn it, Lucas, I didn't know that guy," I said, gesturing with the card deck I still held.

He pried it out of my fingers and looked through the pictures. "My, my. Such a happy welcome from a total stranger."

"He's in some kind of contest," I protested. "He wants me to vote for him."

Lucas quirked an eyebrow at me. "Hell of a way to campaign."

"It's not like that. It's—"

Clair snatched the cards out of my hand. "It's the Mr. Boddy contest." He sorted through the photographs. "Ooh, these are good. I'm collecting sets from all the models." When George glared at him, Clair shrugged unapologetically. "Just because I'm on a steady diet, it doesn't mean I can't look at the menu. And this is such a tasty menu."

"You look thinner." I longed to touch Lucas' face, but I was aware of the avid glances cast our way from curious onlookers.

The harsh lines around his eyes relaxed. "I've missed you, Bea," he murmured. "You look good. It's been too long since I saw you."

"Now that we've ascertained that everybody is pining for everybody else, can we talk about Mr. Super Model and why he was kissing you?" Clair asked.

"I'll explain later," George said, taking his arm. "Let's give them some privacy."

"It's the middle of a hotel lobby," Clair pointed out. "Privacy is in short supply."

"Then we shouldn't intrude on the little they have." George pulled him to the side.

I barely noticed. "I already checked in to the hotel," I said anxiously. "Earlier today."

He smiled and my heart lurched. His eyes always warmed when he smiled that way, his mustache just twitching at the corners and his dimples barely visible. It made me tingle all the way to my toes. "I figured that. I'm sorry I didn't tell you my plans, but I've been busy. I'm not even sure I can stay for the whole weekend."

"Oh. I hoped we could—"

He put a hand on my arm and maneuvered me to the far corner of the lobby. I heard someone whisper, "*That's him, I'm sure of it. I saw his picture in the newspaper. It's a real life romance. He saved her life and ...*"

Lucas and I exchanged wry looks. "Real life romance?" He shook his head, shaggy curls catching light from the chandelier. "I never expected to be a famous romance hero."

I had no answer to that. He had acquired a certain notoriety because of my book. The hero was so obviously patterned after him and given the circumstances of our meeting and falling in love...well, it did have "Romantic Book of the Year" written all over it.

"Why didn't you tell me you were working again?" I asked as we moved to stand next to an expanse of windows.

"You've been busy."

"Not that busy. Why didn't you tell me?"

He looked at his watch. "I planned to talk to you about it the next time we got together. Then our visit got canceled and...I'm working this weekend. I need to meet someone."

"Working? Doing what?"

"I can't discuss that. I just wanted to check in with you and see if—" He stopped so abruptly I leaned forward, certain I'd missed what he'd said.

"See if what?"

"See if I'd be welcome."

"What?" I was suddenly faint, as though doused in hot then cold water. "Lucas, what's wrong? What's going on?"

He stared down at me, his dark eyes searching my face. "We need to talk, Bea." He glanced again at his watch. "I have to go now. Let's talk later tonight."

"But the conference starts tomorrow. I'm going to be busy. I'm on some panels and I have to give the speech at the opening lunch. I thought we'd have time together before it started."

"I'll try to get back early." He edged away from me, moving toward the front portico.

"Wait—are you staying here? Did you check in?"

Lucas nodded. "I left my bag at the desk." He smiled hesitantly. "I'm staying with you, if that's okay." I wanted to shout *Of course it is!* Instead I just nodded dumbly. He leaned toward me and I met him halfway for a brief kiss. "I'll call if I'll be late." Then he was gone, moving quickly to the front door. I watched as John Brody intercepted him. The two men talked and Lucas stepped back from Brody, hands clenched and his face set. He glanced at me than at Brody and said something that made the Richard Gere lookalike put up a hand defensively.

"Are they going to come to blows?" Clair asked, materializing at my side.

I watched Lucas draw away from Brody, almost running over two women who were approaching the model with card sets in their hands. The last I saw of Lucas was a glimpse of his angry face as he hurried down the front steps to a waiting car. "I don't know what's happening!" I rounded on Clair.

He held up his hands, two fingers crossed in a vampire-prohibiting 't'. "Don't take it out on me, girlfriend. We'll hash it all out over drinks. I'm the master of all things romantic. Trust me. We'll solve whatever little problem you and the hunky hero have."

"Come on." George appeared at my side. "Let's go to that restaurant." He waved a pamphlet at me. "The Hog's Breath Saloon. It sounds perfect for booze, some love talk, and maybe a bit of mayhem. We've recruited some friends to join us."

"I didn't think you knew anyone at this conference," I said as they bundled me out of the building. I saw the car with Lucas in it vanishing into traffic. "Correct me if I'm wrong, but I thought you were only considering changing from romance writing to this genre. How could you know anyone at a mystery conference?"

"That was four hours ago." We joined a milling herd of people in the porte cochere, many of whom turned and called out greetings. George watched with proprietary amusement as Clair was absorbed into the crowd. "You know how he is—there isn't a stranger in the world. As to our knowing folks— you'd be surprised how many people are familiar with Claire George, the writing team. We're somewhat well known in literary circles. Even mysterious literary circles."

A taxi pulled up and George and I dove in along with three other people who introduced themselves

11

around laughs as 'Tom', 'Janet', and another name I didn't catch. I was happy for the chance to huddle back in the seat and let the conversation wash over me as Florida's Emerald Coast sped past our cab windows. Lucas' odd behavior had combined with the mystery man, John Brody, to leave me dazed. Why had Lucas acted that way? Granted, he and I were still figuring out our relationship, but why had he asked if I wanted to see him? Why had he looked so hesitant? Didn't he know how I felt? Didn't he know how much I love him?

I followed the group out of the taxi, my mind awhirl. He was the most important person in my life, but somehow there was never the right time to tell him so. As I entered the crowded bar I tried to push the niggling thoughts into the back of my consciousness. He and I would talk tonight and get it all straightened out. I plopped down in a faux bamboo chair and grabbed a laminated menu from the table holder. We'd get it all figured out.

"Oh, hey. I meant to give this to you." George pulled an envelope out of his back shorts pocket and slid it across the table to me. "The desk clerk gave it to me to give to you."

I looked at the envelope with the Pittman Publishing logo in one corner. I recognized the handwriting on the front as that of Karen Levy, my editor at Pittman. I ordered a mojito from the bikini-clad waitress who bounced over to take our orders then scanned the note between introductions to the late arrivals that quickly filled the long table.

Bea: There's a model contest at this conference and since we're looking for a Cal for your covers, I hope you'll help the conference organizers and do a few publicity photos.

I asked Dana Cartwright, a publicist for Pittman, to give you this note. Dana will be in touch about what you need to do. Thanks! Karen L

I folded the note and stuffed it in my already bulging Sak handbag on the floor at my feet. Presumably this Dana person would be able to tell me why a Richard Gere clone was accosting me in the hotel lobby. I hoped I didn't have to do anything dorky like judge a swimsuit contest or pose with a bunch of hunky guys. My glass paused as I raised it to my lips. Hey, maybe that wouldn't be so bad after all. I examined the menu and had just placed an order for ribs when my mobile phone in my capri pocket thumped then chimed *Try To Love Again*, part of the Eagles ring tone package I had downloaded. It competed with the Hog's Breath band, which had just started to play a raucous set.

I pulled out the phone and turned aside from the noisy voices around me, plugging my free ear with a finger. "Hello?"

"Bea, it's Lucas."

"Lucas? Where are you?" I could barely hear him between static and the noise of two people arguing at the bar behind me. I turned to look at the verbal sparring partners. Patrice Samuels, The Red Nail publisher, and another younger woman were almost nose-to-nose and if looks could kill, they'd both be in the ICU in a few hours. Each woman was tall, big-boned, and somewhat overweight. I noticed the other people at the bar were giving them a wide berth, as though uncertain about the fallout zone. I heard the younger woman yell, "My lawyer will be on this so fast your head will spin, you bitch. You can't..." Then I tuned out the words.

"I'm sorry I had to run out like that," Lucas said, his voice tinny and crackly. "I may have to leave town tonight and I'm not sure when I can get back."

I bent over almost double, trying to find a quiet spot in the decibel-laden environment. "You just got here!"

"I know. It won't be for long, though. I should be

able to get back by Friday."

"Friday? But—" I was leaving town on Sunday. That would mean we'd only have two days together instead of the four I'd planned on when I came to the conference a day early.

"Ask him if he's going to punch Brody," George asked from his spot next to me.

Lucas must have heard him. "I almost did hit that son of a bitch."

"Why? Honestly, it was just a little kiss, it didn't mean—"

"It wasn't that. It was what Brody said when he apologized to me."

I wasn't sure whether to be offended that Lucas didn't care a handsome stranger had been kissing me or gratified he'd been willing to deck the guy anyway. I decided to be gratified. "What did he say?"

"That a middle-aged overweight writer wasn't his type."

I almost dropped the phone. "I'm not middle-aged," I sputtered. "Well, I mean, sort of, but they say that fifty is the new thirty so I guess I'm really thirty-three."

Lucas laughed. "Any younger and you'd be jail bait to me. I have to go now. I'll call if I can't get there tonight. I was looking forward to being with you, too. I'm sorry."

Until that moment I hadn't realized how much I was looking forward to seeing him, holding him and yes, making love with him. I swallowed bitter disappointment. "Just try to join me as soon as you can, okay? We need to make up for lost time."

"Nice line," George said.

Lucas laughed again. "Nothing like having a critique partner there to give you advice."

I grinned, cheered by his light tone. "You know the Boys—often imitated but never duplicated. Hurry back, Lucas. I've missed you."

He said something I didn't catch then the phone went dead in my hand. I folded it and leaned over to tuck it away in my bag, surprising a look of such brooding malevolence from Patrice Samuels that I drew back. The author had left her and the Red Nail publisher was sitting behind me at the bar, an umbrella-decorated drink on the counter in front of her.

I smiled tentatively. The woman took that as an invitation to lean over and extend one hand, the red-lacquered nails looking bloody in the dim light of the bar.

"Patrice Samuels," she said, her turquoise necklace swinging dangerously near my face. A chunky pendant shaped like a cat with arched back dangled hypnotically near me, its rhinestone collar glinting in the light as the pendant swiveled on the neck chain.

I took the hand and gave it a brisk shake. "B.R. Emerson."

"I thought I recognized you." She straightened up, removing the turquoise menace from my immediate vicinity. "You were in all the papers last year when Jan Pritchard got murdered. You can't buy publicity like that."

I considered and discarded some comebacks, finally settling on, "I'm sure Jan would appreciate giving my career a boost."

Samuels boomed out a laugh that made others nearby stop and stare. "I doubt that, but it's a nice thought. Are you still with Pittman?"

I nodded, moving aside so the waiter could set down a steaming plate of barbequed ribs. "My next mystery is coming out in the fall."

She looked beyond me to the others seated at the table and her eyes widened. I glanced to my tablemates and saw two women shooting Samuels dagger-filled looks. It seemed like a lot of hostility was flying around the Hog's Breath.

"Pass the salt?" the man next to me asked.

I turned my attention to dining and when Samuels murmured a polite, 'Nice to meet you,' I just nodded, my mouth full of yummy food. I discovered that my dining companions were also mystery writers. We had a great time plotting how to murder people in the restaurant with deadly implements ranging from poisoned fish, conch shells, and band instruments. The booze flowed freely and I got a few good plot ideas. About an hour after we got there, John Brody came in surrounded by four other amazingly handsome men, all shepherded by three people who had 'conference management' stamped all over them. The entourage mixed and mingled in the crowded room, competing with the dancers on the miniscule wooden floor for attention.

Brody saw me and waved. I waved back then turned immediately to Clair, not anxious to garner more attention than I already had. "Aw, come on," Clair wheedled. "Lure him over here so we can ogle him and his competitors."

I peeked over my shoulder and saw to my relief that Brody had been diverted by another group of writers at a different table. "So how does this contest work?"

"I'm not sure, but I'm certain it'll be interesting." Clair surged to his feet to join a group of people heading for the dartboards, almost knocking over the waiter who was setting a mojito refill down next to my plate.

For a brief minute I had the table to myself, then a new group of people, led by George, joined me and I was tossed into the social whirl again. I was grateful for the distraction and for the alcohol, which would guarantee me a good night's sleep. Another drink later and I headed toward the ladies' room, weaving my way through dancers, dart throwers, and a jammed crowd that spilled onto the porch and the nearby beach.

I peered blearily at myself in the mirror over the sink. I had once been compared to Jane Seymour, but I think I had a few pounds, and years, on Jane. I certainly looked that way tonight. I queued up for my turn in a stall and had just settled down for a good pee when someone turned the lights out. The funny thing was, nobody else seemed to notice.

I called out, "Hey, who turned out the lights?" but the sound never got beyond my stall.

I leaned against the cool metal wall and passed out.

Chapter 2

Voices murmured around me. "Not too much farther now," someone said.

"Is she all right? I hope you'll let us know if we can help, we pride ourselves on our customer service here. Anything we can do…"

I had the sensation of movement, a drifting feeling that made me yawn lazily. I tried to stretch but hands held me firmly. When I wiggled it was like fighting warm molasses. Complete lassitude gripped me.

"No, no. You can't sleep yet," the voice said.

"Soon?" I mumbled.

"Yep. Soon."

I opened my eyes and saw a rectangle of gray light. I squinted, trying to focus. The rectangle stayed a rectangle, though, and didn't materialize into anything definite until I turned my head and saw it in context.

I was in a hotel room. I propped myself up on my elbows, belatedly realizing I was lying on a bed. I peered groggily down at myself and discovered I was fully clothed in my Happy Bunny T-shirt and denim capris. Only my sneakers were missing.

I took a deep breath and sat up, swinging my legs over the side of the bed. A brief pounding in my temples subsided as I groped for the bedside lamp. I managed to turn it on and stood up, tripping over my discarded shoes on the floor.

I looked around me, swaying unsteadily. It was my hotel suite. My bottle of bourbon was sitting on the table in the corner, the small bag of cracker-snacker I'd brought from home next to it. My brown crocheted Sak handbag was sitting on the credenza next to the TV. I stumbled past the bathroom and into the 'office' portion of the two-room setup. My laptop was on the desk and a draft of my latest manuscript was sitting next to it in the brown notebook I always used. There was the microwave, miniature refrigerator, and small sink. Yep. It was my room. I tugged on my braid, resulting in another brief flare of pain. The clock on the microwave said 5:45. It had to be morning, right? Didn't we go to the restaurant last night? Didn't we go there for dinner?

I tottered to the bathroom, located between the bedroom and the office, where I washed my face, brushed my teeth, and undid my braid, sighing with relief as I brushed out hair that had been too long confined. I wandered back into the bedroom, spying a piece of notepaper at the foot of the bed.

We'll call you for breakfast. Sleep well. George.

What had happened? I sagged onto the bed and stared at myself in the mirror over the credenza. I looked surprisingly rested and refreshed for a person who'd had a brief spurt of amnesia and had no recollection of the last twelve hours. I had only fuzzy memories after sitting in the bathroom at the restaurant—had I really passed out? Good Lord, I'd only had two or three drinks. I was accustomed to a lot more alcohol consumption than that.

Where was Lucas? He said he'd call if he couldn't make it. There was no sign that he'd been in the room. I checked both closets. My suitcase occupied the luggage rack and only my jeans, T-shirts, and one pantsuit hung there. I'd seen no signs of a man's supplies in the bathroom. Where was Lucas? Did he call?

I grabbed my Sak and pawed through it, looking for my phone. Then I remembered and checked my jeans pocket. The phone was there but the battery was low. I plugged it into the charger then changed clothes, stripping out of Happy Bunny and pulling on shorts and my *'Wrinkled was not one of the things I wanted to be when I grew up'* T-shirt. I checked my phone but there were no voice messages—where was Lucas?

I twitched open the curtain. Dawn was breaking over the Gulf to my left and to my right I could see Choctawhatchee Bay, a name that I'd memorized because it rolled so amazingly off the tongue. Fluffy clouds in the distance complemented the white sand beach, giving the impression of a Blue Willow dinnerware world: blue sky, white clouds, blue ocean, white beach. Everything looked warm, tropical, and alluring, a far cry from the snow I'd just left in damp and chilly springtime Minnesota.

I considered calling George for an explanation but immediately discarded the notion. The Boys were not morning people and wouldn't appreciate an early wake-up. I stared down at the beach, which looked pristine and postcard-perfect in the rising sun. I hadn't had time to familiarize myself with the area since I'd arrived late in the afternoon yesterday. Restless and anxious, I grabbed my card key and some cash then slipped on my sneakers to explore.

The hotel was ghostly quiet. We were in the off-season so ClueCon had most of the 20-story building for its guests, the thousand or so attendees scattered around different floors. The lobby appeared empty as did the restaurant although I could see people behind the glass doors, apparently laying out a buffet. I exited the back of the hotel, skirted the swimming pool and passed by the outdoor bar/restaurant, its awnings lowered against the night.

A woman was approaching me from the left where the pool cabanas waited for morning customers. An ugly khaki canvas hat held down a thatch of curly black hair and her clothing, a loose moo-moo with a gaudy tropical pattern, fluttered in the morning breeze. She was about half-a-foot taller than my five-foot frame and almost as round as she was tall. Her skin glinted with sweat in the dawn light. As she neared I saw the telltale badge looped around her neck, the bright red "First Timer" button pinned to her nametag.

"You're up early," I said with a smile.

She dabbed at her face with a handkerchief. "My doctor put me on an exercise program and the only time I can do my walking without dying of heat is early morning." She grimaced then abruptly stuck out her hand. "I'm Gwendolyn Bandorf. I recognize you from your picture, you're B.R. Emerson, aren't you?"

I reluctantly took the sweaty appendage and gave it a shake. "Yes, I am." I thought of my own First Timer button, sitting on my dresser upstairs. "Are you enjoying the conference? It's my first time at ClueCon, too."

She nodded vigorously, mopping her forehead again. It was hard to determine her age. The rolls of fat around her face successfully hid any wrinkles that time might have given her. She wasn't one of those women of whom people say, 'if she could only lose a few pounds, she'd be beautiful.' No, Gwen Bandorf was unabashedly plain, overweight, and unstylish. Of course, I didn't have room to criticize. I was fifteen pounds overweight, wore a braid because I was a klutz with a curling iron, and confined my style options to jeans and T-shirts.

"I'm looking forward to the workshops. There's so much to learn at conferences like this. Of course, I suppose you find them boring. You've had such success with your books."

I started to take baby steps toward the beckoning beach. "There's always more to learn. It was nice to meet you, Gwendolyn. I'm sure I'll see you around the conference."

Thankfully, she took the hint. "I'm looking forward to getting your autograph on Saturday. See you around." She waddled toward the hotel, moving quickly despite her bulk.

Autograph? I struggled to remember the schedule that had been sent to me by the conference organizers. If I remembered correctly, and I had no hope that I did, I was supposed to autograph books on Saturday before the gala award banquet. I needed to check that. I wanted time to spend with Lucas. Workshops started at nine in the morning, so I'd have plenty of time to check the schedule and map out my day after I had my walk on the beach. I hurried toward the beckoning Gulf, a bright azure expanse in the distance.

An older man stood at the top of the four steps that led down to the beach. He was dressed for business in a lightweight suit, his face deeply tanned and etched by sun and years. His white hair was still thick and full, clipped in a Marine's buzz cut. In fact, he had the look of a retired military man, his bearing erect and his shoulders only slightly stooped. He turned as he heard me approach and smiled.

"Miss Emerson, I'm glad to see you're recovered." He extended a hand. "I'm Saul Richardson, the hotel owner. I helped your friends last night." His dark eyes were polite and curious as he regarded me.

"I don't remember much about what happened," I confessed. "I can't believe I passed out. I only had a couple of drinks. I'm sorry if I caused any trouble for you or the hotel."

He looked past me to the tall building, his expression sober. "You didn't cause me trouble, Miss Emerson." There was a slight emphasis on *you* and I wondered if someone else had caused him trouble recently. "I'm just glad you're feeling better. Going for a walk?"

I nodded. "I'm always an early riser. I thought a stroll on the beach might help jog my memory of what happened." I looked out at the ocean as a fleeting memory ghosted across my brain. "I don't remember ordering more than one drink." But didn't the waiter bring me two or three? I just couldn't remember.

Richardson tensed, his shoulders stretching the suit coat as he straightened. "Really? That is very odd." His flat voice told me he was just being polite to a guest who'd passed out, although he appeared thoughtful, as though this might be a relatively common occurrence.

"I guess I'm not used to mojitos," I said, moving past him to the white iron gate that led to the beach. "I'll be more careful in the future."

"You do that." He opened the gate for me, using a card key withdrawn from his suit's breast pocket. "I would hate to see my guests unhappy. Enjoy your walk."

"Thank you." I walked down to the beach, conscious of him watching me. He'd been so pensive, almost sad—I wondered briefly what kind of troubles he might have then mentally slapped myself on the head. Any hotel owner could have a million and one troubles and I had probably just

JL Wilson

added to his already long list. After all, guests passing out and being hauled unconscious to their rooms was probably not good for business. I resolved to avoid strong drink at this conference unless I poured it for myself.

I took a dozen or so steps onto a pristine white beach and stared at the view ahead of me. I am not a stranger to bodies of water, being a denizen of Minnesota, but the Gulf was impressive, right up there with Lake Superior in my novice estimation. I tested the water with one hand and found it tepid. Of course, I was accustomed to lakes that didn't warm enough for swimming until Memorial Day and where people ice-fished in the winter, so I should have known better. Everything here in Florida was soft, warm, and easy, so unlike the northern climes where the harsh weather kept us on our toes.

I looked to my left and saw a thirty-foot wide expanse of sand flanked by tall grasses and buildings with gates protecting them from touristy riffraff such as myself. To my right was a rockier stretch of beach with a boardwalk that traversed dunes, also covered with waving grasses. In the distance I saw a jogger and a truck, ambling down the strand and pausing at trash cans spotted at random intervals. I took the road less traveled and went left.

The beach was hard packed in spots but soft in others, so I got a good workout. A warm breeze blew the tall grasses, giving a hypnotic swaying effect. I walked for five minutes or so, examining and discarding some seashells while trying to dredge up memories of the previous evening. I'd had two drinks for sure, maybe three. I remembered ordering one and drinking another one set down by the waiter. It seemed to me that there was another drink after that, or maybe I had just sipped that second drink really slowly. That would be out of character for me,

24

though. I wasn't known for stretching out my drinks for an evening, especially when someone else was buying. Granted, I wasn't accustomed to mojitos. Maker's Mark bourbon was my toddy of choice, but surely straight bourbon was comparable in power to some rum, sugar, and mint?

The wind was a bit stronger as I rounded a bend. I fished a scrunchie out of my shorts pocket and bundled my hair into a serviceable ponytail. As I did, I saw a small curious face peeking at me from the tall grasses on my left, the tabby markings on his face reminding me of my own cat, Billy the Kit, undoubtedly snoozing back home in Minnesota with my dog, Buster.

"Hey, there," I said softly.

The cat ducked back into the shelter of the grass but another face, gray this time, peered at me from a foot or so away. I stood very still and soon noticed other shapes moving in the grass like ghosts using cat roads only they could see. I meandered further down the beach and suddenly saw an exodus of cats emerging from the grass to circle around an elderly woman who was spreading plastic bags in a cleared space near a building's back entrance. She looked up as I approached, her tanned face and gray hair belying the sturdy strength of her arms as she muscled an enormous bag of cat food into position.

"Can I help?" I asked, moving near her. The cats skittered away, but a few eyed me warily and stood their ground.

"I've got it, thanks." Proving her words, she upended the bag and distributed the food onto the three plastic bags spread out at intervals in the clearing. She stepped back and cats swarmed out of the meadow, converging like locusts on the food. The woman next to me counted quickly, tallying the day's visitors. "Twenty-three today," she finally said. "Looks like we lost a couple last night."

"Really? How?" I edged closer to the feeding animals, most of whom ignored me. They all looked thin but relatively healthy.

The woman shrugged, her baggy T-shirt sliding around narrow shoulders. "Hit by a car, picked off by a bird, killed by one of the stray dogs, illness, old age. It's a hard life." She hitched up her equally baggy shorts. "Of course, there'll be more to take their place. Poor things are always producing litters."

I thought about it for a long moment, looking up and down the beach at the resorts, apartments, and hotels. There was an abundance of trashcans for the scavenging around here. "There's probably a lot like this, aren't there?" I asked, realization sinking in.

"Oh, yeah. Folks just abandon them, figure the cats will get along fine because it's so warm here." The woman's voice held a faint trace of bitterness, as though she'd had this argument too many times to muster energy now. "Stupid humans."

"No shit," I muttered. I made a mental note to send a healthy monetary donation to the local Humane Society. I wondered how I could get this Good Samaritan's name without being nosy. I glanced at the nearby high-rise building. "Do you live here?"

"Yep. We moved down here from Detroit about ten years ago, bought a condo." Again that shrug of one bony shoulder. "It's okay. Morrie, my husband, he loves it, but me…I sort of miss wintertime, you know?" She looked past me to the hotels lining the beach. "You visiting?"

I nodded. "I'm at the Sandy Shores hotel, down that way." I gestured vaguely back the way I'd come.

"Ah, Saul's place. Nice man. He's been in business since forever. I heard some developers were looking to buy his place. He and his boy don't want to sell, but I know Saul would like to retire."

"I talked to him this morning. He was up early."

"Saul takes business seriously." She smiled at two of the smaller cats who were dashing in and out of the weeds. "I told David, his son, I'd try to capture a couple of them for his kids. There are two who are pretty tame. That black one there and the yellow one."

I followed her gaze to the two kittens, one blond and one as black as night. "Crockett and Tubbs," I muttered.

As though recognizing their names, the kittens paused and regarded us before dashing off into the weeds again. The woman laughed. "Good names. I'll come out here tonight, they're skittish now because of you being here."

A faint shout wafted to us on the air. We both looked past her building down the beach where we saw two people, tiny silhouettes in the distance. Beyond them I saw another indentation of the shoreline, making the people appear as though they were dancing on top of the Gulf waves. From this distance it was hard to see details. They were just two shapes, probably both adults since both appeared to be about the same size.

"We get lots of joggers out this early," the woman said, folding the empty cat food sack into a lumpy one-foot square. "It gets hot later in the day and runners don't like to be out then. I see the same folks, every day, running along the beach. I told Morrie, what's the difference if you got to stay indoors because it's too hot just like we had to stay indoors because it was too cold up north? He says, 'Becca, I'd rather be too hot than too cold any day.'" Again that shrug of fatalistic diffidence. "Men. You can't live with 'em."

I laughed. "No kidding."

The Good Samaritan shuffled back along the sandy path to the back gates under an elaborate

27

'Tiffany Square' sign. "Nice talkin' to you," she said over one shoulder. "Enjoy your stay. Say hi to Saul and David for me if you get the chance."

"Sure will." I doubted I'd get the opportunity, but it seemed the polite thing to say.

"And don't worry about the bums. They're always out sleeping on the beach. They won't hurt you. Just walk by 'em." With these words of wisdom, she disappeared into the gated world from which she'd emerged.

I watched the cats for a minute or two longer, but they ignored me in favor of gobbling every last morsel. They were all well behaved and shared with each other, which surprised me, but perhaps they were united in the common cause of survival. I resumed my beach exploration, sobered by this reminder of man's inhumanity to animals. Who would just toss out an animal, especially one that wasn't neutered and of breeding age? I stomped harder, sloughing through loose sand. Damn it, why were people so irresponsible? Why was it that whenever humans were irresponsible, usually something else suffered, like a baby or an animal or the environment? Why couldn't people just think before they acted and try to be...well, human?

I spied a blanketed figure ahead, lying atop a pile of chaise lounges like the princess on the mattress, unable to sleep because of a pea. The mound of chairs was apparently comfortable because the figure didn't stir as I passed by. The chair legs were looped through with a chain to a post in the ground with a sign affixed, the words "Property of" in black letters at the top. I couldn't read the rest of the faded lettering from this distance. It was hard to determine if the sleeper was male, female, old or young. A patchwork blanket covered the lumpy shape from ear to ankle, with only a thatch of gray hair sticking out at the top like fronds on a carrot.

I took the Good Samaritan's advice and kept walking, hands jammed in my pockets. Like most Americans, I am embarrassed by poverty and this was no exception. I passed another resort's cache of beach gear, this time circled by plastic orange snow fence and covered by a rust-colored towel or tarp, held down loosely by thin white rope. The chains on this pile wound through the fence like a many-segmented caterpillar to emerge at the lock, which drooped near the ground under the towel. I continued my walk, deep in thought, and passed another pile of beach chairs, also locked with chains. This stretch of beach appeared to be the province of resorts, which apparently stored their beach equipment on the strand.

I was nearing a turn where the shore dipped inward to the left, making it hard to see what was around the bend. Glancing at my watch, I saw it was almost seven. The Boys would be waking soon and if I wasn't in my room, they'd be worried. I decided to head back.

I heard a cat mewling from the grass in front of me. I rounded the outcropping of sandy dune and saw another expanse of beach with sparse grasses and yet another pile of beach accessories piled high with the ever-present chain and lock looped through the webs of the chairs. There was no cat in sight but another bum was lying on the pile of chairs, a stiff-looking tarp covering the body and a stocking-capped head poking out at the top. I heard the mewling sound again and walked slowly toward the grass, not anxious to go into its maze-like thickness and perhaps emerge with cooties or worse.

I hesitated, not sure what to do. The mewling noise came again and I realized it came from the water. I went to the edge, skirting the sleeping bum, and peered out at the waves. Gulls were bobbing in the ocean, sleek white bodies like frothy accents to the waves. That must have been what I heard. Satisfied with that explanation, I turned to walk back to the hotel.

A gust of wind eddied up from the beach, probably pushed along by the ocean currents. I passed the stocking-capped sleeper, who was snoring loudly, and stayed near the shoreline, dodging waves as they came in. I glanced at the orange open-topped enclosure as I passed and was surprised to see someone there now. Or perhaps the person had been there before and the rusty towel had been removed by the wind. That's how it looked—the towel flung aside and the person lying awkwardly on top of the admittedly hard-looking chairs. Something looked wrong but I couldn't quite put my finger on it.

I approached, dipping and peering at the piled-up mess of chair webbing and aluminum frames, trying to get a good look at the figure sprawled there. Why hadn't I seen the shape just moments earlier? Then I realized—the person was sunk into a pile of chairs, as though the webbing had given way. The sagging had made it look like the person was just another lumpy piece of beach furniture when covered by the towel.

I slowed as I approached, conscious of a sound intruding on the gulls and wave noises. The put-put of an ancient motor was popcorning the air. The truck I'd seen earlier was bouncing down the strand toward me, pausing at the first set of chairs I'd seen and the grouping of trash cans there. I turned back to the figure atop the chairs and realized then what was wrong.

He was on his back, arms outflung. The towel had shifted away from his face and upper torso but it still covered most of his body. I could tell by the outline under the cloth that his lower body was splayed in one direction and his head pointed the opposite way. It was an awkward position at best and probably painful at worst.

I inched closer. Something was not right. Nobody would actually choose to sleep in such an uncomfortable position. I was about eight feet away when a sharp report, like gunfire, sounded behind me. I jumped so high I stumbled as I came down, slipping then landing with a thud on the hard pack of the beach, my hand coming down on a sharp shell.

"Ow. Son of a bitch." I grabbed the unoffending shell with the muddled idea that I should have it in case I got an infection. Vague visions of a puffed-up hand and gangrene flitted through my brain. I scrambled to my feet, scraping my knees in the process and whirled around, looking for the source of the noise.

The black pickup truck was trundling toward me on the shale, sunlight reflecting off the windows and giving it a blind-eyed cartoonish look. It stopped about thirty feet away and a man leapt out, striding across the sand to a cluster of cans near the grass at the inland side of the beach. The truck rumbled and belched as it waited, probably the source of the noise I'd heard.

I turned back to my original mystery, the man on the pile of chairs. A little voice in my head was clamoring for me to get the hell out of there, and fast. It all felt wrong and I didn't really want to be in the vicinity. But it was too late. The maintenance worker blithely slinging trash into the back of the truck had already spotted me. If I bolted and something was wrong, it would definitely look suspicious.

I took a hesitant step toward the reclining man, the shell still clutched in my hand. I looked at the shell then did a double take—I was bleeding from a short but jagged cut on my palm. Damn. The stupid shell had indeed inflicted a wound and I probably would get some kind of obscure blood poisoning from whatever creature used to inhabit the carapace. I spied what looked like a roll of paper towels on the ground near the enclosure and snatched it up, unrolling several layers before getting to some that appeared dry and clean. I tore off strips and made a makeshift bandage, tucking the ends in to make a bulky mitt then picked up my shell again in my now bandaged hand.

I sank into the soft sand around the snow fence and used my good hand to steady myself, grabbing one of the enclosure's poles to drag me up the last foot or so of the small slope. "Hey, mister," I called out softly. "Hey, are you okay?"

There was no answer. To my left the truck started up with a belch, slinging sand as it rattled down the beach. The man in front of me didn't stir, didn't wake up, didn't show any sign of…life. In fact, he appeared abnormally tight, as though his arms and legs were locked in position. Holy shit. Was he really…?

I edged closer. The reclining figure was about four feet away and three feet above me on top of the pile of chairs. He wore light blue denims, leather loafers and what had once been a white shirt, now stained with something dark. I walked slowly around the enclosure as the truck meandered toward me, stopping just a few feet away at the oil barrels that overflowed with picnic leavings and charred hunks of wood.

I took a step closer to the man. I recognized him. His gray/white hair was thick and he'd once had dimples that flashed when he smiled. He was—had been—one of the handsomest men I'd ever seen in my life.

John Brody.

"Holy cow," someone shouted. "What's going on?"

I turned, overbalanced, and grabbed the snow fence to steady myself. My bloody hand tangled in the mesh and I almost tugged the whole thing down.

"He's dead," I said breathlessly. "Call the police."

"Dead? How do you know?" A wizened little man pushed past me and peered up at the body. "What happened?"

I shook my head. "He's dead, trust me. I recognize the symptoms." I stumbled away and sat down on the beach.

It looked like I could add another murder to my resume. At this rate, I'd never be asked to speak at another writing conference again.

"Oh, shit," I muttered. I flopped back down on the sand and waited for the police.

Chapter 3

"Not another murder? Good God, are you Typhoid Mary or something?"

"Keep your voice down, Clair," I muttered. "Geez, it wasn't my fault. Besides, I'm not even sure it was murder." I looked around but no one was paying attention to us—yet.

As soon as the truck driver called 911, the beach became a hub of activity. I'd given a brief statement to the uniformed officer who arrived first, then was 'escorted' back to the hotel's beach area where I now sat on a chaise lounge, waiting to be 'interviewed' again by the detectives who'd been called in on the case. In the distance I could see the flurry of activity around what had once been John Brody.

Clair's perpetually mournful face saddened even more. "Not murder? An apparently healthy man is found lying dead on the beach. Looks suspicious to me. Yep. Typhoid Mary. Or should we call you Typhoid Ralph?" He held out my cell phone. "There you go. Good thing you gave us a copy of your room card. I told you, it pays to be careful when you travel. Always give a fellow traveler a copy."

"Yes, mother," I muttered, checking the charge

on the phone.

"Speaking of which, I'm surprised your mother hasn't called yet," Clair continued, watching more police personnel swarm around the area down the beach. "How is Mavis? Still praying you and L.J. will get married?"

I winced. He'd hit uncomfortably close to the truth. "Mavis is doing fine. And no, she's not praying I get married. She just wants me to be happy." That sounded pompous, even to me.

Clair sipped from the paper cup he'd brought. "I'll bet. She's probably attending daily masses and bruising her knees praying to get you wed."

"You have to admit, Bea, murder seems to follow you wherever you go," George said from his spot next to Clair on a chaise lounge near me. His pale blue eyes took in everything around us, including the uniformed officer who stood inconspicuously nearby, listening to every word. "Cherry danish?" George held out half of the pastry to me.

I shook my head. "Where'd you get that?"

"They were setting up the breakfast buffet when we came by. I talked them into the coffee and danish."

I sipped my paper cup of coffee gratefully. "You've got your priorities straight, George."

"Enough social chitchat. What the hell happened? Why did you pass out last night? Did you really drink that much?" Clair peered past me to the activity around the body then glanced at the young officer behind us, smiling politely.

I could feel the cop's eavesdropping presence but I gave a mental shrug. I had nothing to hide. Let the cops take all the notes they wanted. "I only had a couple of drinks. What happened? I don't remember a thing after going to the bathroom. How did you guys know I needed help?"

"We wouldn't leave you high and dry," George

said practically. "We were keeping an eye on you. When you didn't come back, we deputized a waitress and made her go in after you." He shuddered dramatically. "No way was I entering that bastion of femininity."

Clair took up the tale. "She found you passed out in a stall and came to get us." He laughed. "We tucked you back in and bundled you out the back door. It wouldn't do to have a famous author caught with her pants down—literally."

"Although I think finding a body on the beach tops being drunk in a bar," George said, his gaze on the ambulance that moved slowly through what appeared to be a public access gateway to the orange snow-fenced area. From this distance it looked like miniature toys being maneuvered into position.

"Bea? Are you okay?"

I twisted on the chair, upsetting my coffee cup at the sound of that sweet Texas drawl. "Lucas?" I was up in a flash, pressing my face against his chest. His arms enclosed me and his smoky sage aroma made me feel immediately safe, protected, and loved. I nestled against him, willing to relinquish responsibility for the moment.

"What's going on?" He bent over slightly to give me a quick kiss. "I was at the airport and saw a news story on TV about an accident at this hotel, that someone was found on the beach. I turned around and came back." He held me tighter. "Good thing I did, too. I get the feeling the local police want to talk to me."

"Airport?" I peered up at him. "Why were you at the airport?"

"Did you really get in a fight with Brody?" George asked.

I dropped out of Lucas' arms in shock. "What? A fight?"

"Just tell the world," Clair muttered, glaring at

the police officer nearby.

George shrugged. "If the hotel staff knows, the world knows." He sipped his coffee and regarded Lucas with shrewd blue eyes. "So? Did you?"

Lucas nodded, releasing me but keeping an arm across my shoulders. I leaned against his long, solid torso. "I came back to the hotel last night and he was in the lobby. We talked."

"Talked?" I sagged with relief. "Well, if all you did was talk—"

"It was a bit more than that." Lucas' voice was quiet and perhaps only I heard the anger in it. "He said some things that—" His gaze swung to the cop. "We'll talk about it later."

"Damn it, Lucas, you keep saying that!" I pulled away to confront him, my fists clenched on my hips. Then the pain in my hand reminded me that I'd sustained a shell wound during my benign walk on the beach. "Ow. Damn."

"Did he hurt you?" Lucas put his hands on my shoulders and stared intently at me.

"That was my question, too," a female voice said behind me.

Lucas released me and I turned to find a tall, slender woman gazing impassively at us, her eyes a startling hazel in the Hispanic brown of her face. She had shoulder-length straight black hair, a wide-hipped figure and tight black pants paired with a snug white blouse that did wonders for her meager bust. I judged her age in the mid-to-late thirties although her businesslike manner and appearance made it hard to judge. I stifled my jealousy at the sight of her long legs. Long-leg-envy is a chronic problem with me because I am vertically challenged.

"I beg your pardon?" I asked. "Who are you?"

She flashed a badge. I reached for it but she pulled it back too soon. George stood up and smiled. "Allow me." He held out a hand. The woman glared at him but he met her stare with one that was equally implacable. She finally handed him the badge case. He examined it, removed a business card then handed it back. "It would appear that Detective Ramone has some questions, B.R." His glance flicked to Lucas. "For all of us."

"Starting with you first," the woman said to Lucas.

I looked up at him. Lucas just nodded, his face revealing nothing. I knew that look. This was his *'I'm a cop and don't fuck with me'* look. I was reassured to see it in place. "Why?" I asked the woman.

"I think I can guess." He smiled briefly at me. "I'll be right back. We can continue our talk later, if I'm not arrested."

I gaped at him as he followed the woman to another set of beach chairs set apart from ours. They were already deep in conversation. "What the hell?" I muttered, sinking back onto the lounge chair I'd previously occupied. "Arrested? Why would he be arrested?"

"He did have a fight with a man who was just found dead," Clair pointed out.

"Lucas is a cop," I sputtered.

"Ex-cop," George said, polishing off the Danish pastry. "Professional courtesy only goes so far. Besides, everybody knows what a powerful motive jealousy can be."

"Jealousy? Of what?"

"Brody planted a big kiss on you in front of everybody." Clair lounged back on the chair, head tilted to one side. I recognized the ploy, but he was too far away to eavesdrop effectively on Lucas and Ramone.

"It was just a kiss," I protested. "Besides, I didn't even know the guy."

"Those little facts may not be of great

importance to the local fuzz. She must have a partner around here somewhere." Clair looked at the other people on the beach. "Him, maybe," he said with a nod to a group of people approaching us.

I followed his gaze and saw a stocky man talking to the truck driver, who was walking toward us. "Maybe. Who do you think is in charge? Her or him?"

"The raven-haired dominatrix," George said. "Look—she's even got L.J. toeing the line."

He was right. Lucas regarded the authoritative woman with wary respect, his eyes never leaving her face. L.J. nodded once then looked at me. From this distance it was hard to read his expression. The woman said something and he nodded again.

"How did Brody die?" George asked.

"How would I know?" I snapped, intent on trying to lip read the conversation between Lucas and the detective.

"You found the body," he said patiently. "Gunshot? Knife? Come on, Bea. Think like a mystery writer. You've researched more ways to kill people than fleas on a stray."

"Oh. That reminds me. Becca. Maybe she saw something." I reached for my handbag and my ever-present Palm Pilot, only to realize I didn't have the bag with me. "Make a note. Check with Becca. Maybe she saw something on the beach."

Clair sighed dramatically but pulled out a small memo pad from his shirt pocket. "Becca who? Saw what? When?"

I explained about the Good Samaritan, finishing with, "She said that a lot of folks jog there in the morning. Maybe she knows the regulars." I looked up as the stocky man stopped next to my chair, his body blocking the morning sun.

"You should have been a cop," the man said. "That's a good idea about the regulars."

"Nah. Being a cop is hard work. I'd rather be a

writer. Who are you?" I already knew, but I wanted confirmation. He was the 'good cop' part of the 'good cop/bad cop' pair.

"Detective Pete Martinelli." He handed me his badge case, which I examined then passed to the Boys for further scrutiny. Martinelli was probably near my age, in his fifties with thinning dark hair traced with gray, a solid build and a crooked smile and nose that gave him a boyish look. I wasn't fooled, though. I saw the way his dark eyes examined us all, assessing and re-assessing our body language, interactions, and words. "I need to talk with you." He smiled politely at Clair and George. "In private."

"Maybe we should call Margaret," Clair commented. "Her lawyer," he said to Martinelli, who'd flashed him a puzzled look.

"That won't be necessary, will it?" Martinelli gestured to the gate leading to the hotel. "Why don't we go in and sit down and chat?"

Said the spider to the fly, I thought. I got up reluctantly while looking at Lucas, who was still deep in conversation with the other detective.

"Miss Emerson? Can we talk over there?"

It wasn't a question. Martinelli touched my arm, nudging me toward the white iron gate I'd passed through just an hour earlier. "Can you explain the circumstances in which you found Mr. Brody?" He pulled out a small wire bound notepad and waited, pencil poised.

I leaned against the gate and crossed my arms. "Circumstances? He was dead." I looked past him, trying to see Lucas but a palm frond hid him and Ramone from view.

"Can you give me a few more details?" Martinelli looked expectantly at me, a smile firmly in place, a smile that didn't reach his eyes.

I knew this routine. I gave him my movements,

step by step. "The other sleeper must have seen something," I finished, shifting my weight to one side in order to peer past him. I caught a glimpse of Lucas, talking to Ramone and a man.

Martinelli examined his notes with what I thought was a bit too much diligence, a stalling tactic if ever I saw one. "Other sleeper?"

"The person sleeping further down the beach from where Brody was. Maybe he was sleeping off a hangover. He was really snoring loudly."

"Are you sure there was someone?" Martinelli was already gesturing to a uniformed officer, who hurried to join us.

"Of course I'm sure." I ticked off the people I'd seen on my uninjured fingers. "There was Becca the Cat Lady. Then I passed someone covered by a blanket. I passed Brody, but of course, I didn't know it was him yet. In fact, I didn't know it was a person. I thought it was just a pile of chairs or something. That towel covered everything." I paused, suddenly remembering how the towel had looked. "It was reddish colored. Was it blood? No, wrong color. Anyway, I thought I heard a cat crying, so I went a bit further on and saw another guy sleeping sort of around the bend. He had on a stocking cap. I remember thinking how hot it must be to wear a stocking cap in Florida. I mean, he must have really been sweating. Unless of course he was an addict. They often get the chills." As though in sympathy, I felt a shiver along my spine. Poor man, to have to sleep on the beach. I thrust the thought away for later study. "Then I turned and started back toward the hotel. That's when I passed the snow-fence thing and saw Brody."

"Check with Ramone about the other people who were outside," Martinelli told the uniformed officer. The man nodded and hurried off. "Snow fence?" Martinelli's pencil paused over his notebook.

"The orange plastic fencing stuff. Snow fence." I shifted position again and this time saw Lucas, Detective Ramone gesturing and him glowering at her. She turned aside as the uniformed officer said something to her.

"We call them dune barriers here," Martinelli said.

"Whatever." I watched as Lucas ran a hand through his hair. I recognized that angry gesture. "Damn," I muttered. "He's a cop. This is crazy."

Martinelli looked over his shoulder. "Cops have been known to get a bit crazy."

"Not Lucas. You don't know him. He'd never do anything like that."

"Like what?" Martinelli tapped his notepad against his left palm. "As I recall, you never answered your friend's question. How did Brody die?"

I threw up my hands in disgust. "I don't know. It wasn't anything bloody, unless the towel absorbed it all, but I think it was the wrong color..." I considered the dark stain I'd seen on Brody's shirt. It hadn't looked like blood, which should have been bright red on the white fabric. It would be rusty-looking, of course, if it had been dried for a long time. I wonder... "When did he die? I suppose given the warmth of the air temperatures here, you have an entirely different way of figuring rigor than we do in Minnesota." I thought furiously, trying to remember what I'd read about rigor in tropical climates. "He appeared to be in full rigor when I saw him, though, so he must have died—"

"What? How do you know what full rigor looks like?"

"Please. I'm a mystery writer. Doesn't rigor usually start within three to four hours after death? But with the warmth, perhaps it started earlier. Or would that delay rigor? I can't remember. Anyway, I thought he looked too—excuse the expression—rigid when I saw him. His arms and legs didn't look natural. I found him around seven in the morning. That means he was probably killed—"

"Okay, okay. You've made your point." He grinned at me. It was meant to be charming but his cold eyes mitigated the effect. "What else did you notice? Anyone else?"

"I've told you everything I remember."

He appeared to take this under advisement. Then he smiled suddenly, a real smile. It was like sun breaking through the clouds—dazzling and almost painful. "How'd you hurt your hand?"

I looked down at my left hand, which had been bandaged by a member of the ambulance crew when they'd first arrived on the scene. "A shell. It's over there." I gestured vaguely toward the beach, using the motion to give me a better view of Lucas. He was striding toward George and Clair, anger evident in every gesture. "It's one of the conch things, I think, all hollow inside but sharp on the outside. Damn shell. With my luck, I'll get cooties or something from it."

Martinelli looked where I pointed. "Looks like your gentleman friend is upset."

"What a quaint expression. Gentleman friend. Yes, he is upset. I can't say I blame him. Why would somebody think Lucas is—"

My phone, stuck into a shorts pocket, chimed *Good Day in Hell*. Were the Eagles prescient? Or was it just a happy coincidence my ring tones matched my mood? "Can I answer this?" I asked Martinelli, pulling the phone out of my pocket.

"I have a few more—"

I glanced at the display. "I need to take this." I didn't give him a chance to nay-say me. I flipped open the phone.

"Good God. You're at a conference and someone

dies again."

I closed my eyes, prayed for satellite interference then said, "Hi, Mom."

"Beatrice, why does this happen to you? We raised you and Angie right. You had a good education. I'll grant you, there were some unconventional moments, like the time you chained yourself to a tree to protect the forest and the whole jail thing because of supporting Nixon's impeachment. But those were tame compared to this. This is the second time you've gone to a conference and people die."

"It's not my —"

"When you met Lucas I was so relieved. He's a policeman. I realize he's retired, but it's just because of his injury. Otherwise he'd still be on the job."

"What does Lucas being retired have to do with this?" I smiled briefly at Martinelli who was starting to look pissed off.

"You and he are involved. I thought that would give you..."

"Immunity?" I supplied when she appeared stalled for a word.

"Exactly. It's like getting a vaccine. You're dating a detective, although at your age 'date' is probably not the most appropriate term. But still, it should be like getting immunized."

"My immunization apparently didn't take," I said, watching as the vaccine portion of our conversation talked to Claire and George.

"I'd appreciate it if I could have your undivided attention," Martinelli said, stepping closer. He wasn't smiling. Now his expression matched his cold eyes.

"Who is that? You let me talk to him, I'll give him undivided attention."

"It's one of the detectives on the case."

"Oh."

I could almost see the gears turning in my mother's head. I edged away from Martinelli because I knew what was coming.

"Is he married? What does he—"

"For heaven's sake, Mother, I have more important things to consider right now." I ran my fingers over the phone. "The signal's breaking up, my satellite must be moving out of range." I glanced at Martinelli, who appeared bemused by this ploy. "I'll call as soon as I know if I'm going to be tossed in jail or not."

"What? Beatrice, you had better not—"

"Talk to you later." I turned the phone off and tucked it back in my pocket. "My mother," I said to Martinelli.

"She gets the news fast," he commented as Lucas strode into sight, trailed by Clair, George, and Detective Ramone.

"Knowing her, she had a GPS chip implanted in my neck at birth in order to track my movements. What's going on?" I asked Lucas.

"I'm free to go. For now." He didn't slow his pace but continued walking toward the hotel, where we could see a group of people avidly watching the goings on. I recognized Patrice Samuels from the previous evening as well as a couple of the authors with whom we'd dined.

I hurried to catch up to Lucas. "Wait—what's happening?"

Clair handed me my seashell. "You left this behind."

I considered tossing it then decided I'd kept it this long, I may as well put it on my desk back home as a memento of this trip. "Lucas, what do you mean, 'free to go for now'?" We rounded the perimeter of the swimming pool where the crowd was thickest.

"Just that." He glanced at me and I was surprised by the anger in his brown eyes. "I'm in a bit of trouble, Bea."

Unspoken but heard was *'Because of you'*. He hurried ahead of me, disappearing into the crowd. I stopped dead in my tracks, stunned by the animosity I sensed.

"I'll go with him," George murmured, giving my arm a squeeze.

"It would appear Mr. Remarchik is upset."

I turned at the low, cool voice. Detective Ramone was about a foot behind me. She was smiling, her perfectly lipsticked lips looking like the Cheshire cat. Her eyes were on Lucas and the look I saw in them was not that of a cop eyeing a suspect. The look was that of a woman evaluating a potential available male.

Clair looked from Ramone to me. "Yep," he said glumly. "Trouble in Love Land."

Chapter 4

"L.J?" I hurried to catch up to him, attempting to avoid a crowd of people gathered to watch the show.

"What happened?" Patrice Samuels asked. She easily peered over me. Understandable since she topped me by at least six inches. "Who's that? Another author? She looks familiar."

I glanced back at Detective Ramone. Her predatory smile hadn't faltered, but now it was matched by a disdainful expression when it touched me. If I hadn't been in a hurry, I would have been annoyed. As it was, I filed her look away for later consideration. "I'm not sure what happened. I found John Brody on the beach."

"Brody?"

The name rippled through the crowd, coupled with startled exclamations. I saw L.J. ahead of me, George talking to him and gesturing.

"Brody? The model?" Patrice started to push forward. She's a big woman and I was afraid she was going to push through me so I sidestepped her, almost taking an elbow to the chest. There was a look of fierce determination mixed with either anger or fear on her heavily made-up face. She seemed to quiver with suppressed energy or maybe it was rage. "What's wrong with him? Where is he?"

"Do you mean John Brody?" She paused long enough to glance at me. "He's dead."

She looked as if I'd hit her. "What? Dead?" Her face went totally still, only her pale green eyes darting about like a trapped animal's, seeking escape. "Where?"

"What happened to John Brody?" A woman stepped in front of me. She was at least two hundred pounds heavier than me so I had no choice but to stop or bounce off. Good Lord, another overweight attendee. This woman was Gwendolyn Bandorf's twin except for hair and age. She also had better taste in clothing, dressed stylishly in a lightweight white/navy skirt and top with matching blue pumps.

"I found him on the beach. He was dead." I jerked a thumb over my shoulder. "Ask her. She's the cop in charge."

My words had the effect I desired. Like sharks descending on a bloody morsel, dozens of mystery writers converged on the local constabulary. Clair laughed out loud. "Good work. Come on." He led the way through the crowd, muscling people aside.

"B.R.—hey!"

I paused. The overweight woman was following, panting. I slowed lest I be accused of causing a heart attack. "I'm sorry—have we met?"

"Mary Carr. I'm with Pittman's, too. James Scarlino is my editor. Listen, what happened? Wasn't Brody one of the models who's up for the Pittman contract?"

"You're Mary Carr?" Clair grabbed the woman's hand and gave it a firm shake. "I love your books, you are so good."

"You like cozy mysteries?" the woman asked, head tilted to one side and regarding Clair like a plump bird eyeing a tasty morsel. "You don't strike me as the cozy type."

"Not those books." Then he realized what he'd said. "I'm sorry, I mean, I'm sure they're good, but I meant your Marty Mayeye series." He put a hand over his heart and rolled his eyes. "You are so hot—so hot."

Carr grinned. "It's nice to meet someone who appreciates the art form." Then remembering me, she said, "Was Brody a finalist for your hero?"

"I don't know anything about it. I know there's some kind of contest and Brody is—was—a contestant. That's about all I know." I caught a glimpse of Lucas' silvery head as he disappeared into the hotel. "I'm sorry, I have to go."

"I saw the fight last night between your boyfriend and Brody."

I stopped in my tracks, torn between catching Lucas or catching gossip. Clair saw my indecision. "You go on. I'll get the scoop."

I gave his arm a grateful squeeze and pushed past Ms. Carr, ducking into a hallway that led past the hotel gift shop. Lucas was ahead of me, striding down the faux marble corridor. He limped, which told me that his leg, which had been badly broken last year, was bothering him. His limp was always more noticeable when he was tired or upset.

George was standing by the gift shop, watching Lucas in disbelief. "What's wrong?" I demanded as I hurried past.

He shrugged. "Take my advice. Don't talk to him now. He's too pissed off."

I, of course, ignored him. "Lucas!"

I didn't think he'd heard me until he stopped and turned. I hesitated when I saw the cold expression in his eyes but then I gathered what remained of my courage and approached. "What's going on? What did that detective say that has you

49

so mad?" I skidded to a stop in front of him.

The harsh expression didn't alter, but I did see a flicker of something—anger? sadness? wariness? in his eyes as he reached out a hand to steady me. "I'm supposed to be working, Bea."

"Doing what?" I threw up my hands, almost tossing my shell in the process. "I'm sorry you've been delayed, but I don't understand any of this. What kind of work? Why were you leaving? Why are you so upset? What's going on? What did the police want?"

Lucas shook his head and I saw a smile twitch his mustache. "I swear, you can make me forget to be pissed off faster than anyone I've ever met."

"Good. So talk to me."

His expression sobered again. "I've already screwed up big time. I don't want to compound it."

I stomped my foot. "Damn it, if you don't tell me what's going on, I'll scream. I will."

He held up a hand. "God forbid."

"No shit. This isn't my fault. I just found the guy on the beach." I reached for my braid to tug then realized I had my hair in a ponytail so I twisted that instead.

He pulled me away from the flow of people in the hall toward a nook containing several miniscule tables and metal chairs. The instant we sat down a waiter materialized at our side. Lucas started to wave the man off but I reached for the menu he held. "I haven't eaten."

"Just coffee for me," Lucas said, impatience clear in his voice.

I took the hint. "English muffin and coffee for me." I sat back as the waiter ambled away, scribbling furiously on his notepad. "What has you so upset?"

"You mean besides the fact I'm under suspicion for murder?" He tapped the table with my seashell, which I'd set down next to the sugar packets in their little plastic holder. A few sand grains dribbled out from the hollow interior, but the inside remained mostly packed with wet sand. I decided to soak it in my room sink at the first opportunity. God knew what was in it.

I put my hand over his to still it. "You know as well as I do that's bullshit. Once the evidence comes in, you'll be cleared completely."

He regarded me, his craggy face as impassive as always. It had been almost a year since we'd first met during a murder investigation in Texas and three months since I'd seen him, but I still thought L.J. Remarchik was one of the handsomest men I'd ever known. He wasn't pretty boy handsome like John Brody had been, but rugged handsome like Sam Elliott or Harrison Ford. It still amazed me that he had fallen in love with me. "I was on the beach last night," he said, his voice low. "They'll match my footprints to the ones near the body."

I sat back so fast I almost tipped the chair. "What?"

"Brody and I argued in the lobby then he called me later and asked me to meet him on the beach." Lucas frowned. "So it's not all bullshit."

"But he was alive when you left him?" When Lucas didn't reply, I prompted, "Right?"

"I never found him. I walked down to the area he mentioned but he wasn't there. Yet." He glanced beyond me to the hallway. I could imagine him visualizing the beach scene we'd just left. "He must have showed up after I left."

"When was that?"

"I was supposed to meet him at midnight. I waited twenty minutes but he never arrived."

"You were meeting him out there? At night? I mean, isn't that—" I stopped, for once thinking before I spoke.

"TSTL? Isn't that what you writers call it? Too Stupid To Live?" He nodded. "Yeah, in retrospect, it was. But it seemed to make sense at the time. We had a full moon, there's light from all the buildings, and there were quite a few people out on the beach, partying." His broad shoulders shifted in his charcoal gray suit coat. "It seemed sane enough."

I twisted my ponytail, trying to squeeze intelligence into my over-worked brain. "So you were supposed to meet him at midnight and I found him at around 6:30 a.m." I swallowed the sudden lump of fear I felt. "Where were you all night? Do you have an alibi?" I hated thinking that he might have one (was it a woman? Was he with someone last night? L.J. wouldn't do that. But where was he?) yet I wanted desperately to know that he had one.

"You might say that." He sounded and looked disgusted. "I was in jail."

"What?" My startled shout drew looks from the couple seated at a table on my right. I smiled apologetically then leaned forward and whispered fiercely, "What? You were under arrest? Why?"

"I wasn't under arrest." He tapped my seashell again, a staccato rhythm that matched my accelerated heartbeat. "I was taken in for questioning. I entered the beach at the public access point but I tried to leave at the resort's gate—or what I thought was our resort. Turns out I wandered into a private home. Their alarm went off, the police came, and I was taken in for questioning. It took about a half-hour to get to the station, another hour to be interviewed, another hour to get lost on the way to the airport in Pensacola."

"Pensacola? Why didn't you just come back here?"

"I tried calling and you didn't answer." He held up a hand when I started to speak. "After what Brody said—"

"What did he say? Lucas, what's wrong?"

He ignored my questions, looking past me to the doorway. I recognized this avoiding tactic, but wasn't sure why he was employing it. "My flight was due to leave at seven," he continued. "I figured I could get back to Abilene, be deposed, and be on another flight back here by later on today. You wouldn't even know I was gone."

Something in his tone of voice bothered me. He sounded too flippant or unsure of himself, as though he was asking me to confirm something. The problem was, I didn't know what I had to confirm. "I'm glad you came back." I touched his hand again. "I've missed you so much."

"Have you?"

Was this what he needed confirmation for? That was easy. I nodded. "Yes."

"That's not what Brody said."

"Brody? I barely knew the man. Why would he say something like that?"

Lucas' dark eyes examined my face and I knew he was doing a cop thing, looking for any telltale lie. "That's what I wanted to talk to him about."

I shook my head, trying to will intelligence to replace my befuddlement. "Is that why the police talked to you? But that doesn't make sense. You didn't have any reason to kill him."

"The police think I did. Jealousy." His dark brown eyes searched mine.

I blew out a raspberry noise. "Brody kissed me. Big deal."

"Was it a big deal?" Lucas' hand tightened on mine.

I met his gaze squarely. "Not at all. You're the only man in my life, Lucas. The only one."

He released my hand as the waiter came to the table with a tray. The man set down two cups, a carafe of coffee and my English muffin. "Enjoy," he murmured then drifted off, ignoring the couple near us.

Lucas busied himself with pouring us both coffee then said, "I wasn't sure."

I almost choked on the bite in my mouth. "What? What gave you that idea?" I dabbed at the butter oozing down my chin.

He ran a hand through his hair, mussing his already tangled curls. I longed to follow suit, pull his head down to me, and kiss him. He must have seen the look in my eyes because he smiled that slow, sweet smile that warmed me all the way to my toes. "I don't see you enough," he murmured. "When you look at me that way, I don't believe what she says."

"What she says? Who?"

"I got a letter from Karen Levy, at Pittman. She said you and she had talked and decided it would be better for your book tour if you didn't see me. She said it would be good publicity for you to come here and be seen with the entrants in that contest they're having. So when I saw you and Brody together, then when Brody told me—" He shrugged.

I almost dropped my coffee cup. I saved it in time to rattle it down into the saucer. "She said what? Let me see it—I don't believe she'd do that!"

His face relaxed so fast that I knew he'd believed it. "Then it isn't—?"

I stood up. "Let me see it. This is crap. If she actually sent you that letter, I'm firing her." I tossed my napkin down and grabbed my seashell, brandishing it. "I'll fire her."

Lucas stood, too, putting a ten-dollar bill on the table. "You can't fire her. She's your editor not your agent. "

"You know what I mean." I looked around. "Come on. We'll call her right now. This is such bullshit. I'm not—"

"Wasn't your breakfast to your liking?"

Our waiter blocked the exit. I tried to dodge past him but he shifted position. "It was fine," I said, edging around him. "We're busy. Excuse me but—"

"Would you like to make a statement for the press?" he asked, gesturing to the couple at the table near ours. They were already standing, heading toward us.

"Damn." Lucas put a hand on my arm. "Let's go."

"Were you spying on us?" I demanded, pulling back as Lucas tugged me forward.

"Bea. Come on." His last tug jerked me past the waiter, who followed us. The man and woman behind him formed a little procession as Lucas and I made for the staircase.

"Just a few words." "Can you tell us where you found the body?" "Aren't you a detective in Texas? Why are you here, Mr. Remarchik?" "Miss Emerson wrote a story about your relationship, didn't she? It's a best seller, right? Is it true you and she…"

Voices faded behind us as Lucas sprinted up the shallow stairs two at a time. Luckily he released my hand, otherwise I'd have been dragged. Double-stair-jumps, regardless of how shallow the steps, were not in my repertoire. Behind me, I heard George shout, "I've got 'em blocked. Get out of here!"

"Friends like that are worth their weight in gold," Lucas muttered, looking around the lobby. "Come on. Over here."

"Let's just go up to the room," I said, heading for the elevators. "We can talk in private there." I grinned over my shoulder at him. "Or do more than talk."

"Damn it, Bea, don't try to seduce me at a time like this." He pulled me toward an alcove near the front door, an area like a mini-lobby where people could talk in private. "I've got to leave. I'm booked on another flight in a few hours. The police gave me permission to go but I'm being monitored and I have to come back tonight." He gave me a gentle shove and I landed on an overstuffed couch. Lucas settled next to me and put an arm around the back of the couch, cocooning me against the high couch arm. An overhanging palm tree effectively screened us as long as neither of us sat up straight.

"I'll call Karen," I said, reaching for my cell phone. "I want to get to the bottom of this. She had no right to say such a thing to you."

Lucas leaned close to me. "No need. After seeing your reaction...well, I guess it must have been some malicious prankster. Unlike the person who drugged you last night. That was no prank."

"Drugged me?" I leaned into his solid warmth. "Lucas, what's going on?"

He shook his head. "I'm not sure. I think someone drugged you last night. The way Clair described it, I wonder if it wasn't one of those date rape drugs."

"But nobody took me or—"

"Because the Boys were watching out for you." He looked grim. "I owe them a big one for that." He hurried on, not letting me speak. "I'm working for Margaret Troolin's law firm."

"Margaret? In Abilene? They do corporate law, right?"

He nodded. "They have a group that does corporate, but they also have a criminal division. I'm trying to track down some people to testify in a fraud case they're litigating. The short version of the whole thing is that a corporation is being sued for breach of promise, but I think I've found some witnesses who will say otherwise. They're in Pensacola, just up the coast from here."

"So you were combining business with pleasure. I mean, I hope it was pleasure," I added, suddenly unsure of his feelings.

He leaned even closer. "You know it is. And yes, I was combining both. That's why I was at the airport. I'd interviewed the people I was looking for and wanted to get back, be deposed, then get back here. Especially after what Brody said."

"What did he say? You mean that crack about an overweight writer?" I had to admit, that remark still rankled a bit, especially after seeing the leggy Ms. Ramone and the way Lucas had accorded her such respect.

"Not just that, although that was annoying enough." Lucas winked at me. "It was later, when I came back to the hotel, looking for you. Brody said that you had asked him to join you. He said my services weren't needed."

The harsh anger in his voice told me how that barb had hurt. I knew Lucas was still ambivalent about the money I'd shared with him from the sale of my romance book. The novel was lucrative and some of Lucas' old cronies had made snide remarks about how he'd 'earned' his money. Brody must have picked up on those innuendoes. I decided to try again to put that to rest.

"Lucas, you know how much I care for you. I would never have said anything like that. I wish now I'd stayed behind and we could have talked. I went out because you said you'd be gone. I'm sorry, if I knew you were coming back I'd have waited and—"

He placed a finger on my lips. "Hush. It's okay. I didn't know you were already in your room, sleeping off the effects of...whatever." He frowned. "I need to tell Sereta Ramone to get a blood sample from you."

I pulled back and looked up into his face. "Sereta?"

He nodded, either ignoring or unaware of my suspicious tone of voice. "If they can analyze your blood, we might get an idea of who did it. I don't like this. Somebody is trying to drive us apart and I'd like to know why."

I looked around as loud voices reached us from the main lobby. "It sounds like the waiter called in reinforcements."

Lucas glanced at his watch. "It was inevitable, I suppose. A mystery conference and a murder—it'll top the noon news."

"You'd better get out of here. Those reporters will be on us like a duck on a June bug if they see you." I pulled his face to mine and kissed him—really kissed him—for the first time since I'd seen him. When we finally separated, I was hot and bothered and it wasn't from the Florida heat. "Call me as soon as you can," I murmured, staring into his eyes.

"I've missed you so much." His fingers traced the line of my face then he kissed me quickly. "I'll call later. I promise we'll talk. We have a lot to discuss."

"No kidding." I stood and glanced to my left. An open door beckoned, leading to what looked like a ballroom. A French door in the distance led to a small patio outside the hotel that in turn led to the street. I'd seen it when we'd arrived the day before. "You go that way. I'll head 'em off in the lobby."

Lucas stood and put his hands on my shoulders. "I'll see you soon." I saw his eyes flicker to the people behind me who were already crowding into the small area. He kissed me then strode away.

"Mr. Remarchik! Can you tell us—?"

I turned to face the reporters who swarmed into the tiny foyer, blocking their access to Lucas. "Mr. Remarchik had to leave. Perhaps I can help you?"

Chapter 5

I skimmed through my notes then rose as polite applause started. Katherine Maxfield, the president of the ClueCon organizing committee, smiled apologetically and adjusted the microphone for my vertically challenged self. I cleared my throat, tossed back my braid, and faced the eight hundred people gathered in the ballroom.

"An odd thing happened on the way to the conference..."

Titters broke out. I smiled. "I'm sorry. I had to say it. Although I didn't know the man who died, I'm sure he would not have wanted us to ignore the odd circumstances. You have to admit, a suspicious death at a mystery conference is just too convenient."

I paused. The words resonated in my head. What had started as a flippant opening remark seemed to have a deeper meaning, but I wasn't sure what meaning I could find. I didn't have time to consider it now—I had several hundred people staring at me, waiting for pearls of wisdom to drop from my lips. I launched into my canned speech, pulled out whenever anyone asked me about my apparently meteoric publishing career, concluding with, "So you see, I'm an overnight sensation, as long as you consider a seven-year night a normal occurrence. I've had a lot of support and I've been very lucky, I admit that. The only advice I can give you is to keep trying, keep at it, and don't get discouraged. I've got a folder of rejection letters at home the same as you all do. Eventually you'll get an acceptance letter that makes it all worthwhile."

I stepped back from the podium, thankfully not tripping or making a fool of myself. Applause broke out and it wasn't just polite this time. I took a hasty sip from the glass of water on the table near the podium. I had given this speech a few times before but not at a mystery conference where an attendee had just been murdered. I'm glad it went over as well as it did, judging from the audience response.

Katherine stepped up to the microphone. "Check the bulletin board outside this room for any updates to the schedule. Have a good conference everyone!" She turned to me. "Good work," she said as we both smiled at the attendees, who were standing up and gathering their belongings. "I'm glad you mentioned Brody. So many rumors have been flying. It's good to get it out in the open."

"I figured we had to talk about it." Katherine and I made our way across the low stage then through the lunch crowd, joining the queue at the ballroom doors. Afternoon workshops would start in a few minutes and I wanted to get upstairs and change out of my navy blue pants into my jeans. "Dress-up" is not normal in my repertoire and I wanted to get back to normal as soon as possible.

I also wanted to make a call to Karen Levy and for that I needed some privacy. Who had sent a letter purporting to be from her, telling Lucas to get out of my life? Why had Brody made such a snide comment to Lucas last night in the lobby of the hotel?

Why would someone be trying to drive us apart?

I had no answers to those questions but I figured Karen was a good place to start. I'd called her earlier and left a message. I wanted to get back to the room and call again. Maybe I could figure out at least part of this whole confusing mess before I saw Lucas again.

People oozed toward the doors with agonizing slowness. I kept one ear tuned to Katherine, who filled me in on upcoming conference events, and let the prattle of others wash over me. "I was shocked when I heard about Brody and especially how he died," she said.

"The police told you how he died?" I asked. "I thought that would be privileged information."

"I told them I had to know. We're running a conference here. If our guests are in danger, I have a right to know. Mr. Richardson, the owner, was there and he agreed. The police had to tell him." She hustled toward the exit, her speed belying her white hair and cane. Winking at me, she said, "Old age has its privileges. Most folks younger than me can't say no to somebody who looks like Jessica Fletcher."

I laughed out loud. She did, indeed, bear an uncanny resemblance to that revered mystery icon. "So how did Brody die?"

"You don't know? You found the body."

"I didn't get so close." I elbowed aside a few folks to give Katherine more room to maneuver, although she was pretty deadly with that cane of hers, jabbing at the floor and making some of the younger attendees dance out of the way.

"He was choked."

I stopped, causing a momentary backup of the crowd. "Somebody strangled him?"

Katherine continued onward, leaving me in her wake. "Nope. They choked him with a rope. At least,

61

that's what I heard." She touched the hearing aid in her right ear. "People say all kinds of things when they think you can't really hear."

"You're good," I said with sincere admiration. I spied George in the distance, talking with a crowd of women who stared at him with rapt attention. I made a mental note to fill him in on the latest development.

"The rope is the Miss Scarlet," Katherine murmured.

"I beg your pardon?" I was jostled away from her and caught only a piece of her answer.

"…Scarlet is the award for sexy mystery. The prize is the Golden Rope." My befuddled look must have spoken volumes. "Then there's the Reverend Green for Inspirational and the Mustard for amateur sleuth. You're up for the Professor Plum and the award is a Silver Pipe. "

I thought for a minute she meant a bong then I realized she meant a piece of pipe, emblematic of one of the clues in the game.

"The Miss Scarlet is for steamy mystery, the Mrs. White is for Best Cozy, the Miss Peacock is for best historical." She raised an inquisitive eyebrow at me.

I hastened to nod, not wanting to admit I didn't have a clue (excuse the pun) about the contest in which my publisher had entered me. I vaguely recalled seeing descriptions in the conference program and I vowed to bone up on the details as soon as possible.

"…gay, wasn't he?"

Someone's voice intruded on my guilty thoughts, jerking my attention from Katherine.

"…bisexual, maybe. Trudy said he rose to the occasion with her."

"Really? I didn't think the models were supposed to do that."

"How do you think they get…"

I tried to see who was talking, but the crowd was meandering forward and I lost track of anyone who might have been dishing dirt.

"…and all of the workshop rooms are named after locations in the game," Katherine said, unaware of my wandering attention.

"Game?" I asked, leaning closer to hear.

"The Clue game." She stabbed at a man in front of us with her cane and he adroitly moved aside, giving her safe passage through the crowd. I followed in her wake. "Thank God Brody wasn't killed in one of the workshop rooms. That would have been too much. I can just imagine the headline: 'Mr. Boddy killed in the dining room with the rope by'—" She shook her head. "That's the question, isn't it? Who would want to kill a model?"

"Another model?" Then I immediately corrected myself. "No, it's too obvious. Besides, I doubt the contract is worth much. Do you know what's at stake? I confess, I haven't had a chance to read much about the contest, I've been so busy lately."

"Well, it's a big contract and I suppose it would help some of these men break into New York modeling circles, but that seems pretty flimsy to me." Katherine and I stopped, constrained by the press of people at the main doors to the ballroom. "I'm sure Mr. Richardson was relieved the man was found off the hotel property. From what I've heard, he's had some financial problems lately. It would certainly hurt his business if a body were found in the hotel. Of course, it adds a certain cachet to our conference," she said as we started to inch forward again. "We go to a lot of trouble to make this an authentic mystery conference, but even we don't go so far as to plan a real murder."

"Authentic?" I made a mental note to check with Karen on the modeling contract involved in the contest. Was that really motive for murder?

"We have staged forensic displays, we bring in a lot of top-notch speakers, and we try to set the scene as best we can. For example, all the rooms are named after game locations. The 'conservatory' is where forensic talks are being given. The 'billiard room' is where murder weapons are discussed. The 'dining room' is for panelist talks and the 'hall' is for plotting and craft discussions. It's in your program." She beamed at me, her tanned and weathered complexion contrasting with her pale gray eyes. "We do it at every ClueCon—try to set up things according to the game. That's why our award ceremony is so unique."

I nodded inanely. My years of playing Clue were long behind me, but I remembered the basics. I wondered if I could buy a Clue game somewhere then remembered seeing different versions in the bookstore (the 'Library') earlier. I'd have to buy one or else I'd be opening-mouth-inserting-foot for the next few days.

"I told her if she did it, I'd kill her."

I stopped again, but the crowd moved me forward, carrying me with its weight like a lava flow. I looked around, but everyone was talking. It was impossible to tell who had said it.

"I can't believe they're trying to do that. Isn't it illegal?"

"...can't afford to find out. If enough of us..."

"We have a contract. They can't do it. If they try, I'll go to the newspapers. I'll make sure everybody knows what Dunross..."

"I'll see you during the panel discussion," Katherine said, angling away from me. "I'm looking forward to it. Don't forget, we'll be in the Dining Room."

That's right. She and I, along with K.L. Lonigan and Aidan Lindsey, were scheduled to participate in a panel on 'What makes a murderer tick.' I hoped the other authors on the panel were verbose since I had no idea what I would say.

Dining Room? I nodded as she meandered off, already surrounded by conference goers who were anxious to bend her ear. I dug into my book bag and pulled out the conference schedule, which I had festooned with color-coded sticky notes to help me navigate the three days of workshops. In the center of the schedule was a map of the workshop rooms. The Dining Room was on the mezzanine level, one floor above.

"Mapping out your strategy?" Clair caught up with me outside the ballroom.

"Trying to," I said, exasperated. "These people are too clever for their own good. Why can't they have workshop rooms with numbers like every other conference I've ever attended?"

"Where's the fun in that?" He fell into step beside me as I spied an escalator in the distance. "You've got to get in the spirit of the game, B.R."

"Spirit schmirit. Where's George?"

"Pitching to a publisher."

I blinked in surprise. Literary agents and editors all had to accept pitch appointments in compensation for their conference fee. Aspiring authors got ten minutes to sell themselves and their books. George and Clair weren't novices, though. They were a prolific writing team, penning historical romances under the pseudonym Claire George. "Why are you pitching to a publisher? I thought you were happy with National?"

"We are, for our historical romances. But if we're going to branch into mystery, we need a different publisher. National doesn't handle thrillers."

"You're going to write thrillers?"

He laughed. "I have no idea what it will end up being, but it doesn't hurt to pitch. George is talking to Dunross now about a book proposal. I suppose if they want it, we'll have to write the book. We'll have to come up with a new pen name, too. Something dark and thriller-ish."

"I think you can probably get a few people together and come up with a suitable name. You know how authors love to invent characters."

"No kidding. By the way, that was a good speech, even though I have heard it before. I thought your mention of Brody was a nice touch."

"I did, too."

I turned at the unfamiliar voice. Two men were behind me, both of them buff, tanned, and movie star handsome. I didn't have to see their nametags to recognize more entrants in the Mr. Boddy contest. Next to me, I heard Clair hyperventilate. "Cool it," I muttered.

"I'm J.J. Butterfield," the tall blond one said, extending a hand I automatically shook. "John was a friend of ours."

"Tony Jackson," the tall, dark, handsome one said, also extending a hand. Both men were tall, although Butterfield was slightly shorter, probably in the five-foot-ten range. Each had chiseled good looks, although Jackson had a slightly bumped nose and a hard look, like Bruce Willis in the Die Hard movies. "Thanks for mentioning John. You were right. He wouldn't have wanted his murder to be ignored."

"Murder?" I was jostled forward and for an instant, Tony Jackson and I were almost cheek-to-chest, my cheek on his chest.

His dark eyes examined my face. "Of course he was murdered. It's too obvious." My blank stare must have spoke volumes. "He was killed with the Miss Scarlet."

"That's the second time someone's mentioned that," Clair said, breaking up my tête-à-tête with

Mr. Jackson.

"What do you mean?" I backed up.

"Someone at lunch mentioned it." Clair started moving toward the open atrium where sunlight streamed in, dancing off the two-story waterfall in the center of the space. Although the ballroom was in the lower level, the open space above reached up into the heights of the hotel and the skylights on the roof, giving the feeling of open sky. A dizzying circle of balconies overlooked the atrium and I could see small faces peering down at the ballroom attendees milling around and queuing up for the elevators.

"Someone at lunch mentioned the awards and the prizes associated with them. They said something about Brody being killed with the Miss Scarlet." Clair nodded toward the elevators across the open space. "Going up? Or are you going right to the workshops?"

"But—" I snapped my mouth closed. Was this really an open secret? Katherine made it sound as though only she knew about the cause of death.

J.J. Butterfield nodded. "It's the talk of the conference." He and Jackson exchanged looks. "There're bets on who's next."

"What?"

"Sure. Sort of like *Ten Little Indians*. Oops. I mean, *And Then There Were None*. I want to be politically correct." His cynical smile told me how sincere his political correctness was.

"But why would—"

A strident voice interrupted our conversation as well as the conversation of anyone in the vicinity. "I told her it didn't matter. She can talk all she wants to, but it won't change facts."

We all turned to see Patrice Samuels, her red face clashing with her ginger-colored hair and trademark turquoise necklace, this time shaped like an elaborate cross. She and another woman stood in the middle of the atrium, the sunlight glinting off the silver on Patrice's necklace.

"Not that again," Butterfield muttered. "They've been arguing about it since they arrived. You'd think they could put it to rest for a while."

"They'll come to blows if they aren't careful," Jackson said.

"What's the deal?" Clair asked, his attention oscillating between the two handsome men and the potential gossip surrounding a publisher.

"Rumor has it there's a merger in the works," Butterfield said. He looked past Clair to Patrice Samuels, who was being placated by the heavyset woman with long dark hair. "That's the publicist for Red Nail, Holly Newcastle. Patrice probably had too much to drink at lunch and Holly is probably trying to calm her down."

"I didn't have too much to drink at lunch," I said indignantly. "I didn't have anything to drink at lunch. That's not fair." Then I belatedly remembered my internal promise to avoid alcoholic beverages I didn't control. Oh well. No harm, no foul.

Jackson grinned at me, two magical dimples creasing his stubbled cheeks. "You have to know who to ask. Patrice always has a toddy or two at lunch."

"You guys know a lot about the inner workings." I started to edge my way toward the elevators that were even now whisking conference-goers back to their rooms. "Why did you say that about *Ten Little Indians*? You don't think there's another murder in the works, do you?"

He shrugged, visible muscles rippling in the thin linen of his shirt. Clair sighed so deeply I thought he'd pass out. "It's just odd, that's all," Jackson said. "John's death was so convenient."

"In what way? Why do you say that?"

"I'm sure you don't care about a lot of idle gossip," Butterfield interrupted smoothly. "After all, it's all just rumor."

"Damn straight I want to know about idle gossip," Clair said. "That's how contracts are signed and deals are negotiated."

Jackson laughed. "Funny you should say that." He looked beyond me and I followed his gaze, glancing over my shoulder at Patrice and Holly Newcastle. "I'm sure some people won't miss John, but he was a decent guy. It's not fair he should have died like he did." He turned his back on the two women and exerted the full force of his personality on me. "I hope we can talk more tonight at the banquet."

I stopped in my meander to the elevators. "What banquet?"

"You're one of the judges for the Mr. Boddy contest," Butterfield said. "There's a banquet tonight where you get to meet all the contestants."

"I didn't know about a banquet." I felt the first prickling of anger. "Nobody told me about any banquet. Is it in the program? I was supposed to meet—" I looked at Clair, who was shooting me a warning look. "I'm supposed to dine with a friend."

"Nope," Jackson said cheerfully. "You're dining with us tonight. Pittman, Dunross, and Red Nail all have book series coming out and we're all vying for spots as your cover models." He smiled at me, a mischievous little wrinkle to his nose. "There are three contracts and eight models. Seven now. Competition is fierce."

I longed to slap the smirk off his pretty-boy face. The only person I wanted to dine with that night was Lucas. "I need to talk to that woman. Cartwright or whoever she is. I'm supposed to have a schedule or something." I bumped into someone and turned to find Patrice Samuels crossing my path behind me. "I'm sorry," I said, reaching out to steady her as she tottered on her high heels. "I wasn't looking where I was going and—"

"Watch out!"

I whirled at the loud shout then looked up from whence it came.

"Ralph!" Clair grabbed me by the arm and jerked hard. I stumbled, my book bag flying out of my hand and landing on the carpet at J.J. Butterfield's feet. He bent to get it just as a bottle came sailing down from above, exploding like a bomb between us.

Chapter 6

"Holy crap," I yelped, jumping backward.

Blood-red fluid and pieces of glass liberally splashed J.J. Butterfield, Patrice Samuels, and me as the bottle exploded on impact. A shard nicked me and I jerked away. Clair still held my arm and he steadied me, pulling me back from the widening puddle on the royal blue carpet.

I looked upward. Twenty stories of balconies rose above me into the aerie of the hotel in a concentric circle, disappearing into the heights. On one floor near the top someone was leaning over and staring down at us. From this distance it was hard to tell if it was male or female, young or old, although the fleeting impression I had was of dark hair. As I watched, the face disappeared. Other faces peered over lower balconies as an excited babble of voices broke out.

"Are you okay?" Clair asked, releasing me and stepping back. "Good Lord, you're cut."

I looked down at my shin. A bright trickle of blood was oozing down my leg and now that he mentioned it, my leg stung, as though an unseen insect had gotten me. "I think that's it." I twisted, checking the rest of my exposed flesh. "Damn. These pants will never be the same. And this blouse—" I pulled what had once been a white-and-red blouse away from my skin, wrinkling my nose at the odor of merlot. I turned to Patrice and Butterfield. "Are you okay?"

Patrice Samuels was so pale I was afraid she'd pass out. Her pallor was emphasized by her pastel peach pantsuit, giving her a sickly appearance. The splashed red wine made her legs look bloody and mangled. J.J. Butterfield's pale green shirt was also dotted red in a random pattern, most of it on his back where he had bent over to retrieve my book bag. Butterfield gingerly picked up my bag, which was dripping wine. "I'm fine, but your papers are a mess."

"Is everyone all right?" Saul Richardson hurried across the open atrium to us, another man by his side. Richardson went to Patrice and the other man, a younger version of the hotel owner, came to my side.

"Are you okay?" he asked, looking down at my bloody leg then up at the balcony. "Good God, you might have been killed."

A sudden hush greeted those words then a buzz of conversation broke out. "I'm fine," I said. "Just a bit shook, that's all."

"With good reason." He looked at Richardson and some unspoken message passed between the two men. "Let me escort you to your room, I'm sure you'll want to change clothes. I'll have the hotel doctor meet us there to check your cut. The hotel will, of course, pay for your cleaning and see to it your clothes are cared for promptly."

"That's it? That's all? I was almost killed and you'll pay for my dry cleaning bill?" Patrice Samuels' shrill voice cut through the assembled throng like a bullhorn. "Those balconies are a menace. I'm going to report you to—"

"We've never had a problem in the sixty years my family has run this hotel. I'm sure it was an accident." Saul Richardson and I exchanged a look and I shook my head slightly. This had been no accident. All of the balconies overlooking the atrium were about four-feet high with an open ironwork grill adding another foot on top of it. My room was on the ninth floor, and I had peered over the edge yesterday when I checked in. I had to stand on my tiptoes to look through the top part of the grill, and I was five-feet tall exactly. There was no way someone could accidentally knock a bottle of wine off that ledge. "The police are on site and I'll let them know about this, of course," he continued smoothly, watching with solicitude as Patrice shook one arm, red wine dribbling down the sleeve like a wound.

"On site?" Clair asked, taking my bag from Butterfield and twisting it, letting the wine ricochet off in a circular pattern.

"I'll need a new bag," I said morosely then I brightened. "At least I was holding my conference schedule with my workshops marked." I gestured with the 30-page document, which had sustained only minor splatters. "Thank goodness for small favors." Then Richardson's words sunk in. "The police are here?"

"Investigating the unfortunate problem on the beach last night," the man with me said. "Please, let me escort you upstairs." He pulled a ring of keys from a suit pocket. "We have an express elevator we use." He glanced at Butterfield. "Are you staying in the hotel?"

"Who are you?" Clair asked as the man started to shepherd us toward the elevators on the right side of the room.

"David Richardson. My father and I own this hotel."

"I'll be fine," Butterfield said, breaking away from us to join Tony Jackson and three other men who had materialized from one of the adjoining conference rooms. "I'll talk with you tonight, Bea." He smiled at me and slipped away.

I frowned at his merlot-stained back. I didn't share my first name with everyone, and I disliked having it bandied about like that. I caught a glimpse of Saul Richardson still trying to placate Patrice Samuels. Holly Newcastle, the Red Nail publicist, had joined them. She dabbed ineffectually at the stains on Patrice's jacket but only succeeded in smearing the liquid more deeply into the fabric. Her face was neutral but I thought I saw a flicker of sympathy for Saul Richardson as he spoke and Patrice responded, her face now a mottled red color.

"You really don't have to escort me," I said as David Richardson gestured me into a small corridor with a door marked "Employees Only."

"It's the least we can do." He inserted a key into a panel outside an elevator. "I apologize for what happened. I don't know how a bottle could have fallen off a balcony."

"That's pretty obvious, isn't it?" Clair asked as we all got into the small cubicle. "Somebody tossed it."

Richardson paused, his finger hovering over the control panel. He was tall like his father, his hair longer and dark with streaks of gray at the side giving him a distinguished, 'gentleman about town' look. His dark gray suit emphasized his broad shoulders and the crisp white shirt and dark tie set off his tanned good looks. Like his father, he had a chiseled, rough profile making him appear like a tough guy with a civilized façade. In a businessman sort of way, Richardson was as sexy as the boy toys in the model contest. "You're on the ninth floor, aren't you, Miss Emerson? You're in one of the suites?"

"Yes." I leaned back against the wall of the elevator, which had serviceable brown paneling and faded carpet unlike the more ornate elevators in the main part of the hotel. "Clair is just down the hall from me. You didn't answer his question."

Richardson turned to look at us. His eyes were very pale blue rimmed by darker blue around the iris. The startling contrast had the effect of disguising whatever he was thinking. Either that or he was such an accomplished businessman he had no difficulty hiding his true emotions. "I have to agree, it does seem...odd. But then, several things have happened lately that have been unusual."

"You mean besides a body on the beach?" Clair's placid expression successfully disguised the excellent mind working behind his homeboy front. I'd seen Clair pull this impersonation before and was always impressed by the results he garnered.

"If I didn't know better, I'd say we were haunted—or cursed," Richardson muttered. "Fire alarms going off for no reason, the pool shut down last week because of a chemical problem, our waiters walking off the job two weeks ago." He frowned. "It seems like we've had nothing but bad luck in the last couple of months."

"Interesting. It's been my experience that bad luck usually has a cause. Does anyone have a grudge against you?" Clair smiled innocently when Richardson looked up, startled. "A hotel is vulnerable to anyone who wants to be malicious. Perhaps it's an idea to consider, especially if it might put your guests in jeopardy." He paused long enough for his meaning to soak in. "Of course, it's hard to tell who the intended target was today."

"What do you mean?" I asked. "I don't know anybody here. I couldn't be the target."

Clair gave me a patient look. "As we well know,

you don't have to know somebody to incite jealousy or anger."

"Hey, now, wait a minute, I'm—"

"I'm speaking in general terms, not specifically about you," he said, putting an arm around my shoulders and giving me a brisk squeeze. "We all know you could never incite jealousy or anger in anyone."

I shot him a suspicious look. "I think that's an insult."

He released me. "I know it is." The floor indicator chimed. "Looks like we're here." Clair extended a hand to David Richardson. "Thanks for the escort. I'll take it from here."

"Are you sure?" Richardson shook Clair's hand then turned to me. "Miss Emerson, please contact the front desk if there's anything at all you need. I'll see to it a maid comes to your room for your clothing. Plus I'll make sure the doctor stops by to check your cut."

I looked down at my wound, which had stopped dribbling. "I've hurt myself worse when I've shaved. No need to bother the doctor."

"Are you sure? I'm so sorry this happened during your stay with us."

"It wasn't your fault." I stepped out of the elevator and looked around, getting my bearings. We were in a small cul-de-sac at the far end of the building, away from the main elevators in the center. "But I appreciate the gesture."

"I'm sure the police will want to chat with you," he said, holding the elevator door open with one hand. "I'll have them call you to arrange a time, is that all right?"

"I'd rather not —" The door was closing even as I spoke. "Damn. That reminds me." I turned to Clair and held out a hand. "My cell phone was in the bag."

We exchanged items, him holding my schedule

book as I rooted in the book bag while meandering down the hall toward our rooms. My phone was damp but undamaged. I flipped it open and my message ring tone chimed out *Wasted Time.*

"What do you have Mavis's ring tone set to?" Clair asked as I maneuvered open my hotel room door while juggling book bag and phone. "*Desperado?*"

"I don't have personalized tones for people," I said, tossing the book bag toward the bathroom. "I prefer to be randomly surprised."

Clair 'tsked' and scooped up my book bag. "I'll bet we can salvage some of this." His voice faded as he disappeared into the bathroom. "Hey, your seashell is congealing."

"Hmm?" I examined my messages. Karen Levy had called me, as had my mother. No surprise on that one. In fact, I was surprised she didn't have me paged at lunch. Mavis was something of a celebrity with her bridge club back in Washburn Creek, Iowa, due to my publishing fame plus the fact I'd been involved in a murder investigation last year. I'm sure my finding a body on the beach had provided endless fodder for the girls. Wait until they heard a bottle of Merlot had almost beaned me. I'd have to call Mom back in between workshops in the afternoon and give her the scoop. Mavis' phone wouldn't stop ringing for a week once news got out.

"There's gunk inside the shell and it's hard." A rattling sound issued from the bathroom. "I can't quite see what's in there. Was it empty when it stabbed you?"

I closed the phone, disappointed Lucas hadn't called. "Of course it was empty. I wouldn't pick up anything slimy." Then I remembered the chaos on the beach when I found John Brody. "I mean, I thought it was empty. Is there a critter in there? What lives in seashells?"

"How would I know? I'm from Kansas City. Hold on, I think...yeah..."

"What lives in a seashell—giant snails?" I peered around the doorframe to see Clair poking at the long oval opening in the shell with the handle of my hairbrush. "Hey, put that down, I don't want it covered with snail slime. I have to use it."

"It's dead," he said confidently, picking up the shell and peeking into its depths. "I'll bet it got filled with sand then got wet and dried out. Sand can be like concrete once it dries." He shook the shell and something echoed in its depth, a hollow tinging sound. "Whatever is in there, it's suffocated. You might want to soak it and clean it out before getting on the plane. I'm sure the airline has rules about transporting mollusks across state lines."

I took the shell from him and examined it closely for the first time. It was about six inches long in the fat part and my fist barely closed around its nubby circumference. The thing was pale white on the body and pinky-brown at the top. It was also fluted, tapering to a long tail at the bottom with part of itself flared open, as though a woman's skirt had blown back to reveal the pink interior. "It's kind of..." I searched for a word. "Sexual."

Clair barked out a laugh. "Only if you have alabaster womanly parts." He waggled his eyebrows at me and turned his attention to the book bag, grabbing a washcloth, dampening it then scrubbing at the red-and-black harlequin exterior. "Thank goodness the conference theme is blood. The merlot will blend right in."

"So you think somebody was aiming for me?" I left him to his task and took my shell back to the office, putting it on the coffee table in front of the couch in case something truly was living in its depths. Finding a slimy critter there was better than finding one in the bathroom.

"I doubt it." I heard water running then he emerged, book bag in hand. "I left the damp books and papers in the tub. Seriously, Ralph. I don't think you have an enemy at this conference. Which sort of begs the question—does Butterfield? Or Samuels?"

I thought of the arguments I'd seen Patrice Samuels engaging in. "Maybe. What was the talk about a merger? Didn't Butterfield or what's-his-name mention that?"

"Tony Jackson? Mr. Tall, Dark and Handsome?" Clair peered into the fridge while I rooted in the closet. "Anything good in here? I can't believe we chose a murder conference that also has a male beauty pageant going on—talk about dumb luck!"

I grabbed my '*National Sarcasm Society: Like we need your support*' T-shirt from a hanger. "I don't know which one said it, but somebody talked about a merger. Is Red Nail being sold?" I took a clean pair of jeans from the TV dresser and went into the bathroom, leaving the door open to hear Clair's reply.

"George heard from Dotty Sanders—you know Dotty? She writes for Signature? Anyway, Dotty's daughter Marlene has a critique partner who writes for Red Nail. This critique partner knows somebody who works in the head office. That person —"

I missed part of his sentence as I shed my wine-soaked luncheon clothing and dragged on my T-shirt and jeans. "Marlene?" I transferred my Necessaries to the jeans: business card/credit card case, cell phone, and room card, all tucked into pockets.

"No, the head office person. Anyway, what has been said is Red Nail is going into a merger with Dunross."

I dropped the stained pants and shirt in a heap on the floor and frowned at myself in the bathroom mirror, noting once again I only vaguely resembled Jane Seymour, who never had such flyaway hair or blotchy skin. I grabbed my face powder and started dabbing. "Why would Dunross merge with Red Nail? Red Nail publishes soft porn. Dunross is one of the old New York houses." I dotted on some earth-tone eye shadow the store lady had told me was 'perfect for someone with such green eyes'. Since I'm a complete klutzoid when it comes to makeup, I was willing to take a total stranger's advice.

"Not porn," Clair said with a laugh. "Erotica."

I blew out a juicy raspberry noise. "Give me a break. It's porn tarted up to look nice so people aren't ashamed to be seen holding the book." I rinsed potential seashell slime off my hairbrush and considered my lopsided bun.

"Want me to fix your hair?" Clair called out.

"Please." I emerged from the bathroom and handed him the brush. He gestured to the desk chair and I obediently sat. "So you think Dunross and Red Nail will merge? What happens to the authors involved? Do Red Nail authors automatically get a Dunross contract?"

"Not sure. From what the Red Nail person said, it may not be the case. Some authors are going to be dumped. There's a clause in their contracts about it." He plucked out my remaining hairpins and unwound the loop of hair balanced precariously on top of my head.

I regarded his reflection in the faux hunting print over the desk, watching him manipulate my waist-long locks. In Clair's pre-published life he'd been a hair stylist and he still had the touch. "If they signed the contract, then ..." I shrugged.

"Maybe, but Red Nail used to give each author a contract, which the author then used for the life of her work with Red Nail. Just recently they redid all contracts, giving the authors a cover sheet with a brief summary of what changed. Many of the long-time authors just signed the contract after skimming. The buy-out clause was buried."

"So not illegal, just unethical," I murmured. "Or possibly immoral?"

"Or all three. Marlene told Dotty who told George that a lawsuit might be in the works." He stepped back and surveyed me. "There you go."

I went to the bathroom and checked my look in the mirror. My hair was upswept and pinned into place. "Thanks. You're a lifesaver." I headed for the door. "How much could an author sue for? I mean, what kind of money are we talking about?"

"Big bucks, from what I heard."

"No offense, but how big could it be? Red Nail isn't as big as Dunross."

"But if you have eight or ten authors, all suing? What if the deal falls through?" He handed me my schedule. "Possibly millions. Since most of the officers of the company have a share in stock and since the stock will take off once the deal is announced..."

I added it up in my head. "So who would benefit if Patrice Samuels was killed? Her heirs? Or the company?"

"How would I know? I'm just a lowly writer from Overland Park, Kansas."

I snorted. Clair and George were hardly 'lowly writers'. In addition to their publishing income (which I suspected was quite healthy) they'd invested in real estate and stocks. The Boys were well off. "Guess."

"I'd put money on the company. It's a small firm and I'll bet all the directors had to sign an agreement, naming each other as beneficiary."

"I suppose that's good business sense." As I put my hand on the door handle, someone knocked. I stood on tiptoes and peered through the spyhole. Detective Ramone was standing outside my room.

"Damn. It's the fuzz." I pulled open the door.

Today she was dressed in a low-necked lace-edged black top covered by a pale green jacket with black slacks emphasizing her long legs. Stylish pumps edged out from the cuffs of her pants. They probably added three inches to her already five-foot-eight-ish height. She either had a flawless tan or impeccable makeup. I was betting on the makeup, since her hazel eyes were artfully highlighted by shadow and eyeliner.

Her glance flicked past me to the office then the bedroom beyond and I saw her eyeing the assorted effluvia I'd left lying around. I realized she was looking for evidence of Lucas' sojourn there. Damn. Where was a pair of size fourteen cowboy boots when you needed them?

I smiled politely. It was an effort but I managed. My mother's long training on etiquette stood me in good stead. "Can I help you?"

"Going somewhere, Miss Emerson?" She made it sound like I was skipping bail in order to avoid a hearing.

I held up my conference schedule like a shield. "Sorry. I'm busy. Workshops. We are at a writing conference, remember?"

"I didn't think events started until two o'clock. You've got plenty of time." She moved forward but I didn't budge.

"I'm directionally challenged," I countered. "I need ample time to find the room."

She started to edge past me. "I'm sure you have time for a couple of questions."

I held my ground. "I'm sure I don't."

She gave a sigh. "Why don't you let me in and we can talk about this?" Her eyes went to Clair, who'd walked up to stand behind me. "Privately."

"I'm her business advisor," he said.

I kept my face still at this blatant lie. She looked like she wanted to argue the point, but I didn't give her the chance. "If you want to chat, Clair stays in the room," I said.

She shrugged, the camisole under her jacket dipping and showing a curvaceous expanse of brown bosom. If she was trying to impress either Clair or I, she was playing to the wrong audience. We both remained unmoved. I stepped aside and she came in. I saw her eyes catalog the desk, my seashell, my open closet door, and the king sized bed, barely seen through the open doorway. There wasn't a sign of Lucas in sight, damn it.

"I'm surprised you're in such a hurry." She turned to me and I thought I saw a smirk on her smoothly tanned face. "Don't you want to know who's trying to kill you?"

Chapter 7

Curiosity waged a fierce and silent battle in my psyche with my desire to appear cool and unruffled.

Curiosity won. "What do you mean, kill me? Are you talking about that bottle?"

"Was there another incident at this conference where your life was in jeopardy?"

"Well, no, but—"

"Other people were standing in the atrium," Clair interrupted. "Myself included. Why do you think Miss Emerson was the target?"

Ramone didn't reply. She walked toward the doorway and looked into the bedroom. "Why were you on the beach so early this morning?"

"I took a walk before breakfast." I exchanged a look with Clair. This woman was starting to annoy me. Without "Good Cop" Martinelli, her "Bad Cop" style was coming across as plain rudeness.

She moved, leaning to supposedly look toward the window. I suspected she was just trying to catch a glimpse of the bedroom area. "You had some trouble in Abilene last year, too."

"What's that supposed to imply?"

"I'm not implying anything. I just checked up on

Detective Remarchik—or, rather, ex-Detective Remarchik—and found out that you were involved in a murder last year. He was the officer in charge of the case. You and he became...friends during the investigation."

I wasn't sure which part of this innuendo to tackle first. Luckily Clair thinks faster on his feet than I do and said, "It was two murders, actually. What's your point?"

She turned and her frosty glance shifted to him. He smiled, his best 'aw, shucks, I'm just Jimmy Stewart, you wouldn't beat me up, would you?' look. Her bright hazel eyes narrowed in suspicion. "Detective Remarchik retired right after that."

Clair gave her a look of wide-eyed innocence. "And...?" he prompted.

Her glance shifted to me. "I talked to some friends on the Abilene P.D. They said you gave Remarchik quite a lot of money."

My face got hot. "I shared the profits of my book with him and a woman's group. What are you trying to say?"

Her eyes were impassive. "So you have a business arrangement with Mr. Remarchik? Is that why he was upset last night when you and Mr. Brody were intimate?"

I started to sputter. "Intimate? What? Who said—"

"I think you've got the wrong set of friends in Abilene, Detective Ramone." Clair picked up the schedule I had dropped on the coffee table. "It's time to go. We'll be late for workshops at this rate." He put a firm hand on my arm and started moving me toward the door. "If Detective Ramone has any more questions for you or L.J. Remarchik, she can talk to your lawyer in Abilene."

I heard the finality in Clair's voice and knew he was right. "Yeah. Talk to Margaret Troolin." I lifted my chin defiantly.

Clair pulled open the door and I went past him to the hallway. He stared at Ramone, who was still standing in the doorway, staring into my bedroom. "Detective? Are you coming?"

She sauntered to the door and went by us in a haze of spicy perfume. Clair closed the door and led the way down the hall to the elevators, Ramone trailing behind us like our own personal black rain cloud. "Did you know that Brody was into BDSM?" she asked.

"Bondage, domination, sa—" I shut my mouth quickly. "No, why would I?"

"Since you were friends with him, I thought you might know his preferences."

I hazarded a glance at her where she dogged our heels, an evil presence casting its shadow on our day. "We aren't—weren't—friends."

"You were seen kissing yesterday."

"He kissed me." I caught Clair's warning look and said no more.

"How do you know Brody was into BDSM?" Clair asked as we stopped in the small elevator foyer. Bright lights bounced off the mirrors that faced the elevator doors. I eyed myself, scowling when I saw the svelte Miss Ramone watching me with that amused look on her perfectly browned face. I reached around her and pressed the 'down' button.

"The rope," she said. "We ran some forensic tests on the rope and on the abrasions found on the victim's neck."

I raised my eyes to hers in the mirror. "And?"

"It wasn't just used to kill him. He had sex before he died," she commented.

I stabbed the elevator button again, praying for promptness. "Really?"

Her gaze shifted to Clair. "With a man."

"Really?" His coolly disinterested voice was

masterful. "I've heard some people enjoy that. Bondage, I mean. Not necessarily sex before death, although I suppose that might be enjoyable, too." His sly look skipped over to me but he kept his face impassive. "I've heard some people enjoy handcuffs, for instance."

My ears flared hot. "Really?" A maid came trundling down the hallway, cart preceding her. "I left my clothing in the bathroom," I babbled. "Mr. Richardson said to leave them there so they'd be cleaned."

The woman gave me a blank stare. Ramone spoke a few words in Spanish and the woman nodded. The elevator dinged and I lunged on board. Ramone followed Clair and I more sedately. "Mezzanine, right?" Clair asked.

I nodded. "I need to go to the Library to get a Clue game. I need to bone up on the rules, not to mention the characters."

"Are you meeting Mr. Remarchik's plane?" Ramone asked.

"Hunh?"

"He lands in a half-hour. I thought you might be meeting him at the airport."

Damn. How did she know? Then I remembered. He probably had to give her his schedule since he was under suspicion for murder. "No, I can't. I have to speak at a workshop."

"Really? About what?" Her tone of voice clearly said that no topic I spoke about could be of the slightest interest to a person with a modicum of intelligence.

"What makes a murderer tick."

"Maybe I should sit in. I might learn something."

"You might."

We all moved to the back of the elevator as more people joined us. "At least the bottle proves it wasn't all part of the game," Clair murmured.

"Game?" Ramone leaned around me to look at him.

"You know—Clue. As far as I know, there's no 'Ms. Merlot killed Mr. Boddy in the atrium with a bottle'. Butterfield mentioned that he thought it would be *Ten Little Indians* all over again, but I think the bottle proves otherwise."

"Ten little Indians?" The look of suspicious bewilderment on Ramone's face was priceless. "Mr. Boddy?"

The man who'd just gotten on the elevator glanced back at her. "Agatha Christie," he said, deadpan. Then he looked at me, a mischievous look in his dark gray eyes. "Glad to meet you. We're on the panel together."

I belatedly recognized K. L. Lonigan, the author of the 'Dead Poets Society' series of mysteries. He was a bearded, bespectacled middle-aged man with an engaging grin and a short, paunchy build. I extended a hand. "It's great to meet you. I enjoyed *Final Frost* so much."

He shook my hand. "And I loved *Devils in the Dust*, Rafael."

"Rafael?" Ramone asked as the elevator doors opened.

"Pen name," I said airily. Lonigan gestured me ahead of him, blocking Ramone to emerge immediately behind me.

Clair said, "If you need to contact us, you can check with Margaret Troolin, she's with Spencer, Parker, and Howells in Abilene."

"Miss Emerson?"

I paused and looked back at Ramone.

"Don't leave town," she said.

I laughed out loud and next to me Lonigan made a choking sound. "Sorry," I said. "It's just too cliché."

Her eyes narrowed. "Not really."

"Oh, please," Lonigan muttered. He gestured to the crowded lobby. "Shall we? I'm glad I had a chance to talk to you. I've started a blog with some other authors and I'd like you to join us. It's called GreenBookFriends and it's on MySpace. We're going to talk about the environmental impact of the publishing industry. What do you think?"

"Sounds interesting." I fell into step with him, Clair by my side. I hazarded a glance back and saw Ramone watching us with a malevolent expression.

"What did you do to deserve such a charming police escort?" Lonigan steered me toward a hallway to the right of the lobby.

"I found a dead body on the beach."

"Oh, yeah. Plus you were almost beaned by a bottle of wine. I don't know, B.R., sounds to me like somebody's got it in for you."

"Miss Emerson? Here, you'll need this."

I stopped in my tracks as a chubby man leapt in front of me, brandishing a new ClueCon book bag. He wore a red-edged conference volunteer badge, but I couldn't see the name because the badge was pinned on upside down. "Thanks." I took the bag he thrust into my arms. "I cleaned the other one, but this will come in handy."

"We want our guest speakers to be happy." He sped away.

"So now you have the police sniffing at your heels," Lonigan commented as we entered a long narrow hallway.

I glanced down at the schedule in my hand then transferred it to my new bag. "Should make for interesting plot fodder."

"Actually the cops are sniffing at her boyfriend's heels," Clair commented. "Isn't this the one you were going to?" He gestured to a room with big poster board above it showing a blowup of the "Lounge" card from the Clue game. The sign near the door announced "Female P.I.s: Toughen Up Those Girls".

"Yep, this is it."

"Let's try to get together before our panel discussion," Lonigan suggested. "Can you duck out of this workshop a bit early?"

"Sure. Where do you want to meet?"

"Here is fine." Lonigan moved down the hall. "Our panel discussion is in the next room. See you in an hour." He went a couple of steps then three women descended on him, talking eagerly. Lonigan had nine books out in the series and was an old pro on the promo circuit. I resolved to pick his brain for tips later.

"Are you going to be okay?" Clair asked in a low voice.

I looked up at him, startled by the concern in his voice. "I'm fine, really."

"Okay. If you need anything, just call. I'll have my cell phone on. I'm meeting George at the coffee shop then we'll swing by your room later and we can all go to the banquet together. How's that sound?"

That damn banquet. "I'm not sure. I need to talk to that Cartwright person and find out what's expected. I'm hoping to see Lucas tonight, so I may skip it."

"I don't think you can." Clair waved to someone as he walked away. "You're one of the judges. We'll talk later." He was gone before I could pump him for information.

I slipped into the crowded room and took a seat near the back wall. The speaker was already expounding on her topic to a rapt audience. I took advantage of my first undisturbed moment to dig out the conference schedule and examine the agenda.

Yep, there it was. My name was listed as one of the 'preliminary judges for the Mr. Boddy contest'. I breathed a sigh of relief. Tonight was the 'Theme contest' and tomorrow was a swimsuit competition poolside where conference attendees could vote. Yikes. I'd been to one Chippendale's show in my life and I had a good imagination. I'd probably faint from the lure of so much beefcake.

But what was this 'theme' contest? I read further, listening with half-an-ear to the speaker discuss how to create believable kick-ass heroines, an oxymoron if ever there was one (believable and kick-ass, that is). Then I saw it: 'Each contestant is assigned a major character from an author's book and must portray that character believably, as judged by the author.' So presumably some guys would dress up like Cal, the hero in my books, and I'd have to judge who was the best one.

Of course, the best one was Lucas J. Remarchik. He was exactly who I thought Cal Delvecchio should be. It was hard to write about Cal any more because Lucas kept intruding on my thoughts. Which reminded me—had Karen Levy really told Lucas to back off in order to generate better publicity for my books? I almost pulled out my cell phone to call her again before remembering I was in a workshop room with forty other people.

I slipped out during the question-and-answer session and pulled my phone out of my jeans pocket. I had twenty minutes before the panel discussion started and with luck I'd catch Karen in her office. I moved away from the flow of traffic as the workshop rooms emptied and found a quiet nook near the public telephones. Karen answered on the first ring.

"How's it going, Bea?" she asked. "Getting a chance to relax?"

Apparently our body on the beach hadn't made big headlines in New York. I could picture Karen sitting at her desk in a skyscraper, coffee mug nearby and a stack of manuscripts on a slush pile so high it threatened to tip over and bury her. I liked Karen and I dreaded the thought of terminating my relationship with her. A good editor is worth her weight in gold. Karen's a hefty woman, bulky and solid, so she'd cost me a lot, but if she was dictating behavior to Lucas, I could do without her. I took the plunge immediately. "Karen, Lucas told me something that's disturbing."

"About what?"

Her guileless tone of voice reassured me. "He said you'd contacted him and told him not to see me any more, at least until the book tour was done."

There was a long pause. I held my breath. "Say what?" she asked.

I breathed again. "He said you sent him a letter and thought it would be good publicity if I came here and hung out with the contestants instead of him."

"That's bullshit. If anything, your relationship with Lucas is a godsend, publicity-wise. I'm sure it's a godsend for you, too. I mean—oh, shit, you know what I mean. No, I didn't send him a letter. I'd like to know who did, though."

"I'll tell him that." I was so relieved I leaned against the wall, my knees weak. "I told him it was crap and if you did do that, I'd fire you, but he was still unsure. I wanted to verify."

"You can't fire me, I'm your editor." She laughed ruefully. "Although I'm sure some of my authors might enjoy the thought. I wonder why someone would do that. What purpose would it serve?"

"Lucas thought someone was trying to push us apart." I saw movement out of the corner of my eye and turned to see K. L. Lonigan gesturing to the workshop room where we were to meet. I nodded my understanding.

"I think it would take more than a letter to make L. J. Remarchik leave you alone. That man is in love with you. You're lucky to have found each other."

I felt a pang of regret at that thought. She was

right and I didn't reflect on that fact often enough. I vowed when I saw Lucas again I'd let him know how I felt, show him I appreciated him. We were indeed lucky to have found each other.

"Listen, Karen, I have to go, I'm in a workshop on a panel discussion. I just wanted to clarify the whole letter thing."

"It wasn't me. Make sure you tell Lucas that. Take plenty of pictures at the banquet tonight. I wish I could be there to enjoy the show. Bye."

"That reminds me, I haven't talked to —" I was talking to empty air.

I folded the phone and went to join Lonigan but before I'd gone far a tall woman with killer fashion sense approached, clipboard in hand. She was totally color-coordinated; everything matched from her dark green pumps to her svelte green suit to the green clips in her dark blonde hair. "Miss Emerson? I'm Dana Cartwright, I'm glad we finally got a chance to talk. Here's your schedule for the conference, I apologize for not getting it to you sooner, but it's been hectic. I've had to coordinate a lot of the contest events because the person running it...Well, I suppose I should be charitable, they're all volunteers and I know they mean well, but it just isn't as organized as it could be. Then I suppose you heard about the fuss with Mayhem Manor. They wanted to have a spot in the contest, too, but Red Nail got their dibs in first, so MM was out. Boy, are they peeved. They've asked that the contest be redesigned and I was involved in discussions into the wee hours of the morning. Then we had the disturbance about the model found on the beach and, well, it's just been crazy."

She thrust a stapled sheaf of papers at me, which I automatically took. It appeared to be a daily calendar, broken down by hours, and possibly color-coded. Several entries were in red, some in blue and quite a few were in green. "I'm not sure if I can go to the—"

"If K. L. Lonigan mentions the nonsense with Mayhem Manor, just play dumb. MM is his publishing house and he might try to get some information from you about it. It's best just to stay off that subject. Now about the banquet, it's not formal, so there's no need—" She started to steer me back toward the workshops, talking a mile a minute about contest rules, a PR interview she'd arranged and a warning not to talk to the press any more without her being present. "We don't want them to get the wrong idea and given what happened in Abilene last year, well, I'm not sure what to do about the publicity. I need to talk to Paul Larson—he's head of Pittman P.R.—and get his take on it."

I looked from the papers in my hand to this young bundle of energy who pulsated with impatience next to me. "I think we need to talk in more detail about this."

She looked at a watch dangling from her neck chain. "You're booked into workshops for the rest of the afternoon and I have a press briefing at five o'clock. Why don't we meet before the banquet? Let's meet near the Internet area, what are they calling it? The Study, that's it. We'll meet there at five-thirty. How's that for you? There's Lonigan, you need to get in there. See you later." She hurried off across the lobby, cell phone out and punching in a number with an expert one-handed motion, all the while waving her clipboard at a group of people waiting for her near the front entrance.

I looked down at the schedule in my hand again. 'Thursday, 3:30 PM: Workshop: What makes a murderer tick. Make sure to include references to latest book as well as promo Mary Carr's book, *Armchair Assassin*. See attached blurb and excerpt.' I flipped through the pages and sure enough, there was a two-paragraph back cover teaser and a one-page excerpt from her latest book.

I started to skim through it, but before I could get far Lonigan appeared at my elbow. "Time to prep."

I followed him to the workshop room where Katherine Maxfield was chatting with a thin young woman compulsively arranging and rearranging the name placards on the table at the front of the room. "Aidan Lindsey?" I asked, watching the woman pace back and forth, putting down first her name placard, then mine, then Lonigan's. I noticed she didn't touch Katherine's, which was positioned at the seat next to the podium.

"Yep. She's superstitious about where she sits. It has something to do with Feng Shui or something. I don't know. I think she's trying to decide if she should be between the two writers known by their initials, or if she and Katherine should be grouped together at one end." He watched as a tall man ambled to the front of the room, smiling at Katherine. "There goes our chance to prep. Carl is notorious for getting these things started right on the dot. Oh well, no problem. Carl's a good moderator, I'm sure he's got a list of questions ready to get us started."

We joined Katherine and Aidan Lindsey at the front of the room. I forestalled Lindsey's further rearrangement by plunking down my book bag on the chair next to Katherine's. "How's your conference going?" I asked, folding the bulky agenda Dana Cartwright had given me.

"Pretty good. I was in a great workshop last hour on poisons," Katherine said with relish. "The speaker was a missionary who'd been stationed in the Amazon. Boy, he knew some great arcane facts."

I turned to Aidan Lindsey. "This is okay, right?" I pointed to the chair next to Katherine. "This way we can have initials alternating with full names." I gave her my best 'I'm new at this conference' smile and pushed the agenda into my bag.

The agenda just wouldn't go far. I finally gave up stuffing and opened the bag as wide as I could to peer inside. A folio-sized manila envelope took up most of the interior space of the bag. I pulled it out as I sat down, tucking the book bag under the table behind the white tablecloth that hid our lower halves from the audience.

As Carl the moderator started to shush the people filing into the room, I poured myself a glass of water. "What's in this?" I muttered to Katherine as I tried to unobtrusively rip open the 8x10 envelope.

She glanced at me then at the envelope. "I don't know. It's not something that comes with the bag. I should know, I helped stuff them all with conference gear. All we put in was books, schedules, and some freebie promo items from authors."

I slid a finger under the flap and tugged open the seam just as Carl said, "As we all know, our local panel is composed of experts on what makes a murderer tick. We're lucky to have such distinguished authors with us here today."

I peeked into the envelope.

A thin length of white cord was coiled inside along with a slip of paper. I unfolded the paper. Written on it in block letters was TALK TO PS.

I looked up as Carl said, "...B. R. Emerson, who has had the unfortunate distinction to be involved in a murder investigation last year in Abilene. I guess life does imitate art."

I smiled as I stuffed the envelope back into my bag. I'd seen that cord last night, or one very like it.

It had been lying next to John Brody's body on the beach.

So why was someone leaving me clues in my book bag?

Chapter 8

It felt like I had a ticking bomb on the floor at my feet. I mumbled through my part of the workshop, sure I sounded like an idiot as I babbled on about my book in response to prompting from Carl and questions from the audience.

Gwendolyn Bandorf, the cabana exerciser from the morning, was in the front row, scribbling down every word we said. It was unnerving to know my idiotic ramblings were being preserved for someone's posterity. Her earnest expression and alert look made me feel as though she could use X-ray vision to see into my bag and the clues there.

On the opposite of the aisle from her was her male equivalent, a rotund young man with stringy black hair who alternated earnest looks with fierce nods of his head whenever one of us made a point he agreed with. I found myself watching him, waiting for that telltale agreement saying what I'd spoken had been deathless and profound.

As soon as the workshop ended, I shot to my feet, almost overturning the table in my haste to depart. "Gotta run." I looked down at Katherine as I slung my bag over my shoulder, the incriminating evidence inside.

"No need to rush," she said soothingly, still seated at the table and smiling at attendees who were queuing up to talk to us. "We've got some free time. The conference always cuts off workshops at four-thirty so folks have a chance to hang out in the bar and chat before dinner. Plenty of time."

I patted the bulging bag hanging from my shoulder. "The press woman from Pittman gave me a bunch of stuff to do. I'll meet you in the bar later." I edged away from Gwendolyn, who was approaching me with single-minded determination I recognized from bookstore signings. She probably knew every nuance about my books, what my hero preferred in terms of booze, and why he had a penchant for women in distress. I learned a lot about my plots and my hero from the fans who cornered me at conferences and book signings. I was always surprised at the insights I gained in my writing process from talking to relative strangers.

Behind her I saw the man from the front row peering at me with an unsettling intentness. I was accustomed to fans, but his stare was almost predatory, as though he couldn't decide if I was his next victim or not. When he noticed me watching him he looked away, his face flushing an comfortable pink color.

I successfully dodged fans and burst out into the hallway, hurrying across the lobby. I ducked into the small sub-lobby where Lucas and I sat the day before, extracting my business card case from my back pocket. I sorted impatiently through the cards and found the one I was looking for. I hunched down on the couch and dialed Pete Martinelli's number. He answered on the first ring.

"It's B.R. Emerson," I said. "I've found a clue."

There was a pause. "You're at a Clue conference. Why am I not surprised?"

"I mean it. Somebody put a clue in my book bag."

He sighed. "How do you know it's a clue? How do you know somebody put it there?"

"Because I found it in there—" I stopped myself from saying "Idiot" just in time. "I don't think pieces of a murder weapon are standard freebies at a writer's convention."

"Say what?"

I described the rope, the note, and the chubby volunteer who had pressed the bag into my hands. "Maybe Ramone saw him," I said. "She was lurking nearby. Check with her. Maybe she can describe him better."

He didn't take the bait. "Did you touch the evidence?"

"Well, duh. I opened the envelope and handled the note. Once I saw what was in the envelope, I left it alone."

"Where is it now?"

"Nestled under my armpit in my book bag as I sit in the hotel lobby."

"Charming. Don't go anywhere. I'll be there in fifteen minutes." He hung up before I could answer. I considered ducking into the bar for a quick drink, but decided it might not look good to greet the police with a Cosmopolitan in hand. I called Lucas' mobile number and to my surprise, he answered.

"Are you in town?" I asked. "You won't believe what happened. Somebody put a clue in my book bag."

"What do you mean a clue?"

"My other bag got all stained from the wine bottle so a volunteer gave me a new one. When I opened it I found this clue."

"What wine bottle?"

"A wine bottle fell from twenty stories above me and almost hit me."

"What?"

"Well, maybe it wasn't me they were aiming for. I was with some other people at the time." I decided not to mention I was with two male models at the time. Better not to add to Lucas' aggravation. "Anyway, I got this new book bag and there was…" I lowered my voice, "…a piece of rope inside and a note."

"Rope?"

"Brody was strangled."

Long pause. "How do you know that?"

I waved a hand. "It's all over the conference. There was a piece of rope in my bag."

"Did you tell the police?"

"Of course. Martinelli is coming over here to talk to me. Are you in town? Are you coming to the hotel?" I was suddenly anxious to see him and make sure everything was okay between us. I remembered my resolve to show him how I felt. "I've missed you, Lucas. I talked to Karen. We need to talk, we need to get caught up and—"

"I'm in town but I'm busy right now. I'll try to get there later tonight."

I heard voices behind him. Was he at the airport? I didn't hear any loudspeaker noises but I did hear a man and a woman talking but I couldn't make out the words. "That's okay, I have to go to this dinner." If I were lucky, the banquet would be over by the time he got to the hotel. "It should be over by nine-thirty. I'll be back to the room as soon as I can. Will you—" I stopped, not sure what to ask. Will you be there? Will you forgive me for getting you into this mess?

"I'll see you later. I have to go." He hesitated then said, "We need to talk."

I heard a woman's voice in the background. "L.J., we can go to Pranzo, their lobster ravioli is amazing. Oh, I'm sorry. I didn't know you were on

100

the phone."

"I'll be there in a minute. We'll talk later, Bea." The line went silent.

I closed the phone. The woman's voice had sounded very like Sereta Ramone's husky Latino contralto. What was she doing going out to dinner with Lucas? What was the last comment he made about talking? Usually whenever a man said 'we need to talk' in that tone of voice he meant 'we need to discuss how to change our relationship.' Translation: let's not see each other any more.

I shook my head. I was reading way too much into a simple conversation. Maybe it wasn't Ramone. Maybe he was meeting someone on business. Maybe … I chose a likely fingernail and began to gnaw as I replayed the conversation in my head. If it was Ramone, why did she sound so casual with Lucas? Granted, it wasn't a big deal to use someone's initials but yesterday he'd been a suspect and today...

I looked up as David Richardson approached me from the French doors leading to the outside courtyard. "Just the person I wanted to see," he said, smiling.

He was no longer in his businessman's attire but was dressed casually in light khaki slacks, a darker khaki polo shirt and loafers. He looked like he'd stepped out of an ad for *Yachting Life*, the epitome of the well-to-do, fit, tanned and classy Florida dweller. Even his dark hair, thick and fine, looked a bit flyaway and less manicured as though it, too, was playing hooky from the cares of running a hotel. If my heart hadn't already been promised, I would have given him a run for his money. "Well, you found me."

"I wanted to buy you a drink. It's the least I can do after what happened this afternoon." He nodded to two of the hotel staff who hurried past him out the courtyard door, his pale blue eyes watching them as they hurried away.

"I appreciate the gesture but I'm waiting for the police." I winced when he looked alarmed. "I'm sorry. I think they'll be discreet. I found something that might be of use to them in their investigation and Detective Martinelli said he'd meet me here. There shouldn't be any screaming sirens or anything."

Richardson's face relaxed. "I hope not. We've had enough negative publicity to last us a lifetime. May I?" He gestured to the couch. I nodded and he sat down, turning so he could face me. "I checked with the cleaning staff and no one remembers anyone on the floor where the wine bottle..." He paused then added, "...came from."

"It was tossed. It had to be. The angle, the place where it landed—it had to be tossed. My consolation is the fact I wasn't the only person in the vicinity. I may not have been the target."

"It's a malicious prank." Richardson leaned back and put one muscular and tanned forearm on the top of the sofa. His attention shifted from me to someone behind me.

"Why do you say it was a prank?" a voice behind me said.

I twisted to look over my shoulder. "You set a land speed record," I said to Martinelli.

"I was in the neighborhood. Why do you say it was a prank?" he repeated, standing next to me at my end of the couch and staring at Richardson.

"I find it hard to believe someone is attempting murder here." Richardson's face flushed darkly, making his pale blue eyes appear icy cold.

"Why? From what I hear, this hotel has a reputation for, shall we say, less than savory events. A murder shouldn't be too out of bounds."

Richardson's hand clenched on the back of the sofa, the dark blue stone of the ring he wore flashing in the sunlight that angled in from the open doorway not far away. "Not all reputations are deserved," he snapped.

Martinelli shrugged. He was the antithesis of Richardson, dressed in baggy and wrinkled Docker pants, a shapeless white shirt under an equally shapeless dark jacket, and scuffed tie-up shoes. He reminded me Columbo on a good day except he didn't have Peter Falk's bemused leer. "And sometimes reputations are deserved. I've heard Luca Santorini likes a late night drink in your bar. He also occasionally reserves a room here for some of his more illustrious guests." The carefully neutral tone in his voice was more mocking than anything he could have said.

Richardson stood. "If you don't mind, Miss Emerson, I'll wait for you in the main lobby and we can have that drink. I'm sure the detective would like to talk to you in private."

"Hope I didn't scare you away," Martinelli said, rocking up and down on his heels.

"Not at all." Richardson nodded once to him then left, his rigid shoulders a sharp contrast to the relaxed stance he'd had just moments earlier.

"Well, you put his knickers in a knot," I said as Martinelli sank down onto the couch next to me. I started plotting how I could get him to tell me where his partner was.

"I'm a cop. Putting knickers in knots is my specialty. Is this the bag?" He picked up my book bag from the floor where I'd dropped it.

"Yes it is and I have private things in there." I reached for it but he shifted it to his left side, away from me. "Don't you need gloves or something?"

He gave me a long-suffering look as he pulled a pair of thin, supple latex gloves out of his pocket and put them on. "It's also police evidence."

I watched as he unzipped the bag and reached in

then carefully extracted the manila envelope, pinched between his thumb and index finger like a disgusting bug specimen.

"We may be a hick town but we do know about police procedure," he said as he opened the envelope. He peered inside then looked at me, his dark eyes like bottomless pools of accusation. "So who thinks you're such a hotshot detective?"

"Say what?"

He pulled out the note. "Somebody think you know who PS is."

"Hello? Patrice Samuels? It's either that or Public School and somehow I don't think that's what was meant. So how did you get here so fast? Were you and your partner at the beach, checking out the crime scene?" I silently congratulated myself on the casual way I said it.

"She's busy." He glanced at me then away, staring at the note with studied nonchalance. "She's interviewing a suspect."

My stomach clenched. It was Lucas. I was sure of it. "Really? Where's the police station? Is it nearby?"

"She's not there. Did you touch the rope?"

"I told you I didn't."

He smiled but it was brief and not particularly friendly. "Just confirming." With care he slipped the note back into the envelope then put the entire thing into a plastic bag he drew from one wrinkled suit coat pocket. "We'll need your fingerprints, just for elimination."

"I was printed last year in Abilene, during the investigation at the conference there. I'm sure they'd be happy to share with you. In fact my friend, Mr. Remarchik, was a detective there. Miss Ramone mentioned she also had friends on the Abilene P.D. I'm sure between the two of them you can find someone to send you the fingerprints."

"I'm sure I'll manage without Remarchik's help." The sharp way he said it added fuel to my fiery speculation. Was he jealous of Lucas? Did he have any reason to be jealous? Jealous of what? Why? I longed to grab him by his wrinkled suit and shake the truth out of him. Was Lucas having dinner with Sereta Ramone? Why was he having dinner with her and not me? Why did she sound so friendly?

"I'm certain Lucas will be willing to help in any way as soon as he returns."

"He's back, as if you didn't know."

"I beg your pardon?"

Martinelli stood up. I could tell he was flustered by the way he looked everywhere but at me. "What's in this bag you need?"

"My schedule and my notebook. Why did you make that crack about me knowing Lucas was in town?"

"You just talked to him, didn't you?" He set the bagged manila envelope on the arm of the sofa and peered into my book bag.

"How do you know?" I took the things he handed to me.

"Because I was there. He was checking in with us like he was supposed to do. Now if you're done cross-examining me, I have some detecting to do."

"Who's Luca Santorini?" I asked the question automatically as my mind considered and discarded thoughts.

"Local mobster. He and Saul Richardson go back a long way."

"Go back?"

"Tradition has it that Luca gave Saul the money he needed to get this hotel renovated back in the sixties. In exchange, Saul gives him—and his special guests who come into town now and again—preferential treatment."

"What's Pranzo?"

105

He stopped fiddling with my book bag and stared at me. "That's sneaky."

"What?"

"That way you have of piling up the questions."

"And?" I smiled at him. "Pranzo?"

"Restaurant down on the beach. Nice place to go if you're on an expense account." His sour look told me he didn't have that advantage. "Thanks for calling us so promptly about this." Martinelli held up the manila envelope and my book bag. "As soon as we're done processing it, I'll return it. I'll be in touch if there's anything else we need." He almost bolted across the small foyer. If I hadn't been so worried, I would have laughed.

I really felt like crying. Why was Lucas having dinner at a swanky restaurant with an attractive detective who was eyeing him like a cat eyeing a kitty treat left on an unprotected counter? I stood up, anxious for movement to help my beleaguered brain to think. Maybe I could find out where the restaurant was. I could just drop in and be startled to see him. I headed for the lobby to talk to the concierge.

I had only gone a few steps, though, when Katherine, Aidan Lindsey and some other people I didn't recognize corralled me. "We're going to the bar, come on," Katherine urged, excited voices almost drowning her out. I glanced at the clock over the front desk. I had only fifteen minutes until I was due to meet Dana Cartwright. My plot to sneak up on Lucas behind a potted palm in a restaurant would have to wait.

I looked around the crowded lobby and spied David Richardson. He was deep in conversation with a man in hotel livery and another man, small and swarthy, whose looks almost screamed GANGSTER. Richardson caught my eye and smiled then turned back to his companions, obviously unable to break away any time soon.

"Sure, why not?" I said to Katherine as I was towed into the crowded restaurant bar, following in her wake as she stabbed a path for us with her cane. A table magically opened for her and we sat down. We were barely settled when someone pushed a beer into my hand and I was able to lean back, staring out the floor-to-ceiling windows overlooking the swimming pool to the ocean in the distance. Conference attendees milled around the outdoor restaurant, the cabanas, and poolside, badges around their necks and drinks in hand. The place was jammed with authors and their fans.

"...he said he was a cunning linguist!" The woman next to me threw her head back and laughed uproariously along with her companions. I took a healthy sip of my drink and smiled, wondering what the joke was if that was the punch line.

"Lonigan did a Colonel Mustard, you know," a woman on my other side said in a conspiratorial voice. "When he was trying to get out of his Red Nail contract."

I looked from my right to my left. "I beg your pardon? K. L. Lonigan?"

"He promised a book and didn't deliver. Just like Colonel Mustard."

"Colonel Mustard? In the game?" I looked at her, confused.

The woman looked at me as though I'd sprouted horns. "Of course. Colonel Mustard got advance payments for a book he didn't deliver."

"Just like K L. Lonigan." The other woman nodded, her hair-do threatening to give up the hairpins and tumble around her shoulders in a riot of gray curls. "Patrice Samuels was furious. They went at it tooth and nail at the last ClueCon. Lonigan claimed the contract had been altered behind his back and Patrice said he was lying and just wanted to weasel out on their deal."

"Wow. I had no idea." I sipped more beer, belching delicately under my breath.

Luckily they had no idea I meant my unfamiliarity with the board game and Colonel Mustard's double-dealing. "No kidding. It's a well-kept secret, but you know what publishing is like. It's really a small world. Since then Lonigan and Samuels don't even acknowledge the other is alive. I wouldn't be surprised if he was the one who tossed that bottle over the railing."

The conversation turned to general gossip and I tuned it out. I didn't give the news about Lonigan much weight. After all, a contract dispute wasn't enough to get anyone murderously upset. Yet something about the talk bothered me, reminding me of something I'd heard earlier. I couldn't retrieve the illusive idea, though. My worries about Lucas and the svelte Sereta overrode all other concerns. I finally gave up on socializing and set my beer glass down. "Gotta go. I have to meet my publicist in the Study and I need to drop by the bookstore before they close. Where is it? The Study?"

"Lower level, at the end of the hall near the workshops," one of the women at the table said. "It's open until midnight. I think the bookstore closes at seven."

"Spend early, spend often." Katherine waggled a finger at me. "It's up to us to support our fellow authors."

I smiled but didn't tell her I was out to grab a copy of the Clue game. I needed a roadmap to this conference. I wiggled out of the press of people in the bar and followed signs downstairs to the "Library," a half-ballroom full of tables, books, and people. I managed to muscle my way to the Clue games and found to my relief I could buy 'replacement' parts for the game. I pounced on the rulebook, Clue cards, and, on a whim, tokens representing the characters and the weapons. Maybe I could make a little charm bracelet or something. In reality they would probably be tossed into a desk drawer to languish with other doodads, but it was a nice idea. After a brief internal argument, I also grabbed a book bag with 'There, Their, They're: Got it?' printed on it in bright red letters. One can never have too many bags and I was currently out two bags: one was drying in my room and the other was being dusted by the local cops.

There was a long line for the single cash register. I checked my Timex, relieved to see I still had a few minutes until my appointment with Cartwright. I spent the time wisely, reading the small rulebook to reacquaint myself with the general plot of the game. I had forgotten a whole story revolved around shady financial dealings and the discovery of embezzlement. As a child, I was preoccupied with murder, not money, so that fact had been erased in my remembrances.

I paid for my loot and stuffed my trinkets, rulebook, and notepad into the bag then consulted my well-thumbed schedule. The "Study" was indeed around the corner and at the end of the hallway, past the workshop rooms where I'd sat that afternoon. It was apparently a WiFi hotspot where Internet terminals had been set up for use by conference attendees. I meandered down the hall, sorting through the Clue cards as I walked. The Revolver looked like an old-time dueling pistol while the rope looked chillingly like the one I'd seen last night next to John Brody's body. I shuffled through the cards to the one depicting Professor Plum. I was up for his award. He was an unsavory character, accused of plagiarism and dismissed from his job at the British Museum.

I frowned but was reassured when I noted the

other characters were all as unscrupulous. At least if I won the award I wouldn't have to look for any hidden meaning in the honor. I paused outside the door with the enormous stylized Clue card above it that depicted the small study with couch, red carpet, and desk and tucked my cards in my new bag. Then I pulled open the left side of the double doors leading into the room.

There was a sensation of movement above me, as though something had passed in front of the lights and briefly cast a shadow. Such shadows back home were either bugs or bats, flying around the air over the lake near my house. I instinctively ducked and twisted to the right when a sharp pain crashed into my left arm, making me drop my bag and sag to my knees. I felt the nubby carpet under my hands as I fell face first toward the floor.

I was batting a thousand. For the second time in two days, I passed out.

Chapter 9

It's another Tequila Sunrise ...

I heard the melody from far, far away. I moved my head and the sound became clearer.

... Just another lonely boy in town...

Good Lord, where was the music coming from? It sounded loud, as though it was inside my head. I pried my eyes open, realizing I was pressed against my book bag on the floor. My phone was chirping merrily at me from inches away.

Floor? I pushed aside that question and managed to find the phone and open it. "What?"

"I appreciate you're busy, dear, but I'd like an update. What happened about the man you found on the beach? Did the police—"

"Call 911, Ma." My tongue was thick and wooly, as though someone had put little sweaters on all my teeth. "Tell them to get to the hotel, to the conference Internet room."

"What? Why would I—Beatrice, you're not in trouble again, are you? What's going on? Why do I need to call 911?"

"Just do it, please." I raised my head and tried to focus. After several rapid blinks, I recognized

111

narrow tables and chairs drawn up to a half-dozen computers, their screens all depicting the ClueCon logo.

There was also a woman lying on the floor not far from me. The blood pooled around her head was almost invisible against the dark burgundy carpet. "Call the police."

"Are you all right? You sound funny. Is something wrong? Where's Lucas?"

I warily tried to sit up but the room started spinning. "Please. Call the police."

"We'll talk later, Beatrice."

I sighed. "I know." The phone mercifully went silent in my hand. I had visions of my eighty-something mother, dialing 911 and explaining to the operator she wanted emergency services for Fort Walton Beach, Florida. If anyone could handle a police dispatcher, Mavis could. I pushed up, taking it slowly, and the room stopped its dizzying whirl. I took several deep breaths and got to my hands and knees, then dragged myself upright, holding on to the wall for support. Only then did I look again at the body on the floor.

At first I thought it was Gwendolyn Bandorf. The woman was pointed away from me, her face squished into the carpet so all I saw was her silhouette. She was heavy, a large solid lump of flesh sprawled inelegantly with arms and legs askew. Gwendolyn's hair was dark and curly, though, and this woman had long straight hair. She wore a long linen skirt and matching jacket, both twisted on her body as though they'd been in disarray when she fell.

I took a hesitant step closer, wondering if I needed to check for a pulse. One look at her ruined face and the heavy mechanic's wrench nearby forestalled that idea. If she was alive she was beyond my meager CPR skills. Better to let the police and paramedics handle it. Okay, I'm a coward. I admit it. The sight of blood always makes me wobbly in the knees and there was a lot of blood nearby. The thought of getting nearer made my stomach knot.

I realized I was leaning against the door, so I reached down to pick up my book bag, thinking I'd get out of the way of the cavalry when they arrived. As I stretched out my left arm, a shooting pain ricocheted from my wrist to my neck, culminating in a headache that almost dropped me back to my knees. That's when I saw the blood splattering my bare forearm and dotting the pale blue of my T-shirt sleeve. I touched my shoulder cautiously and my fingers came away sticky with blood.

"Oh, shit." I sagged against the wall, dizziness once again overtaking me.

****

"Will she be okay? It's not serious?"

I opened my eyes at the sound of that insistent voice. Pete Martinelli was staring at the female paramedic who knelt next to me.

"She'll be fine. But we need to get her to the hospital to get X-rays. Her collarbone might be broken." The woman looked back to me and blinked in surprise when she saw me watching her. "How're you feeling?"

"Like shit." I was sitting against the wall, Martinelli looming over me to my right. "What happened?"

"Good question. You tell us." He looked from me to the other side of the room where I was pretty sure a body lay.

"I came here to meet my publicist, something hit me, I fell down, I woke up and found..." I peeked around the solid little woman with the electric blonde hair who was dabbing at my shoulder with a piece of gauze. "Who is it?"

"You tell me."

I closed my eyes. "No games, please. If you won't answer that question, answer this one. What hit me?"

"Probably the wrench," the medic said. "Oh, for heaven's sake. Don't give me that look, Pete. Quit playing the cop."

"I am a cop, Donna."

I opened my eyes to see the small medic shooting Martinelli an exasperated look. "Men," she muttered. "Like being obscure is an art form." Her spiky hair, brightly dyed a stunning white-blonde, seemed to bristle with energy.

"What's that supposed to mean?" he demanded, attention momentarily off of me.

"Figure it out. You're the detective." She smiled sympathetically at me. "We need to get you to the emergency room, have your shoulder checked. Is there anyone you want us to call? Is there someone you want to go with you?"

I thought of Lucas. I could call him but what if he was out with Ramone? Did I really want to know for sure? "I'm supposed to be meeting friends for dinner. They might be worried."

"George Delacroix?" Martinelli demanded.

I nodded, wincing as the medic helped me stand.

"He's been looking for you. Said something about a banquet. I told him you were indisposed. He was insistent."

"That's one way to phrase it," the medic named Donna muttered. "He's outside and threatening to sue unless he sees you."

"That's George." I nodded my thanks to her. She was about my height but a bit more oversized with a chunkier build, a square face, and freckles plastered all over her brown skin. She looked fit in a womanly but athletic way, as though she could run up and down a soccer field all day and barely break a sweat.

I, on the other hand, was not an athlete and I

114

was feeling wilted. "If it's okay, I'd like George to go with me."

"Sure, no problem," Donna assured me.

"That's my call, not yours," Martinelli said, his cheekbones turning a dark red.

"It's my ambulance," Donna shot back.

Martinelli rocked up and down on his feet, hands dug into his baggy pants pockets and glaring alternately at me then Donna. "You always butt in and get friendly with the victims," he finally said.

She shrugged. "I have a heart. Unlike other women I know, one of which could be mistaken for a vampire if she's not careful. Don't take your male ego problems out on me, Pete. You can finish your questioning at the hospital. I'm taking my patient in."

I watched Martinelli process this assertion but he was distracted when one of the crime scene technicians called to him. "I'll talk to you later," he said to me before crossing the room to the body on the floor.

"Yeah, yeah, yeah," Donna said dismissively. "You and your mother. Okay, let's get you to the hospital and make sure everything's intact. Can you walk? It isn't far, the gurney's outside. Mr. Cop didn't want us to bring it into the room." The whole time she talked, Donna had an arm around my waist, steering me toward the door opened for us by a Latino police officer in uniform.

I stepped into the hallway and almost into George's arms, Clair behind him bobbing and weaving to peek into the room. "Good God, another body? What are you, a murder magnet?" George nudged Clair back behind him. "People will start to talk, Ralph."

Clair shuffled closer to the room, peering inside until the door shut firmly in his face. "Are you okay? There's blood on your shirt. What happened?"

Another medic, this one a young black guy, maneuvered a white-sheeted gurney toward me. "One side, gentlemen, I've got the lady's wheels."

"I have no idea." I sank down on the gurney and leaned back carefully. "I went into the room, I got hit and the next thing I knew, there's a dead body on the floor with me."

"One of you can come with us." Donna gently tightened a seat belt around my middle. "The other can follow behind in a cab. We're going to Sacred Heart of the Emerald Coast. Just tell the cabbie, he'll know where it is." She started trundling my gurney down the hall, gesturing to the black man who picked up their cases and followed behind.

"I'm up," George said, trotting beside my chariot. "Clair hates the sight of blood."

"Join the crowd. Maybe he could sit in for me at the banquet. I don't know what I was supposed to do, but I was supposed to be there."

Clair waved a hand. "Say no more. I'll be your sitter. I'll join you two at the hospital later." He and George had a hurried conversation then Clair ambled off down the hall, presumably to be my sit-in judge at the party. Knowing him, he'd be the belle of the ball.

"That was easy," I muttered.

"He really does hate hospitals," George confided as I was manipulated out of the building into a waiting ambulance. "I doubt if we'll see him later." He scrambled in behind Donna, who took up position next to me while her partner went to the front to drive.

"What hit you?" George asked, swaying with the vehicle as we got into motion.

"I'm not sure. It was damn big and heavy, though." I experimentally shrugged my shoulder but quickly stopped when the pain began.

"Probably the lead pipe," Donna said. "It was

big, at least two or three inches in diameter and more than a foot long. You're lucky it didn't hit your head."

"But how—do you mean the killer was in the room? With Ralph?" George touched my hand reassuringly. "She was attacked by the killer when she came in?"

"It was on the door frame." Donna busied herself with some tubes hanging down from the side of the ambulance bay. "It was probably balanced on top, the way you'd do a water balloon when you want to soak somebody. We saw it off to one side when we got there."

"Lead pipe?" I looked at George. "But whoever was in there was killed with a wrench."

"Reverend Green's weapon," George murmured. "Appropriate for Holly Newcastle. She's the publicist for Red Nail."

I stared at him in gape-mouthed astonishment. "How do you know it was Holly?" Then the meaning of his words soaked in. "Wait a minute...the lead pipe is Professor Plum's weapon. I'm up for the Plum, I should know."

"I overheard the description of the woman. It sounded like Holly Newcastle. Did you call L.J.? Where is he?"

I glanced at Donna, but she was talking to the other orderly who was driving, conversing through a small window. "I called him earlier when I found that clue." I gestured when George would have spoken. "I'll fill you in later. I think he and Ramone were going out to dinner. At least, I think that's what I heard."

"Dinner? He's a suspect, isn't he? That doesn't make sense."

"None of this makes sense," I whispered. "Who could set a trap for me? Nobody knew I was going there."

"Nobody?"

I remembered earlier, in the bar. "I mentioned it while I was having drinks with some people but it was just a bunch of conference people there and…"

George rolled his eyes. "Everybody and their grandma was in the bar. Anybody could have overheard and run downstairs. Maybe you were the target. Maybe Holly got in the way."

"But why would I be a target? For crying out loud, I don't even know anybody at this conference, much less have had time to make enemies." I closed my eyes but opened them immediately when dizziness began.

"What did you mean about L.J. and Ramone?"

Damn. I was hoping he'd forgotten. I explained about the envelope in my book bag. "I called Lucas to tell him. I heard voices in the background. It sounded like Ramone."

"Is this Lucas a good-looking guy?" Donna asked.

I peered up. She was leaning over me, once again fiddling with a gadget nearby. "Yeah, in an older, cowboy sort of way."

"Kiss of death from the vampire woman. Sorry. Take my advice. If you love this Lucas guy, get ready to fight for him. If you don't, get ready to lose him."

"That verifies what I've heard," George said with a grim look.

"What do you mean, what you've heard? You're a visitor in town the same as me."

"I have my sources."

"What Sereta Ramone wants, she gets, no matter who she stomps on in the process. This is the voice of experience talking." Donna looked out the front of the ambulance through the tiny porthole window. "We're here."

I realized the ambulance had slowed. "My insurance cards are in my card case." I started to pat my jeans pockets. "It's here somewhere. I don't think I put it in the bag. Where is my bag? Who's got it? And my phone and—"

George held up my cell phone. "I'm guessing the police have your bag as evidence. At this rate you'll leave here with more book bags than brains." He followed behind us then waited as I was wheeled into an emergency room and whisked behind a curtain. After a brief argument, my T-shirt and bra were removed and I was forced into a shabby pink hospital gown. I drew the line at my jeans, though. No way was I shucking my jeans.

The doctor came in, examined me, eyed my X-rays, and determined I had a bruise and possible hairline fracture of my collarbone, which would probably heal on its own if I allowed it to. I promised him I would allow healing to occur then I was wheeled to a different room for 'short-term observation'.

"Where's Donna what's-her-name?" I asked as George paced beside my cart.

"I got her business card and phone numbers. I'm meeting her later to get the full scoop." He watched as a nurse clipped a doodad to my finger.

"What's this?" I asked.

"Oxygen monitor." He pulled up a chair. "They want to make sure you're still breathing."

The nurse gave him a dirty look and left after admonishing me to 'call if I need anything'. "You could lie gasping on the floor like a fish out of water and they wouldn't get here until an alarm went off," George said darkly. "We'll get you out of here in an hour or two."

"You speak with the voice of experience."

"I've sprung people out of hospitals for less than a possible concussion."

"I wasn't concussed. I was piped." Either the drug the doctor had given me in the E.R. was starting to take effect or the snug bandage on my left shoulder was keeping the pain away. My shoulder no longer hurt as much as it had. "At least I didn't break anything."

"It was your left side," George pointed out, settling in the guest chair. "You can still autograph books."

"Damn." I snuggled back in the bed. I enjoyed crisp linens, and hospitals had the epitome of crisp. I poked a few buttons on the bed and it obliged by raising and lowering. "Cool. This could be fun."

"A lot more fun than last year when you ended up in the hospital after the Barf and Ride," George said.

"Please. Don't remind me."

"Oh, and let's not forget getting hit by a police car. That one landed you in the hospital, too, didn't it? Your insurance company must be getting suspicious, Ralph."

"So are you up to answering some more questions?" Martinelli pushed open the door and walked into the room, paper cup of coffee in hand.

I glared at him. "You should knock first."

"It's a hospital. Nobody knocks. Well?" He set the coffee on the bedside table and started rooting in a jacket pocket.

"Where's your partner?" I asked.

"She's on her way." He said it sullenly, as though admitting to an indiscretion. "She'll meet me here."

"So who's Donna?" I asked as he pulled out a notebook.

He shrugged. "I know her."

"In the Biblical sense?" George asked. He held up a hand when Martinelli turned toward him. "It's just good to know who the players are. For instance, I heard you and she used to keep company. At least you did until Sereta Ramone transferred to your station."

I stared at George in amazement. "How the hell—?"

"Please. I called Margaret, who called a lawyer, who called someone at police headquarters. Piece of cake." George's blue eyes turned cold. "It pays to know where the bodies are buried, metaphorically as well as physically. For example, I know Ms. Ramone used to be in the Panama City P.D., but there was a small scandal involving a married police officer. It was suggested she might be happier elsewhere."

"She's a good cop." Martinelli's voice was low but I heard the indecision in it.

"I didn't say otherwise. I did imply her ethics might be less than pristine, however."

The door opened again. "What is this, Grand Central?" I asked. The words died on my lips when I saw who it was.

"Are you okay?" Lucas crossed the room to me, his warm brown eyes bouncing over George then focusing back on me. His limp wasn't as pronounced as it had been earlier, when I saw him in the hotel lobby. He looked less tired, more relaxed, like a man on vacation instead of a man on business.

"Mavis called me and said you were hurt. What happened?" He was dressed casually in a light gray shirt under a dark gray suit jacket and black denims. As always, he wore his black boots with the gila monsters stitched on them. I'd thrown up on those boots last year, something that resulted in the arrest of the man responsible for the death of a colleague. The outfit perfectly matched the salt-and-pepper of Lucas' thick curly hair and bushy mustache. My heart lurched when I saw him. I'd forgotten just how handsome he was, how damn masculine he was. The Marlboro man had nothing on Lucas J. Remarchik.

The door opened again and Sereta Ramone

walked into the room. "Indeed, Miss Emerson. What happened?" She slinked across the floor to stand next to Lucas, almost touching him with one hip. Her pale green jacket was open, her black camisole underneath so snug I saw her nipples poking up at the fabric. She tilted her head to one side, looked up at him then smiled slowly at me. "Trouble just seems to follow you wherever you go." One of her tanned arms brushed against Lucas' forearm.

Lucas looked at her then at me. Our eyes met and he looked away. In that minute I had an answer to the question that had bugged me all day.

They had indeed been together.

But what had they been doing?

Chapter 10

I felt sick. I wasn't sure if it was delayed shock, the drugs, or the sight of Lucas, looking so embarrassed and guilty with that slut standing next to him.

"So nice of you to join us, L.J.," George said, his voice dripping with sarcasm. "After all, it's only the third, or maybe fourth, time Bea's been in danger in the last forty-eight hours. Let's see..." He ticked points off on his fingers. "There was the thing in the restaurant, and then finding the body on the beach, and then the wine bottle and now this. Yep, four times. I think we can count finding a newly dead body on the beach as a danger point. I suppose you can quibble about the restaurant, although I still say it was probably Rohypnol."

"Restaurant? Rohypnol?" Ramone looked at Lucas.

"Surely you've heard of it," George said. "It's known as the date rape drug. Someone put something in Bea's drink to make her pass out. I realize this place is a bit out of the way, but I would have thought the police would know about dangerous drugs."

"I've heard of it." Ramone's cheeks flushed a darker brown as she turned to Lucas. "What are you talking about? L.J.?"

"It happened to me, not him." I was pleased my voice didn't waver. It felt like it should have wavered, a lot. "You should be asking me."

"Bea was slipped a Mickey the other night." George's shrewd gaze settled on L.J., who had shifted position and was now equidistant from Ramone and me. Either he couldn't make up his mind or he was feeling hemmed in. Or maybe both. "Perhaps you haven't heard about that."

"I meant to mention it," L.J. said. "But I was..."

"Distracted?" I finished for him. Anger was unfurling in my gut, replacing my disappointment and hurt. I much preferred anger. I gave Ramone what I hoped looked like a dismissive glance. "I'm glad to see the police believe your story."

"Mr. Remarchik is no longer a person of interest," Ramone said, her tone of voice implying any interest she had was personal.

"Really?" Lucas had once told me something similar and look where it had led us. I shifted my attention to Martinelli, who was standing near the bed with his small notebook open, his eyes ricocheting to all of us like a pinball in a machine. "You said you had some questions? If the rest of you don't mind, I'd prefer to talk to Detective Martinelli alone."

George bobbed to his feet. "Of course. Police business. Understandable." He approached Lucas. "Anyone not involved should leave."

Lucas took a hesitant step back at the sight of the cold fury on George's face, almost stumbling in his haste to move. "We need to talk, Bea."

"You keep saying that, L.J." I deliberately used his initials, putting distance between us. "But it seems like we always get too busy."

He stiffened. "We won't this time. I'll wait outside." His gaze shifted to Ramone, cool and assessing then he turned and walked out, George trailing behind him.

I didn't watch their exit. I turned my attention immediately to my current problem—Vampira and her henchman. "Detectives?"

Ramone crossed her arms under her breasts, giving them a subtle lift that made the camisole stretch. "Miss Emerson, can you tell us why—"

"Why don't you let me continue the questioning I started?" Martinelli wasn't asking, although he did put a polite lilt to the sentence. "Maybe you can check with the crime scene techs and see what they found." He glanced down at his notebook and I think only I saw the slight tremble in his hands. "After all, you haven't seen the site yet. You should get over there and take a look for yourself." He paused. "If you have the time, that is." The sarcasm was laid on thick. I squinched down in the bed, happy to be an eavesdropper.

"I don't think I need—"

He raised his eyes and stared at her, his gaze flinty hard. "I'm the senior investigator. I think it might be wise for you to go to the scene." He smiled, more a grimace really. "It would be good to get confirmation of what I saw."

They locked eyes for a long minute then she unclasped her arms. "Sure. Maybe I'll see something you didn't."

His glance was brief and cold. "Maybe."

She whirled and left, every movement radiating anger. Martinelli watched her exit, his face expressionless. When he turned to me, I saw him take a deep breath, as though trying to force relaxation into a body that was rigid and tense.

"Well, you did it again," I said, casting desperately for something to lighten the mood.

"Yeah? What?"

"You got her undies in a bunch. Underwear-twisting must be your specialty, Detective."

For a frozen moment he didn't react then he suddenly put his head back and laughed. Years seemed to drop away from him. The carefree sound infected me as well. I giggled, probably from shock and painkillers. But it felt damn good after the acid feeling that had inundated me just moments earlier.

"You've got a way with words, Miss Emerson," he said, tapping his notebook with a pencil and grinning at me. It was a real smile this time, one that seemed to light up his eyes and make him look like a mischievous, carefree Tom Sawyer.

"I'm a writer. It's what I do. And you can call me Ralph." I was amazed at the words coming out of my mouth. Only my close friends called me Ralph. This guy was a cop. What was I doing? Then I saw how my casual words affected him. He shifted position and, I swear, he blushed. It was charming in a wrinkled-Columbo sort of way.

"Ralph, eh?"

"A derivative of my pen name. One of my darker secrets." I punched some buttons on my bed control and the part under my shoulders began to rise. "So ask your questions, Holmes. I'm ready for you."

"I can't be Holmes," he muttered. "I don't have a Watson."

"Oh, I don't know about that. Donna strikes me as being a rather capable Watson." I smiled innocently when he shot me a startled look. "Ask away."

He led me through my movements, asking detailed questions about my brief sojourn at the bar with the other writers, my purchases in the bookstore, then my aborted entry into the Internet room. "You didn't hear anything?" he asked, tucking his notepad into a jacket pocket.

"Nope. Although I have to admit I was distracted. I was reading up on the Clue game. I need to familiarize myself with it after all these years." I flinched as a flash of lightning illuminated the nighttime sky framed by the window of the room. "Thunderstorm?"

Martinelli followed my gaze. "It won't last long. They never do." He sounded tired and discouraged. I wondered if his words were a metaphor for something else.

There was a tapping on the door and George poked his head in. "I've sprung you, Ralph. We can go. Your paperwork's at the front desk." He came over to the bed, hefting a large plastic bag with the hospital logo on it in red letters. "I bought you a shirt."

Something in the way he said it made me suspicious. I grabbed the bag. Inside was my bloody "Sarcarsm" shirt and my bra, which I pushed to one side. I pulled out a flamingo pink T-shirt with '*Life's a Beach and then you tan*' in florid lettering on the front. The bosomy babe in the polka dot bikini completed the design, long legs crossed and breasts upthrust in a classic Fifties calendar girl pose.

"Gee, thanks." I wiggled to the edge of the bed, almost catapulting out of it until I remembered the controls. After trial and error, I got the whole contraption lowered. George helped me stand, observed by Martinelli. When I was ambulatory, I asked the question I'd been avoiding. "So where's Lucas?"

"I think he wanted to look at the crime scene, so I told him we'd meet him back at the hotel." George shrugged, his gaudy Hawaiian shirt rippling.

The acid was back. My stomach boiled again. Lucas and Ramone were out playing detective together. Who knew what else they were playing? I snatched the shirt off the bed and headed for the side of the room, pulling the ceiling curtain with me. "I'll be right out."

"Can you do that?" George looked at my bound shoulder then to the T-shirt in my hands.

"I'll figure out something," I snarled. As I struggled with the voluminous shirt I heard George and Martinelli talking, their voices muffled by the curtain and the clothing I was wrestling. I finally managed to ditch the shabby robe and slip the shirt over my head, settling it over my bandage with only a small amount of pain. My bra was beyond my capability, but the shirt was so big it could double as a nightie, so I wasn't concerned about my perky 36Ds being overly exposed.

I came out from behind the curtain in time to see Martinelli leaving. "Where's he going?" I asked, tossing the plastic bag to George who was talking in a low voice to my doctor.

"He's on police business. Come on. We've got some detecting to do."

"This first." The doctor held up a white square of cloth.

"What's that?"

"A sling. Just use it for a few days, until you get back home and have your own doctor look at that bruise."

I grumbled but allowed him to slip the contraption over my head and settle my left arm into its confines. Then I was dumped into a wheelchair and steered toward the front desk. All I wanted to do was go back to the hotel, crack open my bottle of bourbon, and pour a long drink. I longed to forget the sight of Lucas as he stood next to that slinky detective.

I signed assorted forms, read over the instructions for 'after hospital care', and accepted responsibility for a tiny pill in a plastic packet that was my painkiller for the night. I prayed my insurance would cover it all. A few minutes later, George and I were in a taxi and speeding away. He pulled out his cell phone. "You just relax for a few minutes."

I was happy to take his advice. I listened drowsily as he called first Clair, assuring him, "I've got our girl and we'll be there in a few minutes." Then he called Margaret Troolin, my sometime-lawyer in Abilene and filled her in on what was happening. He finished the call with, "Dig up anything you can find about Donna Del Marco. She's an EMT for Fort Walton Beach's ambulance service. Also see if you can get me some more information on Sereta Ramone, Pete Martinelli, and the Richardsons."

"Richardson?" I murmured. "Why them?"

"You may need to sue them," he said in an aside. "I want to know how much they're worth." Then he turned his attention back to the phone, ignoring my protests. There was no way in hell I'd sue them. It wasn't their fault I'd been piped.

Next he called my mother, briskly filling her in on the details of the night's events and putting me on the phone for a brief, "Trust me, I'm fine. I'll call you tomorrow and give you all the details."

"Where is Lucas?" Mavis demanded.

I didn't want to admit I didn't know the whereabouts of my AWOL gentleman friend. "Gotta go. I'll call you in the morning." I held the phone out to George. "You started this, you finish it."

He took the phone and murmured placating phrases to my mother, which lasted all the way to the hotel. "We have to go, Mavis. I'll call you later."

"You don't need to call her again," I protested.

"We'll see." He paid the cabbie and we went inside, pausing at the concierge desk. "You need painkillers," George insisted, waving the papers I'd received at the hospital.

"I have painkillers in my room."

"Eighty-mil baby aspirin for heart attack prevention does not constitute painkillers."

"I'll take a dozen if the pain gets bad." I hated taking drugs and George knew it.

"You need something stronger and they know where to get them." A bellboy was dispatched to the nearest drug store with orders to get the strongest drugs possible to supplement the extra-strength whatever I'd been handed at the hospital.

I grabbed the papers and read through them quickly. "Good. According to this, I can have a drink."

"I don't believe it." He snatched them back. "It says alcohol isn't recommended. It can exaggerate the sleepy effect."

"Good. I need sleep."

"You can't avoid Lucas forever."

I glared at him, momentarily forgetting I was wounded and attempting to put my hands on my hips. My sling and pain prevented me. "Ow. I'm not avoiding him. He's avoiding me."

George threw up his hands. "I give up. You two are meant for each other. I don't understand why the hell you aren't living happily ever after."

I stomped toward the bar at the end of the lobby hallway. "Because that kind of crap only happens in romance novels. I write murder mysteries."

"Thank God, there you are." Clair emerged from the shadowy depths of the room to greet us with a glass in hand. "Are you okay? That's a lovely shirt, Ralph. It's so you."

"Thank your partner. What's that?" I took the drink from him and sipped, grimacing at the sweet taste. "Yuck."

"It's Something on the Beach—Sex, Love, Mollusks. I'm not sure. I've got a table over there with some people. What do you want? No, don't tell me. Bourbon, straight up, right? Don't say a word until I get back. I want the whole story." Clair glided away, waving to the bartender, who nodded and pulled a bottle from the shelf behind him, bypassing several other people vying for his attention. As always, Clair had made a valuable friend.

George steered me toward the large table in the corner. 'Some people' consisted of several publishing luminaries I'd met before: Patrice Samuels, Adrian Ashford, Mary Carr and others I didn't recognize. At the table next to them sat the male models and a gaggle of women. "This explains Clair's choice of table," George said wryly, glancing at the seven men who were signing little card packs, similar to the one Brody had pushed on me the day before.

"Are you okay?" Ashford asked me, glancing at Patrice, whose face was partially hidden by the shadows of the restaurant.

I knew him slightly, having met him at a previous writer's conference. He had a youthful appearance until you got close to him and saw past the long brown-blond hair and stylish goatee. His sleepy-eyed calmness hid a sharp, calculating mind. As a senior staff member at Dunross Publishing, Ashford was an acquiring editor for mystery and romance novels. He'd once suggested I join Dunross and I laughed, albeit politely, in his face. "I'm fine." I sagged back in my deep chair carefully. I saw Patrice Samuels move, leaning over to talk to Mary Carr who was seated next to her. "She doesn't seem upset."

Ashford followed my glance. "There was no love lost between Patrice and Holly, although she did put on a good show for us earlier. Pity you had to miss it." He smiled sardonically. "It was Oscar worthy."

"So it was Holly?" I adjusted my position in the chair, stopping when pain shot through my shoulder. The drugs were apparently starting to wear off.

"That's what we were told. The police just had a press briefing and they also addressed convention people." His gaze shifted to my bulky shirt and the white cloth like a blazon across my front. "They said you were hurt."

I nodded. "Just a bad bruise, really."

"This is turning into a helluva conference for you—again. If you keep this up, you'll never get invited to another writing conference. A mixed blessing." The young woman next to him, a petite little brunette wearing a color-coordinated linen shorts set, laughed at this witticism.

It seemed like Ashford always had some young babe on his arm. I wondered if this was another of the chick lit authors he'd signed. "Is it true Red Nail and Dunross are merging?"

His pseudo-youthful face tightened. "Sorry. I can't discuss that."

I continued as though he hadn't spoken. "What happens to Red Nail authors? Will their contracts be honored?"

George dragged a chair over to sit next to me. "What about Mary Carr?" He nodded toward the plump woman in deep conversation with Patrice. "She's not exactly the Dunross type, is she?" He took the drink Clair offered him.

Ashford's indolent gaze followed George's movement. "Oh, I don't know. I suppose there's a place for porn anywhere, unless it's an inspirational publisher."

"Porn?" I almost dropped the drink Clair handed me. "Her?"

Clair leaned over. "She writes under a pen name for Red Nail. She writes erotic—or maybe I should say neurotic—mysteries."

"Hunh?" I took a long swallow of bourbon, feeling the delicious warmth seep into my bones and making tense muscles sag with weary relief. It wouldn't take much tonight to send me off to sleep.

"BDSM, M/M love, MFM," Clair said.

I struggled with the unfamiliar acronyms. "Bondage, male-male, male-female—what? Her?" I blinked at the middle-aged, overweight, plain woman with the frumpy clothing. "You're kidding, right?"

"Nope," Ashford said. "She's one of the hottest writers on the Red Nail payroll."

"I somehow don't see Dunross needing to renew her contract," George said.

Ashford shrugged. "All Red Nail contracts will have to be renegotiated if a merger does go through. That's the nature of the business."

"And a few writers might get dropped, right?" Clair and George exchanged a look I recognized. They'd dug up some dirt. "She doesn't appear to hold it against Patrice."

He was right. Carr and Samuels were laughing like old buddies, Samuels' trademark turquoise necklace swaying as the heavyset woman leaned toward the table to set down her drink. I peered through the dim light of the bar. "Is that what I think it is?"

Clair nodded. "Yep. We were commenting on it earlier."

"Wow." The necklace was two naked people entwined in a passionate embrace, the man behind the woman with his hands covering her breasts. As it twisted in the light, I saw the man's buttocks clearly.

"There you are! I'm sorry I couldn't meet you before the banquet. How did it go?"

I peered over my shoulder at Dana Cartwright. "I missed it." I took another deep swallow of bourbon and sagged further in the chair.

She leaned over me on the other side from where Clair stood. "You missed it? Miss Emerson, I don't think you understand. You were a judge. You can't just miss an event like that." Her glance went to my stylish pink T-shirt. "Don't you think you should be dressing a tad more professionally? I realize this is primarily a writer's conference, but there are fans here, too." Then she saw my sling. "Are you hurt? What happened?"

I opened my mouth to speak but Clair beat me to it. "I think the police are looking for you. You should probably chat with them. Detective Ramone is in the lobby right now. If I were you, I wouldn't keep her waiting." He started to steer Cartwright out of the bar, glancing back once at me. "I still expect details, Ralph."

I nodded, but the effort was almost too much. The bourbon, combined with the extra-strength wonder drug they'd given me in the hospital, was putting me to sleep. George saw the effect. "I told you we shouldn't have stopped for a drink," he chided. "You need your rest."

"I'm glad to see you're not hurt," a warm male voice said next to me.

I managed to turn my head to the right and found myself face-to-face with J. J. Butterfield. He was kneeling next to my chair, leaning on the arm. His thick blond hair was chunky-cut and tousled, reminding me of Don Johnson in his *Miami Vice* days. Or maybe I just had Florida on the mind.

"Not badly," I said. "Just a bit banged up."

"I need to talk to you. Would it be okay if I escorted you to your room and we could chat?" He smiled, deep dimples appearing by the sides of his mouth. "It won't take long."

George snorted derisively. "Not a chance. Come on, Sleeping Beauty." He put a firm hand under my good arm and gently pried me out of the chair, deftly rescuing my glass before it could fall from my nerveless fingers.

"I'll talk to you tomorrow," I mumbled, barely able to stagger after George. "Slow down, would you?"

"If we slow down you'll fall over." George steered me to the elevators and punched the button. "I'm going to tuck you in then I'll go back and fill in Clair on everything that's happened."

"You're a buddy, George." I must have dozed because the next thing I remember was ricocheting down the hallway and pausing outside my room as George used his copy of my key card to open the door. He steered me inside, flipping on lights as he went.

"I'm going to check on you before we turn in for the night," he promised as he lowered me gently to the big king-sized bed then helped me kick off my sandals.

I waved my good hand feebly. "I'm fine," I whispered around a yawn. "Go party." I didn't even hear him leaving

I don't know how long I dozed but an insistent knocking woke me from my alcohol-induced slumber. I peered around, finally recognizing my hotel room. I inched off the bed, bounced off the wall past the bathroom and went to the door, expecting to see a bellboy with my drugs.

Instead I saw J. J. Butterfield, smiling and holding a bottle of champagne. "I just wanted to drop by and make sure you were okay." He pushed his way past me into the office space. "And to celebrate my win tonight."

I couldn't stop him. I was wobbly, the room was spinning and the lights were exploding like fireworks in my brain. "I'm really tired," I mumbled.

"Just one little glass." He flourished the stemware he held in the other hand. "Come on, just a little sip to celebrate." He grinned at me but his eyes didn't smile. I wasn't sure what I saw there, but whatever it was, it started to frighten me.

"I don't think so." The cobwebs were clearing. Maybe the adrenaline caused by my incipient fright was doing it. "Leave."

"What?"

"Leave. Now." I started toward the door but he blocked my path.

"I don't think so. We have to talk."

I glared at him, fighting the fear pooling in my stomach. "Tomorrow."

He took a step closer to me, his body just inches from mine. His breath was warm as he lowered his head. "Tonight. Tonight we do more than talk."

I heard the sound of someone else at my door and almost wept with relief. Then I saw who was coming into the room.

Lucas paused in the small entryway, card key and overnight bag in hand.

Chapter 11

I said the first thing that came to mind. "Arrest him." I took a step back but almost fell, crying out as my wounded shoulder twisted.

Lucas set his bag down. "Am I interrupting something?"

If I hadn't been so close to tears, I would have laughed. "Damn it, Lucas, I told him to leave and he didn't. Arrest him for trespassing or intimidation or something."

"You're a cop?" Butterfield turned away from me, setting the champagne bottle down on the credenza holding the television set.

"Retired," Lucas said. Although taller than Butterfield, he didn't have the model's beefy, over-muscled build. He put the card key into his inside jacket pocket, pulling back the coat to do so. I caught a glimpse of his gun, carried snugly in the holster under his arm.

Butterfield saw it, too. "I don't want any trouble."

"Then leave." Lucas' voice was low and not particularly threatening, but it was sufficient for Butterfield.

He headed for the door, giving Lucas as much space as the cramped quarters would allow. "Sorry for the misunderstanding." I watched him pause by the champagne bottle then think better of it. "I'll talk to you tomorrow, Bea."

"That's Miss Emerson to you." The door slammed behind him. "Jerk." I blew out a sigh of relief. "What time is it? How long was I asleep?"

Lucas followed me as I walked into the bedroom and sank down into one of the overstuffed chairs near the small table in the corner. "It's almost ten." He pulled a small white package out of his coat pocket. "The concierge asked me to bring you this."

"Oh, the pills." I took the ibuprofen gratefully. My head and my shoulder were hurting. "The doctor gave me a pill but I haven't taken it yet." I considered getting up to get a glass of water and the pill, but the effort seemed too great. "Where have you been?" Then I remembered and wished I could snatch the words back.

He sat down on the end of the bed, a few feet away. "Talking to the police." He glanced at the door. "Did I come in at a bad time?"

"Your timing was perfect. That jerk wouldn't leave. He's one of the models in that stupid contest." I chewed on a fingernail. Lucas didn't deny being with Ramone. Damn. I cast around for a topic of conversation that didn't have the potential to cause an argument. "I have a hairline fracture of my collarbone." Then I decided to be totally truthful. "It's probably just a bruise."

"I know."

"How do you know? You left the hospital." The words and the accusatory tone slipped out. "I thought you were going to wait."

"I talked to the doctor. I knew George would take care of you. I thought it was more important to go to the crime scene."

I didn't want to think about that. I didn't want to visualize him and Ramone, detecting together at my crime scene. "George did take care of me." I struggled to my feet and caught my balance before heading for the bathroom.

As I passed Lucas he held out a gently restraining hand. "Bea, I'm sorry. Maybe I should have waited with you, but it seemed important to get back here to the hotel."

We were about the same height since he was sitting down. I stared into his eyes. "I'm sure it did seem important. Excuse me. I need a glass of water."

He took the drug box from me. "I'll open it for you."

I relinquished the box and went into the bathroom, emotion and pain mingling until I felt weak. Then I remembered I hadn't eaten anything since lunch and factored that into the equation. I found the pill envelope next to the hospital papers George had left. I shook the tiny tablet out onto the faux marble counter and stared at it.

"Do you want one of these, too?"

I looked at Lucas in the mirror over the sink. "I don't know," I said tiredly. I fumbled for a glass and almost dropped it.

"Come on." He put a careful hand on my right arm and steered me back into the room. I didn't argue. I waited passively as he pulled down the covers on the bed. "Can you get undressed?"

I shook my head. "I just need to take off my jeans. This T-shirt is so big I can sleep in it."

He unhooked my jeans and skinned them off of me, steadying me as they pooled around my feet. Then he helped me sit, disappearing into the bathroom and returning with the glass of water, pill, and my hairbrush, which he held up. "I'm not as good as Clair, but I think I can manage a braid."

I plucked out the hairpins I could reach with my

right hand, and he managed the rest, brushing out my long hair and plaiting it. He picked up the glass and pill he'd set on the nightstand and handed them to me. "According to the instructions, you'll sleep fine once you've taken this."

I considered the pill in the palm of his hand. "Will you stay here tonight?" I was mortified to hear a tremble in my voice, but I was tired, scared, and emotionally beat up.

He smiled, that slow, sweet smile I loved so much. "I'll guard all night."

I took the pill. "Good. I'm tired of being knocked out, piped, and accosted."

The warmth in his eyes vanished and for an instant his face had that cop expression I'd seen so often. Then he held out the glass. "Drink up."

I swallowed the tablet with tepid water then settled back carefully on the pillow. The sling kept my arm securely at my side, but it was starting to get sweaty. I had visions of armpit stains plaguing me in the morning. "It's not too bad," I said around a yawn. "I'm just a bit sore."

He sat on the edge of the bed. I longed to put my arms around him and tug him to me, to feel his body against mine, to reacquaint myself with eroticism and lust. Instead my eyelids started to quiver as I struggled to keep them open. "Bea," he said softly.

My eyes shot open. "Hmm?"

"Do you have any idea who's behind this?"

I shook my head slightly. "I talked to Karen. She didn't send the letter..." I yawned again.

"Good." He leaned over and kissed me, his mustache tickling my lip the way it always did. I smiled against his mouth. "What?"

"It's so nice to be with you again, Lucas." I closed my eyes.

At some point he slipped into bed beside me. I heard his murmured, "Good night, Bea," then I was gone again, deep into sleep.

****

The sound of *Love Will Keep Us Alive* woke me.

"Hello?" I heard Lucas' voice, coming from the office area nearby.

I snuggled back into my pillow, willing to let him deal with whoever was on my phone.

"Hey, Mavis. How's it going in Washburn Creek, Iowa?"

I smiled and rolled over. My mother adored Lucas. If anyone could handle an agitated Mavis, it was my guy. I opened one eye. As I expected, the bedroom was empty. I got cautiously out of bed, testing the limits of my sling. Except for stiffness, I felt relatively okay. I moved to the doorway and peeked into the office space beyond the bathroom.

Lucas was dressed and sitting in the chair, his back to me. The TV set in the corner was tuned to a news show and a newspaper was open on the coffee table, a cup of coffee nearby. When I saw the bagel near his coffee, my stomach grumbled.

"She's fine. Just a bit bruised. George was right."

I heard the ebb and flow of my mother's voice, no words discernable but the overall tone indicating her disbelief.

"Now, Mavis, you know I wouldn't let anything happen to your darling daughter." Lucas sipped some coffee, staring at the TV.

I heard more rumblings from the telephone.

"We haven't had a chance to talk about that. She's been busy and so have I." There was a long pause. He glanced over his shoulder at me and winked. "I think we'll make time on this trip to discuss it, though."

Lucas stood and stretched, holding the phone to his ear. I admired the long line of his body. His faded blue jeans and black T-shirt emphasized his height, his broad shoulders and his narrow hips. His white-and-black hair was tousled, the clipped curls lying in ringlets around his face and edging down his neck. He must not have shaved yet. I saw stubble on his cheeks, glinting slightly in the light from the lamp near the TV.

"I'd better go now, Mavis." He crossed the room to me. "Looks like Bea might be waking up. I want to make sure she's okay." He laughed softly at something my mother said. "Okay. I'll tell her." He closed the phone and set it on the counter next to the small sink in the kitchenette area. "Good morning, Princess."

I yawned. "If I'm a princess, does that make you my prince?"

"You know I am." He smoothed my hair back from my face and kissed me, gently at first then with more insistence as my right arm tugged him closer to me. "Damn. For a woman who's injured, you sure know how to get a man hot and bothered."

"I'm not that injured." But when I tried to lift my left arm, the pain from my shoulder made me wince.

"I think you are." He smoothed my hair back from my face. "You need time to recover." His beard scraped my neck as he nuzzled me. "I'll restrain myself like the gentleman I am."

"I'll give you a run for your money later," I promised although I silently agreed with him. My shoulder felt puffy and stiff, as though Quasimodo had taken up residence in my body. Any residual pain-killing effect from the night before was long gone.

"I'll hold you to that." He hugged me to him gently and I reveled in the feel of his body against mine.

All thoughts of slinky Sereta Ramone vanished. This was my man and he was with me, right here, right now. "We need to do this more often," I murmured.

"What? Help you recover from an attack?"

I heard the underlying anger, born of fear, in his voice. "No, be together."

"I promised Mavis we'd talk about that." His heart thumped loudly near my ear. "I told her we haven't had much time to discuss our future."

Our future. Did his stomach dip and twirl the way mine did when he thought those words? In the six months I'd known him, Lucas and I had avoided any talk about a long-term future, limiting our discussion to the next month or, when pushed, to the next season. *We'll get together in February—you can spend winter in Texas.* Or *Let's go to a conference in the spring. The beach should be perfect.* We never said *Let's plan a life together.*

"Speaking of time, what time is it?" I was stiff, sore, and not anxious to face the long-term future. I decided to do a Scarlett and think about it tomorrow.

"Almost nine."

"Yikes. I was supposed to be interviewed at breakfast today." I pulled away from his inviting warmth.

"Someone from the conference called earlier. They said it was going to be postponed to lunchtime. What's it about? They interview you in front of people or something?"

"Yep. Apparently I'm served along with the dessert course." I meandered toward the bathroom. "Have you showered?" I waggled my eyebrows at him.

"Don't tempt me." Lucas settled back down with his newspaper. "Unless, of course, you need some help in there?"

I probably did need help but I also wanted some privacy to think about all that had happened. "I'll call if I get into trouble."

"Bea?"

I paused in the bathroom doorway to look at him.

"We do need to talk about our future." His dark brown eyes were direct and unwavering, snaring my eyes with their seriousness.

"I know, Lucas. We will." I beat a hasty retreat into the confines of the bathroom.

Liar, liar, a little voice chanted in my head as I struggled with my wardrobe, slipping my arm out of the sling and giving it a tentative move. What I felt made me convinced I needed the sling for at least another day. I shed the fluorescent pink shirt and eyed myself in the brightly lighted mirror. My entire left shoulder was purple and yellow and yes, it was swollen. My earlier hunchback analogy wasn't too far off the mark. I gently tugged off the bandage perched on my collarbone, relieved to see my cut had either closed or was hidden in the swollen flesh.

I brushed out my hair then took to the shower, sighing with happiness as warm water sluiced over me. Shampooing was tricky but I did a halfway credible job of that and a body wash. I fumbled the towel twice when I tried to wrap my hair but finally managed it enough to wring out most of the moisture. While I was eyeing the tangled mess, a discreet tap sounded on my door.

"Hey, there, Ralph. Beauty Patrol," Clair called out. "I come in peace and bear salon quality gifts."

I shrugged on the hotel-provided bathrobe and flung open the door, bathing Clair in a fine mist as the heated air surged out. "My hero."

"No shit," he said with a laugh. "You're a disaster."

"Thanks for that little boost to my confidence. In case you've forgotten, I was beaten about the head and shoulders last night. I deserve to look like death warmed over."

"Shh." He looked over his shoulder. "Don't let L.J. hear you. He's upset enough already. It was all George could do to calm him down last night." He pushed past me into the bathroom. "Ready for the Miracle Worker?"

"Lucas and George talked last night?" I looked at the pink plastic bucket Clair set on the counter. "What's all that?"

"Girly things. Don't touch. Yes, they talked last night and this morning while Sleeping Beauty did her thing. I made George keep him occupied while I work." As he spoke, Clair was shoving aside my meager makeup offerings and arranging items on the counter. Powder, eye shadow, blush, hair dealies, tubes, gels, and spray bottles all were lined up like small beauty soldiers ready to go into battle.

I looked at him in the mirror. It would take an army to get me ready for the world. Luckily, I had Colonel Clair to lead the charge. "Where the hell did all that crap come from?"

"Frank's sister is a Mary Kay distributor."

"Frank?"

"The bartender. I called him this morning, he called his sister, and she came over here like an Angel of Mercy."

"So tell me," I prompted as he deftly began separating the tangles in my hair. "What did L.J. tell George?"

"Holly was dead before you got there." Clair toweled my hair then partitioned it into sections for a French braid. "Apparently they did some kind of temperature test." He made a face at me in the mirror. "I don't want to know the details. I'm sure it's nasty. So that means someone set a trap for you after killing her."

"That takes some guts," I thought out loud. "I mean, you're in there with a dead body. What if somebody came in and—" He was shaking his head at me in the mirror. "What?"

"There was a 'Network Outage' sign in the trashcan. Apparently John Q. Murderer put that on the door, set up his booby trap then tore it off when he was done. And no, there weren't any fingerprints," he added when he saw my eager look.

"Damn. Nobody saw anyone in the hall?"

"Nope."

I glanced at the doorway. Lucas was leaning against the frame, watching Clair as he dabbed makeup on my face, George behind him. "You shouldn't watch," I said. "It will ruin the mystery."

"The mystery is why you bother," he grumbled. "You're beautiful without all that junk."

Clair rolled his eyes. "He's too perfect to be true. You'd better hogtie him before he gets away, girlfriend."

"If he's not careful, I will." I squinted at myself in the mirror and Clair made a disapproving noise. "Sorry. So there weren't any witnesses?"

"Nope. Apparently people were either in the bar or starting to line up for that banquet." Lucas tilted his head and regarded me. "You didn't tell me you were supposed to judge a bunch of men in their swimsuits."

"Swimsuits?" I looked up at Clair incredulously. "Are you serious?"

"They don't pull punches at this conference," he said, laughter in his voice. "The swimsuit thing is after lunch. Hold still. We're almost done."

"Believe me, I've heard all about it," George said. He looked and sounded disgusted. I wondered if he was jealous at Clair's obvious interest in the goings-on. "It's like Chippendales, only worse. Avoid the pool area this afternoon unless you want to be involved."

"How bad could it be?" I had to mumble in order to leave Clair undisturbed as he worked his magic.

"How did it go last night?"

"Piece of cake. The different models visited each author's table and gave their pitch. If it was me, I'd vote for either Tony Jackson or Bobby Nelson, but Rob Peters was good, too. You'll be the final judge, of course. They're supposed to come dressed in costume tonight and sit with you again. So you'll have a chance to see for yourself."

I saw Lucas' suspicious look. "I didn't even know there was a contest until I got here."

"That Cartwright woman was supposed to meet you at the computer room, right? She was going to go over your itinerary?"

I looked at Lucas out of the corner of my eye. I recognized that cop-gleam in his. "Yeah, she was. Maybe she killed Holly."

"Why?" George asked. He peered around Lucas. "What are you doing to her? Oh, for heaven's sake. It's a writer's conference. She doesn't have to get all tarted up."

"Almost done," Clair said. "I'm just enhancing the real Ralph."

"The real Ralph is just fine without green eyelids," George said. "Are there any more bagels?" He went back into the kitchenette/office, followed by Lucas.

"They don't appreciate fine art," Clair said with a disdainful sniff. "A true master can turn a pig's ear into a silk purse."

"Thanks for the comparison." I examined my reflection in the mirror. Not bad. At least I wouldn't scare small children if they caught a glimpse of me. I flexed my shoulder experimentally. "I can't wear a bra," I fretted. "The strap would hurt."

"Already dealt with." Clair picked up a plastic bag near the door. I took it from him and peeked inside to see a strapless bra and dark pink tank top with matching floral over-blouse.

"Don't tell me. Frank?"

"His partner's mother runs a boutique. Do you need help with the bra?" He held up a hand at my incredulous look. "Who better to help? I won't be attracted to your womanly charms. Besides, I have four sisters. I've seen boobies."

I glanced toward the doorway. I could hear Lucas and George talking. "Yeah," I said in a low voice. "Come on." I snatched up a pair of khaki capris from the closet then went into the bedroom portion of the suite, Clair following behind me.

We managed to dress me without exposing too much flesh to Clair's delicate sensibilities. "How much do I owe you?" I asked, looking down at the flowers decorating the blouse I wore.

"I'll add it to your bill." He shooed me ahead of him toward the office. "Ta dah!"

Lucas turned at Clair's triumphant shout then crossed the room to me. "I told you that you didn't need any of that gunk," he said in a husky voice, looking down at me.

"The touch of the master," Clair murmured as he edged past us. "What's that?"

I followed his gaze and saw bagels, cream cheese, and … was that … yes, lox, all set out on the counter near the kitchenette sink. "Breakfast? Where'd you get it? No, don't tell me Frank's brother runs the restaurant, right?" I grinned at Clair.

"Becca gave it to me to give to you," Lucas said, giving me a quick kiss on the cheek.

"Becca?" I gravitated toward the food like a lemming toward a cliff, the smell of hot coffee and warm bagels manna to my shrunken stomach.

"The cat lady?" George prompted from his spot on the couch.

"You met Becca?" I thanked my lucky stars I'd decided to splurge on a suite for this trip. There was nothing like a toasted bagel with melty cream cheese topped by lox and onions. Couple it with freshly brewed coffee and heaven was within reach.

"I went for a walk this morning," Lucas said, resuming his seat at the coffee table and turning off the TV with the remote. "When I told her what happened, she insisted on sending you a Jewish Care Package, as she called it." He watched as I plucked up a piece of salmon. "Do you need any help?"

I tested my wounded shoulder. It didn't hurt to hold down a wayward bagel and smear it with gooey cream cheese. "I'm good. These are the best lox I've had since …" I thought about it, the smoked salmon dissolving on my tongue. "I give up. They're the best ever. So was Becca able to remember anything? Did she see something on the beach?"

"Nope. She said it seemed like a morning just like the others, except for you stopping to chat. She's impressed. Seems you're the only person who's gotten close to all those cats." He shook his head. "What a waste. There are times I can't believe how stupid humans are."

I bit into my bagel, closing my eyes in ecstasy as cream cheese combined with onions and lox to provide the perfect palate pleaser. "The two murders must be unconnected," I said when I could finally speak again. I set my bagel on the low coffee table then got my mug and went to the couch to sit next to George. "What would Holly and Brody have in common?"

"They're both here and they both work in publishing," Clair said. He was busying himself at the counter, building a meticulous breakfast sandwich.

"Pretty thin coincidence," Lucas said, sipping his coffee. "How's the wound?"

I shrugged my right shoulder. "Stiff. Sore. But better." I winked at him. "It won't slow me down much."

He blushed and I wanted to laugh at his modesty.

"They were both bisexual," Clair said.

Lucas, George, and I all stared at him, or rather, his back, since he was still at the counter, assembling his breakfast. He sensed the stunned incredulity and peeked over his shoulder at us. "What? Did I say something wrong?"

"How did you know they were bisexual?" I asked.

Clair's dark brown eyes flickered to George then he turned to stare down at his plate, a dull flush moving up his narrow face. "I talked to Brody. That night. He told me Holly had been dumped by her lesbian lover. She was on the rebound and willing to branch out, as he put it. He made some comment to the effect that even though his shingle swung both ways, it wasn't leaning in her direction." Clair smiled mirthlessly.

"What?" Lucas turned in his chair to stare at Clair's back. "You talked to Brody?"

Clair shifted slightly and I could see his profile clearly. "I was on the beach that night, L.J. I saw you."

Chapter 12

"You were?" I almost dropped my coffee mug in stunned surprise.

Clair nodded, finally done with his masterpiece and coming over to take the last chair across the coffee table from Lucas and kiddy-corner from George and I on the couch. "George and I had a tiff and I went for a walk." He nibbled on his piled-high bagel, effectively hiding his face from the rest of us.

"Did you tell Detective Ramone about this?" Lucas asked.

"The Dragon Lady? No way. I'm not going near her. She's a ball breaker." Clair's gaze shifted nervously from Lucas to me. "Metaphorically speaking, of course."

"What do you mean, you were on the beach?" Next to me on the couch, George watched with his typical impassivity. If Clair had surprised him, he was doing a good job of hiding it.

"When we got back from the restaurant and tipped you into bed, George and I went to the bar. I started talking to some of the men involved in the cover model contest and..." Clair's voice trailed off. I swiveled my gaze to him then looked away. His pained expression spoke volumes. "Well, suffice it to say I was having more fun than George."

"Quit being coy," George snapped. "I got fried because you were flirting and I went back to our room. You came up about an hour later after taking a stroll on the beach with some of your new best friends."

I considered probing for more information but saw Lucas' slight head shake. "You have to tell the cops. You can provide Lucas with an alibi."

"Not really. I saw him going in one direction. I was going in the other. We just walked down to the nearest restaurant and had a drink in the bar on the beach then I came back." Clair's overly casual tone of voice told me this was still a sore point between him and George.

"Man, was everybody on the beach that night?" I asked.

"It is convenient," Lucas said. "But yes, you should tell Martinelli you were out there. Even if you weren't there in the timeframe they're considering. It helps them figure out Brody's movements. I know they were trying to fill in some gaps."

I wondered how he knew that, but decided not to press for details.

Clair nodded disconsolately. "I know I should. And I will. Eventually."

"Sooner rather than later," Lucas reminded him.

"Yeah, yeah."

"How was Holly killed? Was it the wrench?" I suddenly remembered the pool of blood and the still figure on the floor. My bagel bites started to congeal in my stomach.

"The autopsy results aren't in yet but that's what it looks like." Lucas was staring at the black TV but I knew he didn't really see it. He was deep in cop-mode. "Holly was in the bar earlier and left about ten minutes before you did. You went down to the bookstore to buy some stuff, so let's say she had a twenty minute head start on you."

"Thirty minutes," I corrected. "It was a long checkout line."

Lucas tapped out a staccato rhythm on the arm of his chair, deep in thought. "Thirty minutes. That's ample time for someone to get there, put the sign on the door, meet with her, kill her and set the trap for you."

"It couldn't have been an accidental meeting," George mused.

"Looed ta ha da," Clair mumbled around a bite of lox.

I unconsciously channeled my mother. "Don't talk with your mouth full."

"Lured to her death," George translated. "Probably correct. But how? Who would Holly go to meet privately?"

We all contemplated the possibilities. "Too many to count," I finally said. "Let's face it, she might have met anyone for any reason."

"Not necessarily." Lucas went to the counter and cut a bagel in half, draping a thin blanket of lox over it. "If what you heard is true, Holly might soon be out of a job." I looked at him in surprise and he nodded. "If Dunross and Red Nail merged, it would affect everyone in the company from the authors on down."

"Smart man," George murmured. "He put authors at the top of the list."

Lucas grinned. "Bea's taught me a lot."

Clair snorted with laughter then put on his best innocent smile when I shot him a quelling glare. "L.J. is right, of course," he said. "Authors are at the top of the heap."

"So let's say Holly's job hunting." George picked up the conversational ball. "There are a bunch of publishers represented here. Mayhem Manor, Pittman, National, Dunross, Murderous Intent, Midnight Hour...If she wanted to approach a publishing house, this might be a good spot to get a feel for her chances."

"Don't forget agents," I pointed out. "Some of the literary agencies might be happy to get a publicist from an established publishing house. There are six or seven agents here, aren't there? Maybe she was interested in one of those spots."

"Or maybe it was sex," Clair said. "Holly was bi, like I said. Or so I heard," he corrected quickly when George turned an assessing gaze on him. "Maybe she was meeting a new fling."

I tried to visualize the plump woman with the long dark hair in a passionate embrace with a man—or woman. I failed but then my imagination usually failed miserably when I considered the romantic choices of others. "Was she promiscuous?"

George grinned. "What a polite word. Mavis raised you right. No, I hadn't heard she was particularly loose in that regard, unlike some of our other esteemed peers."

"Ashford?" I propped my feet up on the coffee table, narrowly missing his coffee cup.

"My lips are sealed." George held up a placating hand when I rounded on him. "I prefer not to repeat rumor and innuendo. I would rather believe the evidence of my eyes or first-hand accounts. I suspect Ashford looks busy, but somehow I doubt he is. I'll say no more," he added when I opened my mouth to protest.

Knowing George, he probably knew a man who knew a man who knew Ashford's personal assistant. I resolved to worm the information out of him later.

"Regardless of who it was, it was someone Holly trusted." Lucas jammed his hands in his jeans pockets and leaned against the counter. I was almost fooled by his relaxed posture until I saw the way his eyes flickered from my shoulder to my face. He was pissed off.

"What I don't get is why somebody put the pipe on the doorframe," Clair said. "That was a really melodramatic touch. Why not just hit Ralph over the head with it?"

I polished off my bagel. "Yeah. Why not just kill me?"

One of those dense silences settled on everyone in the room. We stared at each other and I'm sure everyone was as surprised as I was by my blunt words.

"The pipe could be an accident. It might not have anything to do with you. Maybe it was just a red herring." Lucas sat back down, picking up his coffee cup. "The fact the pipe is associated with the award you're nominated for may have nothing to do with it."

Red herring. There were always red herrings in murder mysteries, at least the ones I read. I doubted if there were really red herrings in real life. Then I remembered. Lucas had thirty years of experience as a cop on various police forces. If he said there were red herrings, there probably were.

"You weren't involved in the attack on Brody," he continued. "You just found the body. Nobody knew you'd be the one to find it. It might be coincidence about the pipe. It might have been set to affect anyone who came into the room, not necessarily you."

That made sense, more sense than someone setting up an elaborate joke on me.

"Let's face it, if the pipe had struck Ralph on the head, she'd be dead. So maybe it was really deadly and not just a prank. Maybe the killer was trying to kill two birds in one room." George looked at me. "The doctor said you were lucky you jumped out of the way."

"I've just been lucky all around on this trip," I grumbled, sliding down on the seat and waggling my sandaled feet. "Get knocked out, find a dead body, get clues stuffed in my bag, have arguments with the man I—" I choked on the words, not anxious to declare my love for Lucas in front of others.

"We haven't argued, Bea."

Unspoken but heard was 'yet'. I smiled at Lucas. "Give me time."

His eyes seemed to drill into me. "Oh, I will."

"To get back to the question of murder," George said, jerking my attention away from the frosty coolness of Lucas' brown eyes. "I had Margaret Troolin do a background check on the major players in our little drama. It turns out Donna, the ambulance technician, used to be involved with Pete Martinelli, the detective. Then Sereta Ramone came to town and love went out the door." George regarded Lucas over the top of his coffee mug. "I was surprised you hadn't already asked Margaret to do a check."

I kept my eyes down, careful not to let Lucas see the small surge of triumph I felt when I heard Ramone outed as a bitch.

"I didn't think it was important." Lucas quirked an eyebrow. "Ms. Ramone didn't mention to me that she and Martinelli were involved."

"Why should she?" I blurted. "I mean, that's sort of a private thing to discuss between two people who are relative strangers."

He flushed but didn't reply. I shot him a dagger-filled look, interrupted by George, who cleared his throat. "Apparently Ms. Ramone has had several less than happy relationships. She was involved with a married detective in Panama City then she was involved with a gentleman in Pensacola, who divorced his wife on the expectation he and Ms.

Ramone would be performing matrimony together. Then she landed here in Ft. Walton Beach, and she got involved with Martinelli, who was inches away from being wed to the lovely Donna Del Marco." George placidly sipped his coffee. "It would appear Ms. Ramone has a problem with commitment. From what I've been able to glean, she and Mr. Martinelli have had some problems lately."

"No shit," I muttered. "He had to bitch slap her yesterday to get her to do her job." I saw anger flare in Lucas' eyes but I barreled ahead anyway. "From what I overheard, Martinelli was a bit worried about her professional objectivity."

"She struck me as being a very capable police officer." Lucas clipped off his words like little bullets tossed in my direction.

"I'm sure you had more opportunity than I did to evaluate her performance."

"Jealous, Bea?"

I was vaguely aware of George and Clair, sitting in frozen silence as Lucas and I flung words at each other. "Not at all," I said, setting down my plate with a trembling hand. "I'm just not a fan of someone who mixes business and ..." I shrugged, unfortunately forgetting my wounded shoulder. I bit my lip to keep from grimacing.

"That reminds me," Clair said hastily. "Fans. Tony Jackson mentioned there's an author groupie here. This groupie collects authors."

I tore my eyes from Lucas, who was glaring at me, to glare at Clare in turn. "What?"

"Don't shoot the messenger." Clare held up a hand. "All I'm saying is, I heard a rumor there's a guy whose goal in life is to sleep with best-selling authors. Female authors," he added when he saw my incredulous look. "I think male authors are off-limits."

"Has the world gone crazy?" Then I shook my

head. "Don't answer that, I don't want to know. So what does this guy do, hang out at conferences and try to seduce people?"

"Apparently."

"That's silly. Who would do that?"

"The same kind of person who sleeps with rock stars just because they're rock stars." George leaned forward to regard Lucas, peering around me. "And apparently he'll do it consensually or not."

"The restaurant," Lucas said softly.

My head whipped back and forth between the two men. "What? What restaurant? Where—oh." His meaning soaked in. "Wait a minute. What kind of criteria does this guy have? Mystery author, romance—what?"

"New York Times bestseller, multi-award winner, ambulatory—I'm not sure. However, I am sure you're one of the few authors at this conference who would qualify. You've got a best seller, you've been top of the charts for months, and you're attractive." George smiled. "You fit the bill, my dear."

"Did anyone try to contact you on Wednesday, before you all went out to the restaurant?" Lucas was back in cop-mode. I could see it in his eyes.

"Just John Brody, in the lobby." I ignored the little voice, clamoring out a warning in my brain. "He's the only stranger I met up to that point."

"One hell of a meeting," Lucas muttered.

"Jealous?" I asked sweetly.

"You met some people at the restaurant," George pointed out.

"They were writers." I dismissed them with a wave of my uninjured arm, using the gesture to gauge Lucas' reaction. He looked mad but he was hiding it well.

"No reason to be jealous." Clair interrupted whatever reply Lucas was forming. "The man was a paid entertainer, after all. It wasn't personal."

"Are you saying he wouldn't have wanted to kiss me?" I demanded.

"You put your foot in it that time," George said, sotto voice.

"Of course you're kissable," Clair hastened to say. "But what I meant was—"

Life in the Fast Lane chirped merrily from the counter near the bagels. I sprang up to answer my cell phone, ignoring Clair's protestation about my attractiveness to strange men in hotel lobbies. I didn't recognize the number on the small LED display. "Hello?"

"B.R., this is Katherine Maxfield. How are you? I hope you got the message I left earlier, saying your interview had been postponed."

I smeared a little chunk of bagel with a lot of cream cheese. "I got the message. Thanks, Katherine. I should be fine by lunchtime."

"Are you sure? We can postpone until tomorrow if you want."

I was tempted but I wanted to get this faux interview over with, so I said, "No, that's okay. I'll be there at noon, right?"

"Eleven-thirty. Your next panel isn't until later on this afternoon. Of course, if you don't feel up to participating, just let me know. I'm sure we can get someone else to fill in."

I walked to the coffee table and picked up the schedule I'd dropped there the night before. I'd scrawled a summary of events on the back cover and I examined it now. *Setting The Crime Scene, Workshop, 3:30 Friday*. It was in 'the Hall', where all panels about forensics were held. Once again I was booked into one of the last workshops of the day. I dropped the schedule back on the table, ignoring the guys who were all talking in low voices. "I'll let you know at noon."

"Good. I'm so relieved you're staying."

I hastily swallowed the gooey morsel of bagel. "Staying?"

"We've had some people cancel and demand their money back." Katherine laughed nervously. "I guess a couple of murders at a murder conference have them scared."

Can't say I blame them, I thought. "Wimps," I said out loud.

"It's tough for Saul and David. The Richardsons," she added, in case I wasn't in with the In Crowd.

"Doesn't the conference have a deal with them or something? I mean, didn't you pay in advance?" I scooped out some more cream cheese, reconsidered then gave a mental shrug. What the hell. I was on vacation. I piled on the lox.

"They gave us a great rate, but we didn't have anything binding. I was under the impression they— well, I think they've had some financial difficulties lately. They were happy to have us here. But Saul mentioned the publicity might be bad for them. Of course, we don't have that problem." Katherine forced another laugh.

"We don't?"

"We're writers—there is no such thing as bad publicity, right?"

A thousand replies flitted through my brain. I settled for, "That's an optimistic attitude."

"Pragmatic, dear, not optimistic. I'll tell K.L. you'll be ready at noon."

"Lonigan?"

"Yes. He's doing the interview. See you then."

I closed the phone and chewed thoughtfully on my inundated bagel morsel. "Did you know K. L. Lonigan reneged on a deal with Red Nail?" I asked the room at large.

Three sets of male eyes regarded me with

varying degrees of interest. "Old news," George said. "He and Patrice hate each other. Everybody knows about that."

"I didn't."

He heaved himself to his feet. "I take that back. Everybody who pays attention to the gossip in the publishing world knew." He put his coffee mug on the counter. "Are you going to be okay for the morning?"

I looked at the microwave clock. It was just past ten. I'd already missed one set of workshops. Unless I hurried, I'd miss another set. "I'll be fine. I may just lounge around and relax until my big interview."

George looked at Lucas, who was still seated. "Good idea. Lounge. Relax. Recover." He nodded to Clair, who bobbed to his feet. "We'll leave you to it."

"If you need anything, you have only to call," Clair reminded me as he put his empty plate on the kitchenette counter.

"I know. Thanks." I walked with them to the door. "You're a lifesaver, Clair. Thanks."

"I exist to serve." He winked at me then glanced at Lucas, who hadn't moved. "Go easy on him, honey. He's worried." With those enigmatic words, he and George left.

I turned to Lucas. "More coffee?"

"No thanks."

His voice was tired and sad. I tried to quell the sinking feeling I got at the sound. "I didn't get you a ticket for the lunch," I said, rushing to fill the void of silence that seemed to suffocate the room. "If I wanted to bring a guest, I had to buy a ticket. I figured you wouldn't want a conference lunch. But if you want to go, I can probably get you a seat. Katherine said people were leaving, so they'll have extra."

"That's okay." Lucas leaned forward, clasping

161

and unclasping his hands. I sank onto the couch to his right and tucked my legs up under me. "It's not going to work, Bea."

I knew what he was saying but I wanted him to say the words. I wasn't going to let him weasel out of being the bad guy. "What won't work?"

"Us." He finally looked up at me, his eyes haunted and sad.

"You're letting a little murder get in the way of true love?" I tried to smile but it was hard. All that yummy cream cheese had turned to lead in my stomach. I plucked at my arm sling, twisting the fabric.

"Is that what it is? True love?" He shook his head. "We're always apart. If it was true love, wouldn't we be together more than every other month or so?"

"I'm sorry. I've been busy, you know that. I have to promote this book and—"

He held up a hand. "I'm as much to blame as you. I'm retired. I could join you." He shrugged. "I just don't want to join you, though. It's boring when you do those book signings. Or embarrassing." He stood up, towering over me.

"I won't be on tour forever," I said, watching him pace the room.

"But you'll always be famous."

"Say what?"

"You'll always be famous. You'll always be the woman who wrote the best selling book about the detective who rescued her." He didn't look at me, just continued pacing back and forth in front of the kitchenette counter, hands jammed into his jeans pockets.

"Well shit, Lucas. I can't very well unwrite the book, can I?"

He paused to glare at me. "I don't know why you had to write it in the first place."

I sighed. "I'm an author. It's what I do."

"You don't normally write books with sex scenes like that in them."

"Uh, yes, I do. My mysteries are pretty hot."

"This wasn't a mystery. It was a romance. And those scenes…"

"What scenes?" I hunched lower on the couch, wishing I could vanish, turtle-like, from this moment. The basis for the argument had been building for months, though, and I knew it couldn't be avoided.

"The scenes in that book. Damn it, Bea, everybody is asking me if you and I—if we—if it's based on fact." He stopped across the room from me and leaned against the counter again, this time crossing his arms defensively across his chest. Even in anger he was so handsome it made my heart ache to look at him.

"What do you say?"

"None of their damn business," he growled.

"Well. There you are."

"Yeah, but …" He looked anywhere but at me.

"But what?"

"There's the money."

"What about the money?" Since my book had hit the best-seller charts, 'the money' had become a touchy issue. Granted, there was a lot of it. Plus I'd inherited some money from Jim Quinn, a fellow author who'd recently died. "I thought you said it didn't matter if I had more money than you."

"You've got a lot more money."

"How do you know?"

He gave me an exasperated look. "I can read a newspaper."

"Don't believe everything you read." My phone chimed *After the Thrill is Gone.* Good God, I needed to download new ring tones. These were playing havoc with my brain.

"Are you going to answer that?"

"It can go to messaging. Are you still mad I gave you a cut of the profits from my book? Are you still getting hassled about that?"

He pushed away from the counter and came back to sit down. "No, I'm not mad. I'm just..." He was silent for a long moment. I held my breath. "I guess I'm just confused. I'm not sure where we should go from here."

"Where are we now?" I smiled even though it felt like all the air had been knocked out of me. "Maybe that's the question we need to ask first."

He raked a hand through his hair. "I'm not sure. I love you. I really do. But it's hard starting over with somebody at this point in my life. I don't want to leave Texas and you don't want to leave Minnesota."

"We talked once about meeting halfway."

He smiled lopsidedly at me, and my heart twisted at the sad quality to it. "Yeah, we did, didn't we? Somehow we've never gotten around to that, though."

The room phone rang and my cell phone rang again, this time chiming *Take It Easy*. Oh, how I wished I could. "You'd better get that," he said, picking up the phone receiver and handing it to me then going to the counter to pick up my cell phone.

It was Karen Levy, my editor in New York. "Bea, are you okay? What happened? I heard you'd been hurt."

Hurt? I took my cell phone from Lucas and thought, *It's only just starting*. "I'm fine, Karen. Really. Can I call you back? I'm kind of busy." I looked down at the LED on my cell phone. I didn't recognize the number.

"Sure, call me back later on today if you can. I need to talk to you about the cover model thing. Have you made your choice yet? It's up to you—and

Dana Cartwright, of course—to pick the model. I think you have to give your opinion by noon today."

Damn that Cartwright woman. I was really in the dark here. "Sorry, I didn't know. I haven't had a chance to talk much with Dana. I'll try to find her."

"Okay. Call me later. You don't sound happy. Is something wrong?"

I looked at Lucas, who had gone to the closet and pulled out his overnight bag. "Yeah, but I can't chat right now. Talk to you later." I hung up the phone. "Going somewhere?"

He hesitated. "I wasn't sure if I should stay here."

"I'd like it if you would." I turned off my cell phone, fumbling the button and probably cutting off someone in mid-message. I really didn't care. "I'd like to try to talk this out, Lucas. I think we have a lot going for us. I'd hate to see it—" I didn't want to voice it.

He stood there, deep in thought then he put the bag back in the closet. "I need to get going. I've got some things to do today."

I ached to ask him what, but restrained myself. I got up from the couch, wobbly with emotion, and snatched my book bag off the table near the door. "I should go, too. I've got an interview."

We met at the door and he smiled down at me. "I love you, Bea."

I leaned against him, hampered by being one-armed. "I love you, too, Lucas. I know we can work something out."

"I'm sure we can." I felt the soft touch of his lips on my head.

I tried to ignore the doubt I heard in his voice.

Chapter 13

Lucas walked with me to the elevator and punched the Down button. "Off on an errand for Margaret?" I asked as we stared at each other in the mirror in the elevator foyer.

"Yeah. I'm still on the payroll." He put an arm gently around my shoulder when he saw my glum expression. "It's not the end of the world, Bea. We'll figure out something. We're both moderately intelligent. There must be a solution."

"Speak for yourself. This conference has me…" I left the sentence unfinished since I wasn't sure how to end it. Lucas and I had never argued before. We'd disagreed, yes, but argue? Never. This was new territory for me and I wasn't sure how to handle it.

We got into an elevator with several riders. As we moved to the back, I saw people looking covertly at us, and me in particular, with my sling. I sidled closer to Lucas and he looked down at me and smiled. The tender look in his warm brown eyes made tears come to mine. I didn't want to lose this man. He was way too important to me.

When we got to the lobby, I moved to one side and he followed. We went into the little foyer we'd used the previous day, where there was some relative privacy. "I'm not scheduled for anything for a couple of weeks," I said. "Maybe I could come down to the ranch and we could be together for a while. Maybe have a chance to talk through some things."

He touched my face, his large blunt fingers gentle, sending shivers down my spine. "I'd like that. I don't want to lose you." He bent to me and our lips touched.

"...told you I saw them. I'm sure it's..."

Lucas and I pulled apart and I looked past him, toward the doors leading to the patio. Gwendolyn Bandorf was peeking in the doorway, another woman hovering behind her like a large gaudy cloud getting ready to rain on my parade. "Your fans," he murmured.

I pulled him toward me as strongly as my one arm would allow. "And yours." I raised my face and we really kissed this time, a good old-fashioned lip lock that made my toes curl. When we separated I was truly hot and bothered. "I expect you to follow through on that, mister."

He kissed me again, quickly this time. "I'll try." His eyes went past me and I turned to follow his gaze. David Richardson was coming into the foyer, making a beeline for us. "Another admirer? Seems like the last time a man headed toward you like that, you got kissed in the middle of the lobby."

"Nah. He just owns the hotel." I moved reluctantly away from Lucas. "I meant what I said. I'd like to be with you, somehow, someway."

"We'll figure it out." He watched politely as Richardson came to a stop in front of me.

"I tried to call you but your room line was busy so I tried your cell phone. I hope that was okay. It was the contact number on your registration card." David Richardson's pale blue eyes went to my sling. "I can't believe this has happened to you. It's terrible." He glanced at Lucas then moved slightly closer to me, shifting position to subtly edge Lucas out of his way.

I shifted position, too, so I was closer to Lucas. "This is L. J. Remarchik."

"Ah, yes. Miss Emerson's guest." Richardson extended a hand and gave Lucas' hand a quick shake. "I'm David Richardson. So glad you could join us." He turned his focus back to me, again moving uncomfortably close.

Lucas' lips tightened. Under any other circumstance, I would have been happy at this sign of possible jealousy, but given our recent talk, I wanted to nip it in the bud. "I'm glad he could join us, too." I touched Lucas' hand.

He visibly relaxed. "See you tonight. " After a brief nod to Richardson, Lucas went out the patio door, smiling at the two women who almost fell down from the proximity to a hero come to life.

I watched him go. When I turned back, David Richardson was watching me. For a second his expression was cool and calculating, then it changed and he was once again the sunny host. "I hope you know if there's anything I can do to help, you have only to ask."

"I appreciate the offer." I started to edge away from him but he followed, touching my unslung arm in a proprietary way.

"I'm so pleased you're staying. These…incidents have been very bad for business."

I saw Gwendolyn coming into the main lobby without her buddy. When she caught sight of me, she smiled brightly. I smiled widely in return and started moving toward her, anxious to get away from the Happy Host who seemed so anxious to corral me. "Katherine mentioned some people were leaving. I never really considered it." Of course, I hadn't considered it because I hadn't *thought* of it. Had I thought of it, I might have bolted out of there.

"It's wrecking havoc with our bookings." Richardson continued keeping pace with me, probably oblivious to the fact I was trying to get away.

"Well, murder can do that." When I saw his pained expression, I added, "Of course, it's not your fault. I mean, it's not like the murders are happening just to put you out of business." I laughed unconvincingly. "Someone must have a grudge against Red Nail."

"Why them?" He ignored Gwendolyn, who had reached us and was waiting by my side, unashamedly eavesdropping on our conversation.

"Holly was with Red Nail, and John Brody was vying for a cover slot with them." I didn't mention he was also vying for one with Pittman. I didn't want to complicate my theory. "It's the only thing they have in common."

"They're both at this conference," Gwendolyn pointed out reasonably.

Richardson finally looked at her, his perplexed expression telling me he hadn't even noticed her earlier. He must have been deeply worried because Gwendolyn was hard to miss in her bright aqua capris and matching floral top and toenails, evident in her faux flower flip-flops. For an instant his face paled and he jerked away, as though she'd spit at him. "There are a lot of people at this conference. Why choose them?"

"Convenience. Proximity. Random chance." Gwendolyn shrugged her massive shoulders. "Why does any murder happen?" Her tone of voice was almost challenging, as though she expected him to have answers.

"Money, revenge, or fear," I said absently, remembering a comment a detective had made to me when I was researching my first book. Could one of those really be a motive to kill John Brody and Holly Newcastle?

"None of that would apply here," Richardson said. "There's no motive like that in relation to those people." He darted a nervous glance at Gwen to see how she took this sally.

"Or maybe there's a motive and we just can't see it." Gwendolyn shot Richardson a shrewd look and changed her stance, stiffening and moving marginally closer to him. He swallowed hard and edged away.

I couldn't fault her reasoning but she wasn't helping allay Richardson's worries. "I'm sure the police will get to the bottom of it all." I looked at the schedule peeking out of Gwendolyn's bulging book bag. "You didn't go to a workshop this morning? Didn't you see one that looked interesting?" I began a meander toward the stairs leading to the mezzanine level and the ClueCon rooms.

"I went to an earlier one but decided to take a break. I'm sorry you couldn't do an interview at breakfast but I suppose you wanted to sleep in." Her eyes went to my stylish sling. "Does it hurt much?"

I was surprised by the solicitude in her voice. "Nah. I'll be fine in a day or so. It's just a big bruise." I swung my scrubbed book bag, much less bulgy than hers. "I was thinking I'd go to the bookstore and browse. Care to join me?"

"Sure, I'll tag along."

"Thanks again for offering to help," I told Richardson, who was looking at the front desk and frowning. I followed his gaze and saw an elderly couple, obviously tourists, who were arguing with the desk clerk about something. The man was waving a piece of paper and even from this distance, I heard, "An outrage—we shouldn't have to pay for..."

"Excuse me," he murmured. "I need to —" He

was gone without finishing the sentence.

"I wouldn't be him for all the tea in China," Gwendolyn murmured.

"What do you mean?"

"Well look at him. He has to handle people who are peeved, deal with the police, and try to make a profit in a failing market." She shook her head. "Poor guy."

Maybe I was being cynical, but I didn't hear much sympathy in her voice. I looked around the crowded lobby. "What failing market?" I went toward the stairwell but stopped when Gwendolyn paused at the elevators.

"Bad knees," she said with a smile. "Sorry. I can't handle the stairs."

"Oh. Sure." It seemed polite to wait with her. "You said something about the market?"

"The Florida market. This part of the coast was hammered by hurricanes in the last few years and the resorts are just starting to rebound. A lot of them were sold to casinos and condo developers. Did you notice all the construction going on down on the Parkway and near Holiday Isle? A bunch of new five-star resorts are going up. Pretty soon there won't be any place for regular tourists to vacation along this strip of coastline."

We stepped into the elevator, forcing the people inside to shuffle to accommodate us. "Are you from around here?" I asked, trying to move into a corner and protect my wounded shoulder. I caught a glimpse of her face in the polished metal walls of the elevator. She looked startled, as though surprised I'd asked the question. "You seem pretty knowledgeable about what's happening."

"I'm from up the Coast," she said. "I know some people in real estate in this area."

The elevator dinged and we led the charge out of the crowded space. "This hotel seems to be doing great business," I observed as we meandered down the hall to the area set aside for the bookstore. "I doubt it's in any danger of closing."

"That's not what I heard." Gwendolyn pushed ahead of me into the room, almost tipping over a display of my books near the front entrance. She managed to catch it in time to prevent scattering the latest Cal Delvecchio thriller, *Devils in the Dust*. "I heard the Richardsons are under pressure to sell."

"Really? From who?" I went to one of the six tables in the middle of the room. Each one had a weapon from the Clue game on a pedestal in the middle. I gravitated toward the rope table, probably due to my recent association with John Brody. I picked up a copy of a rival publisher's book and examined the artwork. Mayhem Manor was known for their gritty covers and this latest book from K. L. Lonigan was no exception. It depicted a woman lying on what looked like a Persian rug, her body twisted awkwardly and a knife protruding from her ample bosom. It was classic MM stuff and had the feel of vintage Forties covers. I'd seen some small faux knives by the checkout counter arranged artfully next to the cash register. It was probably a promo item that went with the book. My Cal cover was tame by comparison. I made a mental note to talk to Karen about cover art and see if I could come up with something that would facilitate a fun promo scheme, even though I knew it would be futile. Authors were the last people in the world a publisher cared to please when it came to covers.

"I heard there's a big consortium moving in on the coast, trying to buy up all the prime real estate." Gwendolyn picked up and examined my book then put it back and moved on to another display. I don't think she even realized the author was standing next to her. "It would be a pity if this resort was sold. It's been around for decades. I'd hate to see it change." She looked memory-struck for a minute then shrugged. "But life goes on, I guess. I'm sure all the negative publicity they're getting isn't helping."

"Has it been bad? I haven't had a chance to read a newspaper." I went to a table covered with Red Nail titles, this one with the Clue wrench on a pedestal in the middle. These covers were what I expected, replete with half-naked men, bosomy women, and draped clothing almost revealing the naughty bits. The inclusion of a mystery element—knife, gun, or blood—was secondary to the flesh.

"It's been terrible." On the opposite side of the table, Gwendolyn picked up and examined Aidan Lindsey's book that had a pair of long legs in stiletto heels on the cover. A gun dangled from one manicured hand of the unseen woman and through her legs we could see a man, lying on the ground, obviously dead from a gunshot wound. Several pairs of stilettos dotted the table. I eyed them warily. Even in my younger days, I wasn't known for my ability to balance on such precarious pumps.

"That one detective was interviewed on TV, that woman. She made it sound like security was bad here and that's why the murders were happening."

"Ramone?" The mention of the slinky detective made my stomach knot, reminding me of Lucas and our earlier discussion. I grabbed a book from the stack in front of me and opened it at random. *His pulsing member entered her engorged...* "Oh, for heaven's sake." I dropped the book back onto the Red Nail stack and hastily moved away from the soft-core porn. "Why would Ramone say something like that? Brody wasn't even killed on hotel grounds and surely Holly's killer was a stranger who ..." I let the words trail away when Gwendolyn looked at me in disbelief. "All right, it had to be someone from the conference. It wasn't a random stranger. But that doesn't mean it was the fault of hotel security."

"You know it and I know it, but tell that to John Q. Public." She looked at the clock above the door. "It's almost time for lunch. Would you mind if I sit with you? I'd love to have a chance to talk plot with you."

I was relieved to have a ready excuse. "I'm supposed to do an interview thing." I saw her disappointed look and added, "But I don't know if I have to sit in any particular spot. Let's check with the organizers and if it works, that'll be fine."

She brightened and I mentally berated myself for even hesitating. I well remembered what it was like to be a hopeful in the publishing world. If an hour's conversation with me would give her a boost, then I shouldn't begrudge her the time.

We headed toward the ballroom where people were starting to queue up at the closed doors. I saw Mary Carr and Clair near the front of the line, deep in conversation. George was nearby, talking to two people I didn't recognize. Several of the male models, J. J. Butterfield among them, were in a small group, talking to adoring women. He glimpsed me and turned away but not before I saw the alarmed look on his face. I silently thanked Lucas for frightening him enough to keep him off my back.

I kept one ear tuned to Gwendolyn, who was chatting with the people around us, and my gaze trained on the people drifting toward the doors. I had to find K. L. Lonigan and figure out what was required of me during this upcoming interview thing.

"Are you feeling better?"

I turned. Tony Jackson, one of the models, had broken away from the crowd of beautiful people. His tough guy good looks were a nice change of pace from the other pretty faces. For the first time I looked at him and the others in the role of cover model, probably because of the covers I'd just evaluated. With a bit of touch-up, Jackson might make a decent Cal. "I'm fine. Just a bit sore."

"You were lucky. From what I heard, it could have been …"

"Fatal? Yeah, I know." I looked at the clutch of male beauty ahead of us in the line. "How's the contest stuff going? I haven't had a chance to get very involved, I've been kind of busy." I lifted my left arm gingerly.

"Okay, I guess." He sounded dispirited.

"I suppose the murders have put a damper on all the fun."

"To be honest…" He leaned closer. "This is the first time I've ever been in one of these things. It's not that much fun. It's just a bunch of schmoozing." He looked bewildered. "I've only done a bit of modeling, but the agency sent me to this thing. They said it could help my career."

I laughed. "Don't tell anybody, but publishing is a bunch of schmoozing. The actual writing is only a small part of it."

"I'm starting to see that."

"So you don't model full-time?"

He shook his head, whispering conspiratorially, "Don't tell anybody, but I'm a construction worker. If the guys in my crew found out, I'd be hounded for a week."

I grinned. "Your secret is safe with me." My phone thumped my butt even as it chimed the opening bars to *Hotel California*. "Excuse me, I'm being paged." I shifted my bag to my wounded arm and extracted the phone as the line started to shuffle forward. "Hello?"

"Miss Emerson? This is Dana Cartwright."

Crowd murmurs around me made it difficult to hear. "I need to talk to you," I said. "Karen said something about the banquet tonight?"

"I had hoped to meet you for lunch, but I got

JL Wilson

sidetracked. I'll …some information … front desk …duties tonight." The cell phone signal started to break up.

"Duties?" The lunch line started moving faster.

"Two models … for your covers will sit …tonight at the banquet…in character as …Delvecchio so you can…"

"How were they chosen?"

"…voted and Clair Delacroix also … the best depiction of…you need to decide…"

There was a stir in the crowd ahead of us. "I'll get us a seat." Gwendolyn flexed her arms, forming a substantial wedge with her overweight torso. "Just follow behind me. I'll wave if you get lost so you can find me."

"I have to go now," I said as the murmuring around me swelled to a muted buzz. "Please call me later so we can discuss this, I may not be able to attend tonight."

"…mandatory…Pittman…contract…six   p.m. with the other authors who…"

I didn't have time to answer because the doors opened and the crowd surged forward around me. "Hang on," Jackson said as he and Gwendolyn moved ahead of me like a solid human shield. I closed my phone and spent a breathless few minutes trying to avoid being trampled as conference attendees spilled into the ballroom and fanned out, people racing for tables and plopping down book bags and tilting chairs to 'save' seats.

I took my time once I got past the initial bedlam to assess the room. Jackson had branched off and was heading to a table with a large placard of a Clue weapon in the centerpiece. I noticed the other models doing the same, moving off toward tables with the gun, rope, pipe, and candlestick on over-sized mockups of the cards from the game. It must have been the organizers' way of delegating them to

176

different spots.

Like yesterday, the room was filled with round tables seating eight with barely enough room to walk between them. I caught a glimpse of Gwendolyn. She was hard to miss due to her bulk and the bright aqua colors of her clothing. She was plowing forward to a table near the stage and speaker's podium, several other women towed behind her in her wake. As I neared them, Katherine Maxfield emerged from a door behind the stage leading presumably to the serving area beyond. She was talking to a man in a starched white coat, probably the headwaiter. When she saw me she held up a hand in a 'wait a minute' gesture.

I saw Gwendolyn had dropped her book bag on a chair at a table in the second row, near the stage. As I joined her, Katherine came over.

"We've got a seat for you there," she said, gesturing to a table with a "Reserved" sign on it. "We'll be giving out some awards at lunch and we wanted everyone who will be going up on the stage to sit at one table."

"Sorry." I smiled ruefully at Gwendolyn. "Looks like I've been delegated to a seat. Can I take a rain check?"

"Sure." Although her voice was discouraged, she smiled gamely as she sat down, plucking up her book bag. Another conference attendee immediately pounced on the empty and unsaved seat.

I felt bad I'd disappointed her. "I'm sure I'll see you at the banquet tonight."

Gwendolyn brightened. "You're one of the judges, aren't you?"

I belatedly remembered I was supposed to find Dana Cartwright and discover just what my role was to be. "I'm not sure. But if I'm not, maybe I'll see you there."

"Good. I'll look forward to it."

I trailed after Katherine to the Reserved table, where K. L. Lonigan and four other people were already taking seats. Lunch passed with the usual small talk and exchange of information between relative strangers. Because we were at the head table, we were served first and thus finished our meals first. Katherine took the stage to make presentations just as many attendees were being served their main course. As she started talking, Lonigan handed me a list of questions. "We do this at every ClueCon," he said leaning over to speak in a soft voice so we didn't interfere with Katherine's speech. "It's just a way for the people to get to know you and provide some entertainment during dessert."

I remembered telling Lucas something similar and felt a pang. Where was he? What kind of work was he doing for Margaret? We hadn't even talked about that. He had flittered in and out of my mind throughout the morning, my concern about our relationship warring with everything else going on around me. I stared down at the questions, not really seeing them, my mind preoccupied with Lucas and all that had transpired between us earlier in the morning.

It wasn't until Lonigan whispered, "Come on, we're up," that I realized I'd zoned out completely and it was my turn to sit on the stage. I followed him up the four steps and we sat down at the rectangular table covered by a white linen tablecloth. I tried to slide my chair under the table, but it caught on the fabric of the cloth and threatened to tip the table, so I desisted, instead leaning back and taking the microphone from the stand on the table. After much tussling Lonigan and I got it out of its holder and I waved it to the crowd, who applauded our efforts with laughter.

Lonigan started by recapping my publishing

career with Pittman and succinctly summarizing the events in Abilene the previous summer, where I'd inadvertently become involved in two murder cases. "We can only hope history doesn't repeat itself here," he finished with a grin at me then the audience.

"I hope not. I was in the middle of a shootout last time. I'd rather not go through again, thank you." That near-death experience in Abilene had taught me with graphic clarity how deadly guns were. Fiction couldn't begin to describe the smells and sounds of a gun battle.

Lonigan asked me the first of the questions on the list: "Tell us how you get ideas for the murders you craft."

I had a ready answer for this and I launched into my modus operandi, which usually consisted of watching the news, daydreaming, reading the newspaper, daydreaming, and surfing the Internet and daydreaming.

We worked through the other questions he'd showed me and I started to relax. Despite having a thousand people staring at me, it wasn't hard. Most of the questions had been tossed at me in other interviews in one form or another, so there were no surprises lurking. Lonigan was a good interviewer, prompting me when I appeared stalled and adding anecdotes of his own to enhance what I said.

As we were nearing the end of the prepared list and getting ready to take questions from the audience, he leaned back in his chair. I saw his attention wander as he shoved his legs under the table. He leaned over and moved the tablecloth so it didn't drape over his sandaled feet. He jerked back and for a minute I thought he'd been stung by an insect. Color drained out of his face, leaving two dark splotches of red on his cheekbones, where his beard didn't reach.

After a brief hesitation, he shifted his chair and

turned so most of his body faced away from the audience. He put his microphone on the floor and leaned over slightly as though to touch his sandal.

"Look under the table," he muttered.

I stumbled over whatever word was in my mouth and opened my eyes wide. I didn't dare say anything because my microphone was still in my hot little hand and I was facing the audience, who stared expectantly at me as I gaped at him.

Lonigan picked up his microphone and fiddled with the index cards in his hand, slipping one out of the stack. "Whoops." He dropped the cards and the mike, the small squares sliding across the rug to my feet. "Sorry," he said loudly to the audience, his voice unamplified but carrying in the quiet room. "Thank goodness that was the last question I had."

As we both leaned over to pick up the cards, he whispered, "Check under the table."

I stretched forward and flicked aside the tablecloth draped down to the floor over the table. For a second I didn't see anything then my eyes adjusted to the darker space.

Patrice Samuels was sprawled under the table, lying on her back. She wore a golden-brown pantsuit and her signature turquoise necklace, this one shaped like a dolphin, was resting on one ample breast.

The chain of the necklace was tangled in the knife stuck in her heart.

Chapter 14

"Oh, shit," I breathed.

Lonigan looked up at me from his bent-over position, where he was randomly picking up index cards. "What do we do?" he whispered.

I thought frantically. If we exposed the body, panic would ensue. Three dead bodies in two days were too much for any group of people to endure, even if some of them were hardened mystery writers. "Finish the interview," I whispered back. "Let's cut it short."

He nodded and straightened up. "I'm afraid I got too nosy and we've run over time so we can't take any questions." There were murmurs from people in the audience. He forced out an unconvincing laugh. "It's probably just as well since I managed to drop all my index cards with the questions on them."

I saw Katherine's startled expression. She looked at her watch and then at us, shaking her head. "Plenty of time," she called out.

"Thanks so much for the chance to chat with you," I said, grabbing my microphone and standing up. "I'm looking forward to the rest of the conference. Don't forget my workshop later today. I'm on a panel this afternoon and I'd love to have a chance to chat with you all there." I watched with satisfaction as people shot to their feet and started gathering their belongings. My conference experience had taught me people were always happy to have a bit of a breather after lunch and this crowd didn't prove me wrong.

Katherine came to the front of the stage, leaning forward. "We have plenty of time for questions and answers if you want to—"

I knelt down to talk to her as K. L. unplugged the microphones and put them on the table covering Patrice. "Call the police," I said in a low voice.

"What?" Katherine stepped back to peer up at me.

Gwendolyn Bandorf muscled her way through the crowd of people moving toward the stage. "That was great," she said. "It was so neat to hear how you plotted your first book. I always thought that having Cal—"

"Could you do me a favor?" I smiled down at Gwendolyn.

"Sure. What?" She looked so pleased to be asked I almost felt ashamed.

Almost.

"I'm not feeling real good." I touched my arm, still in the sling. "Do you think you could ask these people to give me some R&R time? I'll answer all questions at the workshop."

"No problem." She turned and began talking to the people who were lining up to chat with K.L. and me. Waiters started to converge on the tables, probably happy to wrap up their duties a few minutes early.

"Call the police," I said again to Katherine. "We've got a problem."

Man, was that an understatement.

****

Forty-five minutes later I was once again sitting

at the front 'Reserved' table, watching Pete Martinelli on the stage as he watched the coroner examine Patrice Samuels.

Martinelli turned a disgusted look on me. "Bodies keep turning up wherever you are."

"Hey, it's not my fault. I just find 'em. I don't put them there." I took the ibuprofen Katherine handed me and swallowed it with some melted ice water from the pitcher on the table. She was sitting near me, hands folded placidly on her cane as crime scene technicians swarmed around the stage, dusting, cataloging, measuring, and snapping pictures. Her resemblance to Jessica Fletcher was uncanny, especially given the way her sharp eyes took in every detail as the techs worked.

Martinelli walked down the three steps from the stage and pulled out a chair near us. "So tell me again what happened."

I glanced at K.L. Lonigan, who shrugged and repeated what we both had said earlier. "...my foot and realized something was under the table. I checked and saw Patrice."

We all looked up at the stage as the coroner straightened up. "You can move the body now," he told the men who were waiting nearby, holding a black body bag.

Most of this operation was thankfully hidden from our view by the table. I caught a peek of one gold lamè pump as Patrice was unceremoniously zipped up and moved to the waiting gurney at the foot of the stairs. The coroner watched as the body was moved then jumped down from the stage and came to stand next to Martinelli. He held up something in a plastic bag. Martinelli took it and examined it closely.

"That's mine," K. L. blurted.

I glanced at him. He was deathly pale and the lenses of his glasses flashed in the overhead lights, giving him a Little Orphan Annie appearance.

"Really?" Martinelli held up the plastic bag. The small knife inside was slightly curved with a cylindrical handle in the shape of a woman's body.

"I mean, those are my promo knives. I had them made for my latest book. They're not really knives, they're letter openers. I give them out at book signings. They're for promotion. They aren't really knives. They're plastic. I mean, they're metal but they're plastic too. The handle. It's plastic. The blade is metal."

He was babbling, twisting a bit of the tablecloth as he did so. I put a hand on his to calm him. "I saw them in the bookstore," I said. "They had some at the checkout counter."

"You hand out knives?" Martinelli asked.

I squeezed K.L.'s hand when he looked panicked. "We hand out all kinds of crap to entice the public," I snapped. "Quit picking on him."

"I haven't been accused of being a bully since I don't know when." Martinelli appeared amused rather than offended by this.

"Glad to refresh your memory of what it feels like. Anybody could have gotten that knife so it doesn't mean much that it was used as a weapon."

"Anybody? Don't you have to buy a book?"

I looked at K.L. He nodded. "It's a giveaway, right?" I prompted. "They buy the book, they get the knife?"

He cleared his throat and croaked, "I hand them out a signings but I brought some here so they could be included with the sale."

"It's a good promo," I said grudgingly. I hadn't yet found a signature promo item to include with my books. I'd always thought bookmarks were throwaways and other kitsch—memo pads, pens, luggage tags—didn't fit with my books or my main character. That little six-inch knife/letter opener was a great idea.

"I got them through this web site," he said, momentarily diverted from Martinelli, who watched us with an exasperated expression. "I can send you the link if you'd like. They do all kinds of things for—"

"Excuse me? Murder?"

Martinelli's words and cold voice made K.L.'s voice dry up in his throat. With a hacking cough, he fumbled for a water glass. I nudged one nearer to him. "How long has she been dead?" I asked. "She wasn't killed there, right?"

Martinelli eyed me warily. "And you're basing your assumption on...what?"

"Not enough blood. No signs of a struggle. It's an awkward space to kill someone in. It makes more sense to kill her elsewhere and bring her in." I tapped the table, anxious to take notes. "Although it would be tricky, too. Patrice wasn't a small woman. I mean, she's...bulky." I thought that sounded better than saying, 'fat', although Patrice couldn't hear me, so what did it matter? I barreled ahead. "She could have been brought in last night. They used a similar table at lunch yesterday, up on the stage. Did they have the same setup for the banquet last night?" I looked expectantly at Katherine, who shook her silver head.

"We had the banquet in a different room. Yes, this is the same setup. We asked that the table be left in place because we were supposed to interview you this morning, at breakfast."

I turned to Martinelli. "So how long has she been dead?"

"None of your business." He stood and regarded us with a calculating expression. "I think I'd like you all to come to police headquarters and make a statement."

Lonigan moaned softly.

185

"It's just routine," I said with assurance.

"We'd better cancel your workshops," Katherine said. "You and K.L. were both scheduled to talk this afternoon. Although I'm sure word has gotten out already. At this rate, we'll be lucky if anybody stays around long enough to attend the award ceremonies tomorrow night." She heaved herself to her feet, leaning heavily on her cane.

I got up to help her, putting a consoling arm around her shoulders. "Come on, these folks are tough. Surely a little excitement won't keep them away." I looked down at Lonigan, who appeared pole-axed by the knowledge he'd have to give a statement at the local police headquarters. "Come on. No biggie."

"A little excitement?" Martinelli stood, too and gestured toward the exit. "I'd hate to see your idea of a lot of excitement." He nodded to two uniformed officers who came forward to meet us. "Take these folks downtown. I'll be along in a minute."

"Where's the lovely Ms. Ramone?" I asked, walking slowly alongside Katherine, Lonigan on her other side.

"Busy."

"Doing what?"

"None of your business."

It is if she's messing with my man, I thought. The words almost sneaked out but I restrained myself in time. "I may call my lawyer."

Martinelli sighed loudly. "Feel free. Do you need a quarter to cover the call?"

I shot him a haughty look as the two officers started herding us toward the kitchen exit. "I can manage, thank you."

I thought about Ramone's A.W.O.L. status during the entire time we cooled our heels at the Ft. Walton Beach Police Department then gave our statements to Martinelli in the presence of a police stenographer. I gave my statement first then K.L. was called in to talk to Martinelli. While he spoke I called George, who'd left several messages on my phone. I assured him I was fine and would be back at the hotel soon, then settled down to wait for my fellow eyewitnesses.

K.L. took off as soon as he finished, leaving me to wait for Katherine. I had twenty minutes to sit and stew, imagining Lucas and Ramone enjoying cocktails together by the pool. By the time Katherine and I got back to the Sandy Shores Resort almost two full hours after we'd left, I had convinced myself that Ramone and Lucas had run off somewhere and I would find a 'Dear Jane' note in the room, waiting on my return.

I almost fainted with relief when I saw Ramone as I entered the hotel lobby. Lucas was nowhere near the slinky Hispanic detective. She was, in fact, deep in conversation with Gwendolyn Bandorf. The two women stood to one side near the small foyer where I'd spent so much of my conference in conversation with various people. Poor Gwendolyn was probably being interrogated, although from the look on Ramone's face, maybe she was the one undergoing a grilling. Gwendolyn appeared to quiver with anger, her eyes narrowed and her chin jutting out. It looked like she wanted to take a swing at Ramone, but good sense stopped her.

As though feeling my eyes on them, both women abruptly stopped talking and looked at me while Katherine and I walked past. I smiled at Gwendolyn then frowned at Ramone, who returned my look with such a smirky expression I longed to join Gwendolyn in potential hitting.

"Miss Emerson?" The concierge hurried out from behind his faux cherry counter, holding a large mailing envelope. "This was left for you."

I took the plump envelope and stuffed it into the

book bag dangling from my slinged arm. "I think I'll have a breather before the banquet," I said as Katherine and I paused at the elevators.

"I need to talk to the conference committee," Katherine said tiredly. "We need to see if we can salvage anything for the rest of the conference."

"Well, I'm staying even if no one else is." I stabbed the Up button.

"That's good of you." She patted my sling then jerked her hand away. "Sorry."

"It's my shoulder that hurts, not my arm. No problem. Oh, before I forget. Would it be possible to make sure Gwendolyn Bandorf sits with me tonight? I meant to sit with her at lunch, but I didn't know I had to sit at the reserved table."

"That's nice of you." Katherine pulled a small memo pad out of her pocket and jotted a note. "I'll make sure to mention it to Barb, she's in charge of seating. I'm sure Gwendolyn will appreciate it. She's had such a tough time of it. I have to admit, I was surprised when I saw her at our conference."

"How so? Isn't she a MWA member?" The Mystery Writers of America were the parent group ClueCon was affiliated with.

"No, she's not in our chapter. But she is local. I saw her name in the papers a few years ago. Her husband was sent to prison and died there."

"Husband?" I tried to imagine overweight, plain, fashion-wreck Gwendolyn married and failed in the attempt. "Why was he in prison?"

"He was somehow connected to organized crime. I don't remember the details, but I remember the name and her face. It was in all the newspapers down here. I was so surprised to see her sign up for the conference. I didn't know she was a writer."

"Maybe she's trying to exorcise old ghosts." I knew how it went. I'd done that and managed to pen a best seller, the one causing problems between

Lucas and I.

"I'm relieved the press hasn't caught on to the fact she's here. She was such a celebrity a few years ago. That's all we need. Our chapter relies on this conference for a big part of our yearly revenue."

I stepped into the elevator as the doors opened. "I'm sure things will be fine. Try not to worry. I'll see you tonight." Futile words, I know. 'Try not to worry'.

Do what I say, not what I do?

I got to my suite and checked my mobile phone for messages before putting it in the charger. Lucas hadn't called, although my mother had and so had Karen Levy. I took some more ibuprofen, experimented with life without my sling and discovered it was possible, and took a nice relaxing shower and changed into my 'dress clothes', a pair of lightweight summer slacks and a nice glittery top. Without the sling, I felt able to face the world again.

I first called Mavis and gave her the lowdown on the assorted events. "The girls won't believe this," she told me when I finished. "Three murders and you're there again."

"It's a coincidence," I snapped. Clair's 'Typhoid Mary' comment still stung.

"Maybe you're a murder magnet." She sounded cheerful, as though this was a Good Thing. "It's like Miss Marple or Jessica Fletcher. All those murders happened when they were around, and no one ever thought they were clever enough to solve the crime. Perhaps the murderer is underestimating you."

I started to protest being compared to Miss Marple and Jessica Fletcher, both quite older and frumpier than me. Mavis didn't give me the chance, though.

"What does Lucas say about it all?"

I drew on fifty years of experience lying to my mother. "The local police have asked for his help. I mean, let's face it, he's had a lot of experience in this area. I've barely had time to talk to him about it."

"Hmm." There was a long, ominous pause. "Well, give him my regards. Will he be coming with you when you come home for Mother's Day?"

"I hope so. He's working for Margaret Troolin, you know. So it'll depend on his schedule." As I hoped, this diverted her into chatting about what kinds of work he might be doing, why he was working when he was retired, and how busy he was keeping. I finally managed to beg off by explaining I had to make some more calls. Mavis let me go with promises to call her tomorrow before the award ceremony so she could wish me luck.

I took a break and made myself a liquor drink before opening the bulky envelope left for me at the concierge desk. It was from Dana Cartwright and had one sheet of printed information and photos clipped together.

Miss Emerson: Please plan to be at Ballroom B tonight at 5:45 PM. You will be sitting with Tony Jackson and Rob Peters, the two models who are finalists for your Cal Delvecchio covers (note that Mr. Jackson is also a finalist for a Red Nail cover, so he will be splitting time between your table and that of Mary Carr). At the end of the evening, you will decide which man will be the cover model for your next two Pittman books in the Delvecchio series, as well as the model for books going into reprints. See attached biographies and portfolio samples.

I leafed through the 'attached biographies and portfolio samples'. The information sheet for Tony Jackson said he was forty-five, a divorced father of two from South Carolina, and had been in modeling for a decade. The other model, Rob Peters, was thirty-five and from California, and had modeled all his life. I skimmed the pictures, all of them looking like ads for classy menswear. Peters was more classically handsome than Jackson, with chiseled, leading-man looks, sort of like Hugh Jackman or Pierce Brosnan. I couldn't visualize him as my Cal, but to be honest, I was having trouble with Tony Jackson, too. Let's face it—Lucas was Cal in my mind, and had been ever since last year in Abilene.

I stuffed the material back in the envelope and used my cell phone to call Margaret Troolin in Abilene. She didn't answer so I left a message as my room phone rang.

"Ready for some company?" George asked.

"Whenever you are." I folded my cell phone and tucked it in a pocket.

Within seconds my hotel door was flung open and Clair came in, pocketing my room card. George followed close behind. "Where's the booze? I need a nice stiff drink. Tell all and leave no facts unspoken." He strode across the room to the kitchenette and proceeded to rattle glassware as George sat down opposite me on the couch. I told them what had happened, including seeing Ramone and Gwendolyn in the lobby.

"It was odd," I said, sipping my 'Clair-refreshed' drink. It packed a real wallop. "I could have sworn Gwen was reading Ramone the riot act."

"Ms. Bandorf? The large woman in the rather conspicuous aqua outfit?" George asked. I nodded. "She reminds me of Mrs. Beauchamp."

"Who's Mrs. Beauchamp?" I asked, running through a mental list of authors.

"My fifth grade teacher. She has the same look about her, as though she's only acting nice but in reality she could arm-wrestle a person into submission."

I had a sudden memory of Mrs. Stewart, the dragon lady of West Elementary back in Washburn Creek, Iowa. I guess everyone had a teacher like that in their background.

"I mean, let's face it. All she'd have to do is sit on somebody and they'd be wounded." Clair hurried on when I shot him a 'how rude' look. "You'll be happy to know we've been doing some detecting of our own."

"And?" I cautiously lifted my drink with my left arm, pleased there was little pain. Of course, two hefty shots of booze in an hour might have anesthetized me enough not to notice it.

"These were all disguised murders," he announced.

"Disguised?"

"Holly's neck was snapped," George explained. "She wasn't beaten to death with the wrench. Patrice was killed by a sharp object, but not the knife. Brody—"

"Had sex with Holly Newcastle before he died," Clair finished triumphantly.

"What?" I almost dropped my drink. "They did?"

"Yep. The rope was a sex toy, just like we thought. The police don't think that murder was premeditated. It was more of a convenience murder. The rope was an afterthought."

"Where are you getting all your inside information?"

"The lovely Donna Del Marco," George said. "I gave her a call this afternoon and we had a long chat. I invited her over for drinks after dinner tonight, I hope that was okay?" He didn't wait for my approval or disapproval. "Yes, apparently Donna still has some friends on the police force and she called in some favors."

"So how was Brody killed? With the rope?"

Clair looked so smug I knew it had to be something else. "Allergies."

I choked on the sip of booze in my mouth. "Hunh?"

"He was stung by a bee and had an allergic

reaction. His throat swelled up."

"But—but—" Dozens of responses hit the front of my brain, bounced off the bourbon, and spilled out. "Didn't he carry one of those pens—those epi pen things for allergic people? Why didn't he call for help? A bee? At night? How do they know? I saw him. He didn't look swollen. How does somebody look when they've died of allergies?" I looked from Clair to George, who held up a restraining hand.

"All good questions which I think you should ask L.J. when you see him next."

I closed my mouth with a snap, all my earlier insecurities flooding back. "Why ask him?"

"He's obviously working with the police on this," Clair said with elaborate patience. "So go right to the source."

Two pairs of male eyes regarded me with unwavering curiosity. "Sure. I will. When I see him." I glanced at the clock over the microwave. "Oops. Time to go. I'm supposed to get to this banquet thing early."

"That's right, you're Queen for the Day, or at least one of the Queens." Clair picked up our glassware and put them on the counter. "You and some of the male models."

"Meow meow," George murmured.

"Oh, please." Clair followed me to the door and watched as I snatched up my small beaded handbag. "You're not taking that bag, are you? It doesn't match your top."

"It's dressy, it's beaded, and it's small. That's all that matters."

"Honestly, Ralph, you have no fashion sense."

"Well, it beats having no sense at all." I slammed my door and we headed off toward the elevators. "Besides, I've got you guys to tell me what to do. You have more fashion sense than Carter has little pills."

Clair eyed me critically as I strode ahead of them. I could feel his eyes on me. "Not a bad outfit, but a bit casual," he volunteered as we waited for the elevator. "And your hair...well, I could have dressed it, you know."

I checked my look in the mirror at the elevator. A worried, tired, fifty-something woman looked back at me, wisps of hair escaping her French braid. "It's fine. You can play beauty shop tomorrow night for the award ceremony."

"They changed the time, you know," George commented as we stepped into the elevator. "Apparently people were getting nervous about a late evening out, so they're going to do the awards before dinner instead of afterwards. The shindig starts at 5:30 instead of 7:00."

"Like that will matter," Clair said, leaning back against the elevator wall as we lurched downward. "I mean, it's not like a killer needs the cover of darkness to do his dastardly deeds. Look at Patrice."

"Yeah, what about Patrice?" George looked thoughtfully at me and I could almost see the wheels spinning in his closely-cropped head. "When was she killed? If she was killed in place, it must have been during the morning hours. That room was probably empty most of the morning."

I moved back to allow new arrivals to get into the car. "I'll bet changing the time for the ceremony threw the hotel for a loop."

"Nope, from what I heard, people are leaving in droves. I think they're just happy our little convention is staying on. Otherwise it would be a ghost town here." Clair bobbed up and down on his heels. "That has its advantages, of course, but I'm sure it is bad for business."

"Advantages?"

"Faster service at the bar, fewer crowds, more room at the swimming pool."

I snorted with laughter. "You've got the bar taken care of, you love crowds, and I've never seen you at any swimming pool except to lounge and ogle people."

Clair shrugged. "It still pays to accentuate the positive." The elevator door chimed as it opened and we waited our turn to depart. Clair gestured grandly. "After you, Queen Bea. Ha! I made a joke. She's the Queen Bea. Get it?"

George groaned and followed us out. As we emerged I peered around the lobby and spotted a familiar lanky shape dressed in dark slacks and a gray suit coat near the front door.

"Isn't that L.J?" Clair asked.

I did a double take. Was it...? Yep, there was Lucas on the other side of the lobby, leaning against the wall, his arms crossed. He was smiling at someone, his craggy face happy.

I breathed out a sigh of relief. His posture told me all was okay. Whatever had caused him to run off for the day had been resolved and he could relax now. I hurried across the room to join him.

He straightened and I saw who he was talking to.

Sereta Ramone.

I stopped. Logic warred with jealousy. She was a cop and maybe they were talking cop business. The way Lucas had acted with me earlier in the day, his words, his actions—I had to believe he loved me. I had to believe he was anxious to keep our relationship going.

I had to believe...

Ramone said something that made Lucas laugh. She smiled at his reaction and shifted position, her stance now more inviting and open.

That wasn't a cop look I saw in her pale hazel eyes.

Chapter 15

I pretended not to see. "Come on," I said to George, nudging him toward the ballroom. "I don't want to be late."

"What's the rush? Wasn't that L.J.?"

"He's busy," I snapped.

"But why isn't he—"

"I'll explain later," Clair hissed. "Just move along."

I wished Clair would explain it to me. I followed the other people going into the ballroom and hurried to the table with the "Pittman" sign dead center in the middle. Tony Jackson was standing at a nearby table with a "Red Nail" sign, talking to Mary Carr and J.J. Butterfield. He smiled when I noticed him. "I'll be over for dessert," he called. "Save me a seat."

"Ooh. Dessert. I like the sound of that." Clair peered at the place cards on the table. "Looks like you're with the hoi polloi. Us peons will go and have fun without you."

I looked blankly at the cards as he and George waved wildly to friends and took off. Seats to my left were assigned to Rob Peters, Tony Jackson, Bob Marshall (an agent I vaguely remembered) and John

Scarlino, an editor at Pittman. An empty seat was next to mine on the right with "Reserved" on the place card and next to it was a spot for Gwendolyn Bandorf.

Rob Peters materialized at my right side. "Allow me." He pulled out my chair and I settled down, putting my little beaded bag under the chair. "You don't mind if we switch cards, do you?" he asked, reaching out for the "Reserved" sign next to me.

"Is this place taken?"

My stomach knotted at the sound of a husky Texas accent. Lucas smoothly intercepted the chair from Rob. He smiled at the other man then turned to me. "Well, Bea? Is this place taken?" He leaned closer to me, covering the movement as he sat down and scooted his chair in. "The place in your heart, that is?"

I looked into his warm brown eyes, flecked with honey-gold color. Like honey, I melted at the warmth I saw there. "Yes, it is," I admitted. "It's taken by this dumb Texan who keeps vanishing and leaving me alone, only to reappear deep in conversation with a sexy Hispanic woman who's making cow eyes at him."

"Well, you got the 'cow' part right, at least." Lucas leaned even closer, his breath warm on my ear. "You won't be alone tonight. This Texan is sticking close to home."

"Home?" I whispered.

"It's wherever you are."

I looked up at Rob Peters. "Sorry," I said weakly. "Don't want to mess with the seating arrangements."

Lucas snapped open his napkin. "And you also don't want to mess with me."

"Behave yourself," I whispered.

He raised an eyebrow. "Do I have to?"

I opened my napkin. "You've got a lot of explaining to do, buster. I expect answers."

"I'll give 'em to you. Care for a roll?" He held out the basket of buns and winked.

I snatched one and passed the basket on to Rob Peters, on my left. "Damn it, Lucas. What's going on? How come—"

He held up a finger to his lips as Katherine tapped her wine glass and stood. "Be polite," he whispered. "We'll talk later."

"Thanks for getting me the seat," Gwendolyn said as she plopped down next to Lucas. She stuck out one hand, the bright pink nail polish matching her floral pink dress. "Gwen Bandorf. And you are?"

"L.J. Remarchik," Lucas said. "I'm Miss Emerson's lover."

I choked on my roll.

"Ooh, you're the man in her last book, the romance novel." Gwendolyn's eyes glittered with anticipation. "How's it feel to be a nationally known hero?"

Lucas buttered his bread with imperturbable calm. "Pretty good. But I really prefer to just be Bea's hero."

"Wow." Gwendolyn almost melted.

I glared at Lucas. He smiled angelically at me. "I'm just playing my part, darlin'."

True to his word, he was outrageous throughout the entire dinner, charming everyone at the table with stories about his previous job as a homicide detective with the Abilene PD and before that with the Texas Rangers. It wasn't until we were halfway through dessert I realized he'd taken the spotlight off of me, allowing me to relax for the first time since I'd arrived at the conference. I slipped my hand under the table and gave his leg a squeeze. He turned those warm brown eyes on me and whispered, "Is that a promise?"

"You know it is," I replied.

Katherine came over to the table and leaned

next to me, separating us. "Sorry to break up this little tête-à-tête, but I need your vote for the cover model." She handed me a slip of paper and I unfolded it, turning toward Lucas to hide it from prying eyes. 'Tony Jackson' and 'Rob Peters' were typed on the paper. I took the pen Katherine handed me and circled Tony's name then handed both the paper and pen back to her.

"That was fast." She added the paper to the others she held in her hand.

Lucas sipped the bourbon drink he'd purchased at the cash bar. "Good choice."

"You think so?" I asked, suddenly anxious.

Katherine and Lucas both nodded. "Definitely." She winked at me and toddled off, going to the Red Nail table next.

Tony Jackson raised his cocktail. "Here's to Rafael Emerson and the books she pens. Long may she write."

"Hear, hear," John Scarlino said, raising his glass.

I leaned toward Tony. "I hope you won't be disappointed if you win," I said. "The Red Nail contract would probably give you more exposure. Erotica sells so well." I smiled at Rob Peters, who smiled good-naturedly in return.

Tony grinned at me. "I think your covers will have more staying power." He glanced beyond me to Lucas and some message passed between the two men. "That's what women value, right? Staying power?"

I laughed out loud at the solemn look Lucas gave me as he nodded.

"How many books do you have planned in the series?" Gwen asked, peering around Lucas to look at me.

"I have two more drafted and a couple of ideas for a few others." I saw the humor in Lucas' eyes. "At the rate I'm going, I'm never going to be asked back to a conference, so I'd better not count on speaker's fees to pay the rent."

"I think between the two of us, you'll manage to make your car payments," he said wryly.

"Does that mean you're getting married?" Gwen asked. Her dark gray/blue eyes shifted from me to Lucas, anxious and anticipatory.

One of those awkward silences fell at the table. Lucas stared into my eyes. "Does it?"

"Is that a proposal?" I asked, picking up my glass with trembling fingers.

He put his arm on the back of my chair and touched my left shoulder, careful not to rest his hand too heavily on the bruise there. "It's not exactly the way I planned it, but yes, it is a proposal. What do you say we make this whole thing permanent?"

"Tony Jackson will be the next Cal Delvecchio," Katherine boomed into the microphone.

I stared open-mouthed at Lucas as applause broke out. Tony laughed. "I think I've been upstaged."

I looked around at the tables of people, all staring at us. "What?"

"I'm your cover model and L.J. just proposed to you," Tony said, raising his glass again. "Can we have a toast to all of our good fortune?"

I held up my glass and turned to Lucas. "You bet."

"Is that a yes?"

I leaned forward, throwing caution to the wind. "Yep."

"Hot damn!" He took my glass from me and set it on the table, then pulled me to my feet. "Kiss me." He carefully wrapped his arms around me.

I didn't hear the murmurs, laughter, or exclamations as I sank into his kiss.

****

"I can't believe he proposed and we weren't there to see it," Clair complained an hour later. "Honestly, we've been involved in this relationship from the beginning. The least he could have done was wait until we were around. If it weren't for us, there wouldn't even be a relationship. After all, we're the ones who wrote the love letter and sent it to L.J., which prompted him to drive to Minnesota—"

"In a blizzard," I said. "Which almost killed him."

"He's tougher than that. As I was saying, it was our deathless prose that got you two back together last year. The least you could have done was let us in on the proposal."

"Proposals usually occur in private," George pointed out. "Speaking of the prospective groom, where is L.J.?"

We were outside by the swimming pool, lounging on beach chairs in the cool evening and sipping the champagne J.J. Butterfield had abandoned in my room when confronted by Lucas the night before. My newly anointed fiancé had vanished once again, this time with Pete Martinelli, who'd appeared at the ballroom as the dinner was wrapping up and people were starting to straggle out.

"He said he had some business to handle then he'll join us here. Speaking of joining us..." I nodded toward the patio near the hotel, where Donna Del Marco was standing, obviously looking for someone. She wore a peach-colored polo shirt and black shorts. Both emphasized her freckles and somewhat voluptuous physique.

"Come on down!" Clair shouted, waving so expansively he almost tipped his chair. "You're just in time to help us plan a wedding."

"Wedding?" I asked.

"Wedding?" Donna asked as she joined us.

"Who's the lucky groom?"

"Weddings are usually the consequence of a proposal of marriage," George said. He filled a plastic champagne glass and handed it to Donna, who drew up a lawn chair near ours. "Get caught up, we're two drinks ahead of you."

"I thought you guys were already married." Donna sipped the champagne and added, "Or at least as married as gay people can be."

"Not us. Ralph and Lucas are tying the knot, jumping the broom, getting hitched, putting on the old ball and chain." Clair gestured toward me. "He proposed in front of God and ClueCon."

Donna raised her glass to me. "I'm impressed. Smart man."

"Hmm?" I was still bemused by the idea I was an engaged woman. Granted, I'd already felt tied to Lucas, but this was…official.

"Neither one of you can easily back down. You're committed." Donna frowned at the not-so-beautiful people cavorting in the pool. "I should have done that."

"Do tell," Clair prompted. "Dish the dirt."

Donna sipped then settled back with a sigh, crossing her tanned legs in front of her and regarding the tips of her sandals. "Oh, what the hell. Everybody knows anyway, I'm not telling any secrets. Pete Martinelli and I had an…understanding, I guess you could say. We started going out together in the late Nineties, when he was on the Organized Crime Task Force."

"Organized Crime?" I dangled my glitzy shoes. "As in, The Mob? The Sopranos?"

"Yep, the same, except we sometimes have a Hispanic angle to it." Donna took another sip of champagne and eyed a cavorting couple in the pool. "I think he's trying to cop a feel."

I followed her gaze. Yep, she was right. "That's

what swimsuits and pool time are for. Continue your tale of woe."

"Things were going fine for us until about two years ago." Donna glanced at me, saw my sympathetic gaze, and looked away. "Thank God we each kept our own apartment. It would have been a lot worse if we'd moved in with each other. Anyway, we were starting to talk about marriage, and then..."

"The curse of the spider woman?" George suggested.

Donna nodded glumly. Even her spiky blonde hair seemed to droop. "Sereta Ramone came to town. She transferred here from Pensacola. She'd been on the O.C.T.F. there and rumor had it she left under fire."

"The married cop?" George smiled at her startled expression. "Please. When I have a background check done, I make sure it's thorough. She was in the same unit as her lover, it came out they were sleeping together, his wife filed for divorce, it hit the newspapers, a big bust went sour, and...voila, Ms. Ramone is transferred to the lovely Ft. Walton Beach area."

"Where she promptly messed with Pete's life and got him removed from the Task Force," Donna finished for him. "Within a year, Pete was off the O.C.T.F. and back in Homicide. No one ever said he screwed up, but I know he did. He and Ramone were supposed to organize a sting and somebody blew it. The bad guys got away. They both got demoted."

"Holy crap, she really is the kiss of death, isn't she?" I held out my glass for a refill.

"She ruins everyone she touches," Donna said. "Ever since this stuff started happening here, I was wondering if she was involved somehow."

"Not possible," I stated. "Why would she murder anybody? Besides, I think it has to do with ClueCon."

"Well, let's see." Clair refilled my glass then held up one hand, bending a finger for each item he ticked off his list. "John was killed on the beach with the rope. That's the Miss Scarlet award. Patrice was killed in the ballroom with the knife. That's the Mrs. Peacock award. Holly was killed in the study with the wrench." He hurried on when George started to protest. "It looked like she was killed with the wrench. That's the Rev. Green. Ralph was injured in the study with the pipe. That's the Professor Plum."

Donna looked bemused at this recitation of conference fatalities. "What's missing? What's his name, the guy with the mustaches and the fussy housekeeper, right?"

Clair nodded. "Colonel Mustard, whose award is a gun and Mrs. White, whose award is a candlestick. Plus we're missing some locations. The library and the hall and..." He waved his hand. "A bunch."

The mention of Colonel Mustard jogged an errant memory. Someone had said, "Lonigan did a Colonel Mustard", when he didn't produce a manuscript for a contract that was due. Could he be involved in this? Could he be next? What about Mary Carr? She wrote cozy mysteries under one name for Pittman and erotica under another for Red Nail. Was she next in line? She was up for the Mrs. White, after all, for her cozy mystery series.

"But John's murder was staged," Clair continued. "It doesn't really fit in."

"Hell, they all were staged," I said. "None of them really fit a pattern. There's nothing to connect them except for Red Nail. Holly was a publicist, John was up for a cover model slot, and Patrice was the CEO. So why would somebody be killing off Red Nail people?"

"Maybe it's a rabid Christian." George shrugged when he saw my surprised look. "Some right-wing Christian groups really have it in for erotica. They've picketed the Red Nail offices and from what I've heard the staff even received threats."

"But would a radical Christian attend a murder conference? I mean, Red Nail's main readership are people who like erotica. Their mysteries are just a tiny subset. I was surprised they were even represented here."

"They're trying to look more mainstream. They're merging with Dunross so they're trying to look upscale and classy." George snorted. "It's all just soft-core porn, let's face it. I don't know why they try to disguise it." His gaze moved beyond me and I looked up as Lucas joined us.

"Porn? Really? Can we get some?" Lucas' mustache tickled my cheek as he bent down to kiss me. He straightened and looked at Donna. "I'm L.J. Remarchik."

She held up her champagne glass in greeting. "Donna Del Marco. I'm—" The words froze in her throat as Pete Martinelli came into sight. "Just a passerby," she finished.

"She's a stray we found and adopted," Clair said. "When's the wedding?"

Lucas pulled over a lawn chair and sat down. "Pour me a drink, would you?" He glanced over his shoulder at Martinelli as he took the glass from Clair. "Care to join us?"

Martinelli hesitated, standing mostly in shadows cast by the faux Tiki torches that illuminated the fringe of the seating area. "I'd better get back to work. I'll let you know what we find out." He looked intently at Donna then turned and strode off, heading back toward the hotel.

"Find out about what?" I asked.

Lucas took a long sip of his champagne. "Police business."

"You're not a cop any more."

"I'm consulting."

"Since when?"

"You ask a lot of questions."

"I'd like to know everything I can about the man I'm going to marry."

He grinned at me. "You *are* going to marry me, aren't you?"

"Feeling any regrets?" George asked.

"Nope," Lucas said with a smile.

"So you're consulting with the police?"

Lucas sipped again. "Yep. It sort of intersects with the work I'm doing for Margaret Troolin's office."

"Really?" George asked. "The two are related?"

"In a way." Lucas took another long swallow and set his glass down. "Now if you'll excuse us, my bride-to-be and I have some wedding plans to discuss."

"We do?" I peered up at him as he stood.

Clair laughed. "That's a thinly veiled excuse to get you alone, I think."

I gulped the contents of my glass and handed it to Clair. "Sounds good to me. As I recall, he said he was going to answer all my questions." I got somewhat unsteadily to my feet, helped by Lucas who put a guiding hand under my right arm.

"I'll answer your questions," Lucas promised as we started to meander toward the hotel. "Later. Nice to meet you," he said over his shoulder to Donna.

She held up her glass. "Congratulations."

I looped my right arm through Lucas' left. "So tell me," I said as we ambled into the hotel. "Did you really mean to propose or did it just sort of happen?" Several ClueCon guests smiled at us as we walked through the hotel halls to the lobby and the elevators.

Lucas touched the Up button. "A little bit of both." He had the ability to focus intently on a person, making them feel like the center of the universe. He did that now as he smiled down at me. "Somehow it seemed like the right thing to do at the time."

"But just a few hours earlier you were speculating we couldn't make our relationship work." I preceded him into the elevator. "What changed your mind?"

He didn't say anything as the elevator rode slowly upward with other people, waiting until we got to my floor and were walking down the hall in relative privacy to speak. "I was talking to Martinelli this afternoon, after they found Patrice Samuels. He was saying how sassy you were, how unafraid. He looked at me and said, 'It must be tough living with someone like that'." Lucas shook his head as he opened our room door with his key card.

"And that made you think we could get married? Because I'm pushy?"

"Not pushy," he corrected. "Unafraid. You are usually unafraid, and his words made me realize your lack of fear causes me a hell of a lot of fear." Lucas ran a hand through his hair, frowning as he obviously searched for the right words. "I worry about you all the time, I think about you all the time, I imagine being with you all the time. You're part of me, Bea, as sure as if we were married. So why the hell shouldn't we try to make a marriage work?"

I dropped my purse on the credenza near the door. "Even though I'm sassy and I make more money than you do and I write romances with sexy heroes?"

He pulled me into his arms. "As long as I'm the model for your hero, I guess I don't have anything to complain about."

Our kiss ignited a hot glow that made me breathless and weak. We fumbled with clothing, laughing shakily as limbs got tangled and tripping over my slacks as we headed toward the bedroom. By the time the bed came into sight, I was mostly naked and all that remained of his clothing was his shirt.

Lucas winced when he saw the livid bruise covering my entire left shoulder. "I blame myself for that," he murmured, placing gentle kisses on the purple flesh. "If I'd been spending more time with you, someone wouldn't have targeted you."

"We don't know that," I said as I sank down onto the bed. When I tried to put weight on my arm, I realized it wasn't going to work. My bruising was too painful for me to relax back fully. I pulled the covers aside and looked at him.

Lucas saw my uncertainty in my face. "Maybe we'd better take it easy tonight."

I smiled at him and patted the bed. "Why don't you lie down here, cowboy," I suggested. "I'll bet if I get on top, I can manage just fine."

And you know what?

I did manage just fine indeed.

Chapter 16

I awoke at half past six on Saturday, listening to Lucas snore softly behind me. Morning sunlight was whitening the curtains. It was another sunny day in Florida.

Married? I was getting married? I'd been married and divorced after six years of not-so-blissful wedded life. That had been almost twenty years ago and I hadn't seriously considered marriage since then.

Could Lucas and I make a life together? We barely knew each other despite having endured a life-altering experience together last year in Abilene. We'd spent one week together on vacation after Christmas last year, lying on a beach in the Caribbean. And we'd spent several long weekends together, either at his tiny ranch in Texas or my house in Minnesota, getting caught up on life and making long, languid love.

But daily living? In sickness and in health? For better or worse?

Marriage?

"Awake?"

I snuggled into the warmth behind me, feeling

the unmistakable presence of an erect male pressing against me.

"Hmm." I moved carefully so as not to awaken the slumbering bruise on my shoulder. Today I just felt sore, not suck-in-your-breath-ow pained. "Feels like you're awake."

"I've been thinking."

I snuggled against the body part nudging me. "Is that what you call it?"

"The marriage thing." Lucas nuzzled my neck and back, careful to avoid my bruises. "I think I have a solution to our problem." His hand slipped around and slid over my stomach, inching downward. I shifted to accommodate his questing fingers.

"Do tell." I sighed as he began a gentle massage I knew could culminate into something quite spectacular.

"Here's the thing. Neither of us wants to sell our house, right? I mean, I love the ranch, especially in the spring. I know how you feel about being in Minnesota for Christmas and I agree. There's nothing like snow for Christmas."

I drowsed, his words washing over me as his hand slowly manipulated me into a pre-orgasmic state. I paid attention to one or two words in five, just reveling in having him there and enjoying the feelings he was evoking. "...cats and Buster, so we have to ...they'll be fine, I'm sure but...if we could have them with us to...tour will be wrapping up soon, so...and that's when Margaret said...it just came to me."

"Hmm?" I rolled over and looked up into his eyes. "What did?" I lifted my hips.

"An RV."

It didn't make any sense for a second then his meaning soaked in. "An RV? You mean one of those big house trailer things?" I sagged back onto the bed, my mind in high gear.

"Yep. We'll buy an RV and drive it between Texas and Minnesota a few times a year. We'll throw my cats and your cat and dog in the back, hit the road, and take our time traveling from place to place. You can write while we drive and we can visit all those spots we've always talked about visiting."

Who would look after the ranch while we were gone? As soon as the question sprang to mind, I had the answer. Lucas' brother, Larry, kept an eye on the place whenever Lucas was gone. Besides, it wasn't really a working ranch, it was more like a hobby ranch, the same way my house wasn't really 'at the lake' but was just a slice of suburbia with a lot of trees and a tiny lake in the distance. My neighbor Sylvie kept an eye on my pets and my house when I was gone.

An RV? Could it work? I tried to imagine Lucas in the pilot seat of one of those houses-on-wheels and was surprised when a picture sprang into my mind. He was right. I didn't need to tour too much any more. The book had been out for almost three months, so I only needed to do the circuit for a bit longer. It was selling like gangbusters and I didn't really need the money. Once it went into movie production, I'd have to tour again, but that wouldn't be for a year or two.

I could write while we drove and with WiFi I'd have access to my editor and my family as much as I did now. My animals —Billy the Kit and Buster the dog—were seasoned travelers already, having often made the trip to Iowa to visit my mom. I'm sure we could manage an introduction to Beauty and Beast, Lucas' two animals and with a little coaxing, they'd take to life on the road.

"Hello?"

Lucas was smiling down at me. I put my arms around his neck and drew him to me. "You're a genius."

"Glad you noticed. You think it'll work?"

"Work? It's perfect. I'm sure it'll work." He looked so relieved I laughed. "You didn't think I'd agree? I think it sounds great. The first thing to do is to start looking at those RV things. I wonder if we need training to drive them? How do they work? I suppose there's a bunch of stuff to learn about plumbing and —"

"The first thing to do is get reacquainted with my fiancée." Lucas moved on top of me, peering in concern at my naked and bruised shoulder. "Is that okay?"

I shifted my hips so certain portions of his anatomy intersected more firmly with certain portions of mine. "Now it is."

****

"Believe me, I appreciate the diversionary tactics you've been using, but it's time to answer some questions." I was sprawled on the couch in the living room portion of the suite, watching as Lucas made coffee at our kitchenette.

"What questions?"

I recognized his overly casual, bantering tone of voice. I didn't let it fool me. "Let's see, where to start?" I rearranged the overstuffed pillow behind me then leaned back, shifting my *I drive way too fast to worry about cholesterol'* T-shirt away from the bruise on my shoulder. I was in casual wear for the final day of workshops since I didn't have to do any presentations.

"What kind of work are you doing for Margaret? What does it have to do with what's happening here? Why have you been so schmoozy with Sereta Ramone? What kind of consulting work are you doing for the cops? What's the deal with Martinelli and Donna? Did he talk about that? Is Ramone really a bad luck charm? How come—"

He turned to stare at me, coffee pot in hand.

"What did you do, save all these up?"

"We haven't exactly had a lot of time to talk, Lucas. Make me a bagel, okay?"

"Anything else, Princess?"

"Geez, I was demoted. Clair was calling me Queen Bea."

"It sure beats Queen Ralph, which is what they usually call you. Speaking of which, where are your little shadows?" Lucas sliced a bagel and popped it into the toaster before pulling out the leftover lox and cream cheese from the fridge.

"Probably waiting for me to call them." I glanced at the clock. "It's eight. They should be awake by now." I stretched out a hand toward the room's telephone.

"Let me. I'd hate to have you strain. What's the room number?"

I told him and watched as he dialed, talking briefly to whoever answered then hanging up and retrieving my bagel from the toaster. As always, he wore black jeans and today a dark red shirt with his gray suit coat. And, as always, I thought he was the handsomest man I'd ever seen. I smiled smugly, enjoying the thought that I'd have his handsomeness around for the rest of my life.

He moved to the toaster, knife at the ready. I loved to watch Lucas cook, even in such an amateurish space. He took the job so seriously, carefully spreading the cream cheese to the margins of the bagel and arranging the slices of lox in a crisscross pattern. He put the offering on a plate and handed it to me before going to the small foyer.

"Four, three, two, one," he intoned then swept the door open.

"So why are you consulting with cops in the middle of Podunk Nowhere, Florida?" Clair demanded as he strode into the room. "Oh, and you never did answer me. When's the wedding?"

213

"Good morning." George raised his coffee mug to me. "You look well rested." He waggled his eyebrows and plopped down into the chair to my right. As always, he was sartorially perfect in khaki shorts and a darker khaki polo shirt and chunky brown sandals.

"I'm engaged and happy. Sleep can wait."

"So it wasn't just a faux proposal?" Clair grabbed a bagel and popped it into the toaster as Lucas sat down next to me on the couch, nudging my legs to make space as he carefully balanced two mugs of coffee.

"Faux, hell." Lucas sipped his coffee. "We're getting married in October. We'll have a ceremony in Abilene and one in Minnesota, and maybe have one in Iowa, too." He grinned at me. "I figure if we get married a lot, it'll stick."

"Why October?" I asked around a mouthful of cream cheese goodness.

"The weather should be perfect no matter where we go, RVs will be on sale, and your book tour should be wrapping up."

"RVs?" George regarded me over the brim of his coffee mug.

"We're going to do some traveling."

"I know a guy who sells RVs," Clair said, pouncing on his bagel as it spat out of the toaster. "Ow. Hot." He started smearing it with cream cheese.

Lucas snorted. "You know a guy who does everything."

"I try. So why are you consulting with the police?"

"I see where you learned your interrogation techniques," Lucas said to me.

I nodded. "I learned from a master."

"I'm consulting because I'm working undercover for the Organized Crime Investigative Division of the Texas Rangers."

I blinked in surprise. "Since when?"

"Since I retired last fall."

"Why didn't you tell me?"

He sighed. "There's a reason it's called undercover work, Bea."

"Hush." Clair sat down in the remaining chair, bagel in hand. "Let the man talk."

Lucas shot him a grateful look then continued. "I was approached after retirement to help look into fraud and racketeering along the Gulf Coast. Since the big hurricanes came through, there have been a lot of chances for organized crime to come in and get a good foothold. Things have gone okay. We've made some busts and tracked down some solid leads. One of those leads brought me here." He gestured.

"Ft. Walton Beach, Florida?" I prompted.

"The Sandy Shores Resort."

"Not," I said flatly. "Too much of a coincidence."

Lucas shrugged. "Even if your conference wasn't here I'd have found a way to spend some time in this hotel while we were in the area. There are only five big resorts in the Fort Walton Beach area. It was too good a chance to pass up." He leveled a warning look at me. "This is all confidential, by the way. Make sure to keep it a secret if you talk to any other conference goers. Although I doubt the subject is going to come up."

I mimed a zipping action across my mouth then continued gobbling my bagel.

"As I said, one of the leads brought me here, to Pete Martinelli. He'd contacted the Feds last year. It appears he and Sereta Ramone had an affair and during the course of it, he discovered she was on the take."

"What? You're kidding?" I almost dropped my bagel.

"Well, that explains her clothing," Clair said in

the tone of voice of one who has had deep suspicions confirmed. "I mean, nobody on the police force wears Manolos. And that handbag she was carrying was Coach, I know it was."

I polished off my bagel. "Trust you to find a clue in somebody's blouse choice."

He closed his eyes, obviously in pain. "Manolos are shoes, dear. Shoes."

"She's been reporting returns on investments, but some of the companies she's investing in are tied to some pretty big organized crime families. Plus she deliberately blew a sting operation they had going," Lucas said, ignoring our side trip into haute couture. "Pete said he had the evidence on tape. I was asked to come here, talk with him, and make sure he's legit."

"And?" I gestured when Lucas paused to take a sip of coffee. "Is he?"

"Yep."

"Good. So arrest her and be done with it, right?"

Lucas shook his head. "Something's up and we need her to lead us to the right people. No, I can't tell you any more. If I did, I'd be in violation of several Federal laws, not to mention confidentiality agreements and God knows what."

"What about Margaret Troolin?" George asked. "I thought you were working for her."

"It's a cover. Certain people started to notice I was asking some uncomfortable questions. We set it up so it looks like I'm working on a case for her. I did work on it, briefly. That deposition I gave was the real thing."

"What about our plans?" I sat up straighter, suddenly worried. "You can't travel if you're working. What about that?"

"Man, when you get hold of an idea, you don't let go, do you?" Lucas wrapped his hand around my ankle on the couch next to him and gave it a shake.

216

"I suspect by the time this whole thing wraps up, I won't be undercover any more, so I'll probably really retire this time."

George's mug paused on the way to his lips. "Is it that dangerous?"

Lucas shrugged. "Cop work is dangerous, no matter what. This is no more dangerous than most of what I've done in the past." He smiled reassuringly at me and gave my ankle a last shake then he stood up. "Now it's time for me to get back to work. I need to check in with Martinelli. He was going to verify some details about tonight's activities."

"Tonight?" I exchanged a look with Clair. "Tonight's the award ceremonies." I saw the look in Lucas' eyes. "Don't tell me—you may not get there, right?"

"Sorry, honey. I'm just not sure. I'm going to try." Lucas gestured to George. "We need to have a little chat."

I looked up at them with interest. "What are you guys talking about?"

George set his mug down and stood. "Boy talk. Ignore us."

"None of your business, Princess," Lucas said as he paused by the door.

"Queen," I reminded him. "Queen Bea."

Clair laughed. "You won't get anything out of them. George can keep a secret better than anybody I've ever met. So how are you feeling? How's the shoulder?"

I shrugged it experimentally. "Stiff but not broken. I can't lift my arm above my head, but other than that, I'm okay."

"Excellent. Now, listen. About your dress."

"What dress?" I leaned against the arm of the couch, trying to inconspicuously eavesdrop.

"Your wedding dress."

217

"Wedding dress? That's not until October. We've got plenty of time."

He polished off his bagel with a patient sigh. "October is just around the corner when it comes to clothing. Now, I'm thinking burnt umber."

I checked George and Lucas, who were talking in low voices near the door. I couldn't hear a word they said. "Umber? Is that a color?"

"Honestly, where were you when they were handing out style sense?"

"I was in the other line, getting common sense."

"Anyway, I'm thinking burnt umber would be the perfect color." Clair barreled ahead, ignoring my futile attempts to spy on my lover and his cohort. "Attention? Attention?"

"Okay, burnt umber."

"It's a good color. It'll go good with your hair, all those little gold highlights you have. And it will go with your skin tone. Of course, you'll need some tanning ahead of time."

"Tanning? You're kidding."

"Just a touch of tan to give you the tiniest bit of color."

"Allow me to remind you tanning causes cancer."

"Fine. Then go somewhere and have pseudo-tan sprayed on."

"I don't need a tan. I'm not white." I held up one capried leg.

Clair regarded my leg doubtfully. "Well, you're flesh-colored, certainly. Not alabaster. Oh, speaking of which. Did you ever soak your seashell and find out what was inside?"

"Hmm. Hang on. Let me go get it." I used the movement to get up and move closer to George and Lucas just as Lucas turned to me.

"Have fun today."

"When will I see you?"

"I'll try to make the award ceremony if not

earlier. You're autographing this afternoon, right? Maybe I'll show up and have you sign a book for me." He gave me a quick kiss. "I'll see you later, Princess." He pulled open the door and stepped out.

"Queen," I called after him.

He laughed and waved to me as he walked down the hall. I went back into the room and picked up the shell from the bedroom's credenza where I'd left it. I dropped the shell into the ice bucket, which I filled with water from the tap. It could soak throughout the day. Clair was right. I didn't want to be transporting a foreign mollusk, even a dead one, back to Minnesota. God knows what kind of havoc that might wreck on the state's ecology.

"Ready to go to the conference?" George asked, peering around the doorframe.

"Yep." I snatched up my trusty book bag and made sure my Necessaries were tucked into various pockets. "I'm ready."

The first workshop we went to was woefully unattended. There were supposed to be a thousand people at this conference, but the halls were not crowded and the hotel felt like a ghost village. Gwendolyn, however, was there and anxious to talk.

"I can't believe I was there when he proposed," she said excitedly. "Wait until I tell my friends. They won't believe it. It's so romantic."

"It was certainly a surprise." I looked around the room. Only twenty people were sitting in the room, which had been set up for three times that number.

"I'll get us a seat," Clair murmured then he deserted me.

"What a pity he had to propose here." Gwen gestured to the swimming pool and the beach beyond where we could see people walking on the sandy verge.

"Say what?"

"This resort."

"What's wrong with this resort?" I started edging away to join Clair who'd already taken a seat at the back.

"Well, the Richardson family." Her tone of voice clearly indicated her poor opinion of Saul and David Richardson.

"What about them?"

Gwen stiffened and drew away from me, as though I'd insulted her. "They aren't very reputable people." She said it as though they were the de Medici family, capable of anything from poison to blackmail.

"I'm not from around here." I saw with relief that the speaker had come to the podium at the front of the room. "I guess I don't know about their background."

"Trust me. You don't want to have anything to do with them if you can help it. They'll ruin your life." With that condemnation she flounced away to her usual seat front and center in the first row.

"Your proposal is the closest she'll ever get to a proposal," Clair said sotto voice as we took our seats at the back of the room.

I rapped him on the wrist. "Be nice." I belatedly remembered Katherine's earlier information. "She's a widow."

"Not." George leaned back and propped his left ankle on his right knee. "Just look at her. I can't believe she was married."

I followed his gaze. Gwendolyn was a large, lumpy shape dominating our view of the podium, a gaudy geranium in a roomful of more restrained clothing choices. Her curly hair wisped around her head like an aura, and her skin had a blotchy, uneven appearance somewhat like the enormous flowers on her blouse. "Her husband died."

"I know of what," George muttered.

"Hush. She has a good heart."

"That only counts in heaven."

Our second workshop of the day took place in the 'Study', where a pseudo crime scene was set up at the back of the room, complete with mannequin, overturned furniture, and crime scene tape. The lecturer invited us all to examine the scene then submit our own evaluations on the victim and cause of death. It was a bright spot in a dull morning.

Lunch was a sandwich buffet and sparsely attended. "Perhaps people have gone off-site for lunch," I said to Katherine as we nibbled on our ham sandwiches.

"I hope so. Otherwise the award ceremony will be a bust. I'm sorry you won't have a lot of people at the autograph session."

"I'm used to really small conferences," I assured her. "Anything more than a hundred fans will feel like a stampede to me."

She brightened at the thought and I was glad I was able to help her put the whole fiasco into perspective. As we were leaving the room I saw David Richardson in the lobby, conferring with his father. Gwendolyn was walking away from them, smiling smugly. Both men looked harassed, angry, and suspicious. "Did you see that?" I asked Katherine.

"What?"

My phone thumped my butt. I opened it and it chimed *Outlaw Man*. I glanced at the number but didn't recognize it. "Let me take this," I said to her.

She nodded and went to a group of women who were chatting nearby. I pressed the "Receive" button and put the phone to my ear.

"Miss Emerson, this is Detective Ramone. I need to talk to you this afternoon."

Oh, this would make my day. "Of course, what time?"

She paused. I suppose she was surprised I was

being so accommodating. "Three o'clock?" she suggested.

"Can't. I have to do an autograph signing. How about four?"

"This is police business. It's imperative I speak with you—"

"How about five?"

"You don't seem to understand. I can have you come to the station and we can chat there." She stumbled over her words in her anger.

"No, you don't seem to understand. I know the law. You can't summon me to the station without probable cause, and you don't have that." I actually didn't know shit about the law, but I did know about intimidation, and she wasn't going to get away with it.

"I'm surprised you don't want to cooperate with our investigation."

"I've cooperated with L.J. Remarchik," I said sweetly.

"I beg your pardon?"

"He and I cooperated last night. And this morning," I added for good measure. "He's helping the police, right? So in a sense, I've been helping the police, too."

"Four o'clock," she snapped. "I'll come to your room."

I laughed out loud as I closed the phone. Revenge was sweet.

Chapter 17

"Ready for our next workshop?"

George materialized at my elbow. He and Clair had disappeared at lunch, stating their preference for a meal in the restaurant.

"Why are you sticking to me like white on rice?" I asked as he steered me across the open foyer where a few days ago I'd been splashed with wine.

"Hmm?"

"You normally don't attend the same kinds of workshops I do. Confess, George. What's the deal?"

"L.J. was worried, that's all. He asked us to stay close to you until he comes back."

"Worried about what?"

"Which workshop are we going to?" Clair asked, hurrying to join us as we entered the hallway leading to the rooms used for the presentations.

"Just worried in general." George tapped my book bag. "Which workshop?"

"Which one do you want to go to?"

"Anything lively that will keep me awake. You choose."

I pulled out my well-creased schedule book and opened it to the last page of workshop listings. As I did, the original agenda Dana Cartwright had given me fluttered to the floor. George picked it up and scanned through the stapled pages.

"You're due at a photo shoot," he said, handing me the papers.

"Hmm?" I'd forgotten all about the schedule the PR agent put together for me. In fact, I'd forgotten all about Dana Cartwright, Pittman, and the cover model contest. My happiness at being reunited with Lucas had eclipsed everything. "What photo shoot?"

"For your cover. You and your chosen cover model are due in the lobby."

"What? When?" I flipped through the stapled pages, finally spying the entry. *2:00, Saturday afternoon. Photo op, lobby, model & authors.* "Well, damn. I didn't know anything about this." I looked down at my clothing, which was appropriate for someone incognito at a conference but not for someone involved in a so-called photo op. "I need to change."

"Excellent idea but you're already running late." Clair tapped his wristwatch. "Come on. I'll run up to your room and get something while you stall the photographer." I started to protest but they propelled me away before the words could take shape in my mouth.

We arrived breathlessly to find a clump of people in the lobby including Tony Jackson, J.J. Butterfield, Adrian Ashford, and John Scarlino. Dana Cartwright and Scarlino were deep in conversation, and Ashford looked bored, lounging in a chair and talking on a cell phone. When Tony saw me he hurried across the lobby to join me. "Minor catastrophe," he murmured, standing with his back to the others and effectively blocking my view of the action.

George and Clair moved in on the side, forming a small huddle. "What's up?" I asked.

"Mary Carr's missing. She's supposed to have her picture taken with Butterfield. She selected him as her cover model."

I'd paid little attention to the final results the night before, but vaguely remembered Butterfield's name being announced as "The Lord of Seduction" and Paul someone announced as Dunross' choice for their model.

"What do you mean she's missing?" George asked.

"She hasn't been seen since before lunch." Tony looked over his shoulder. "Ashford is pissed off, he said he doesn't have time to wait."

"What's it got to do with Ashford?" I peeked around Tony and saw Ashford staring at us as he spoke on his phone.

"There's no one here to represent Red Nail. Ashford has sort of stepped in."

"So much for secrecy about a merger," I muttered.

"I think Scarlino is upset because Carr writes for Pittman, too, and he's afraid it'll get out she writes erotica for Red Nail."

"Oh, for cryin' out loud. What does it matter—"

"Remember what I said about radical Christians?" George whispered. "That guy is one of them." He nodded toward a pudgy young man standing near the front desk, regarding us all with obvious distaste.

I peered at the culprit. "He looks normal. How do you know?"

George laughed. "Satan has many disguises. Margaret sent me some information about it. I had her do some research. His picture turned up. Apparently he makes it a habit to attend conventions like this and disrupt things whenever an erotica writer gives a presentation."

"Good grief, who made him the arbiter of public

morals?" I peered more closely at the tight-lipped man with the dark shock of hair and pale complexion. "Wait a minute. He looks familiar. I think I've seen him around."

"Of course you have. He paid his money and attended the conference just like anybody else."

"Damn. Now I remember. He and Gwen always sat in the front row and took notes. He looks like Gwendolyn's soul mate." The man was chubby, dressed in a gaudy Hawaiian shirt, baggy black shorts, with white socks and sandals. He was the epitome of geekhood sprung to life with black-rimmed glasses perched on a bulbous nose and an untidy thatch of black hair that was either greasy or just plain dirty. "He sits in the front row and takes notes like a maniac."

"He's probably gathering data for that nutcase religious group he belongs to," Clair said, frowning at the man.

George stood aside and nodded toward Dana Cartwright, who was signaling to me. "I think the party's starting without Mary. Go get 'em, champ."

"Authors! Models! Gather here!" A woman with a clipboard was pointing to a spot near the windows overlooking the beach.

"I'm sorry I didn't dress up," I said to Tony as we moved forward to join the others. "I forgot all about this, Pittman's publicist told me and I just—"

"Hold this." Dana Cartwright thrust a one-foot by two-foot blowup of my next cover into my arms. It showed my hero, Cal Delvecchio, standing under a streetlamp, his face partly in shadow. It was Tony Jackson.

"Man, that was fast," I said as I stared at the cover. "It looks okay. Your hair needs to be more gray, though."

"We'll work on it. Stand over here." Cartwright nudged me toward the window and gestured impatiently to Tony. "Beside her. Hold the poster higher, please."

I took my spot and held up the poster. When I looked across the lobby, the guy George had pointed out was staring at us. He continued to stare throughout our session, standing like Lot's wife, his gaze fixed on me.

Every time I lowered the poster of the book cover, Dana Cartwright gestured urgently to me to raise it. I finally realized she was anxious for me to cover my offending T-shirt. I grinned and complied. We spent a bewildering five minutes posing, smiling, and being snapped then Butterfield stepped forward holding a poster for a book cover with a half-naked clench and himself in the prime spot of studly male.

"Looks like they'll go on without Mary," Tony whispered. He and I joined Clair and George on the other side of the lobby where they were talking with four other conference goers. "So what's up?" I asked.

"It's Mary Carr," Clair said. "We're wondering where she could be."

"Maybe she left early," I suggested. "A lot of folks are taking off."

"No, she's up for an award tonight. She wouldn't leave." This came from a woman whom I'd seen arguing with Patrice in the bar on the first night of the conference. "Mary was working out a deal with Dunross. Ashford said he hasn't seen her. She was supposed to meet him before lunch. They were going to sit together and talk. She wouldn't have blown that off."

I looked across the lobby at Ashford. "But she writes for Pittman," I said. "And Red Nail. You mean she was negotiating a third contract with Dunross?"

"Rumor had it her contract with Red Nail would be null and void once the merger went through. I guess she decided to go right to the source and talk to Ashford instead of waiting to see what would happen once the merger occurred." The woman shrugged. "Mary's a shrewd businesswoman. I'm sure she had several irons in the fire."

As I turned I saw the pudgy man still watching me. "Do I know him?" I muttered to no one in particular.

George followed my gaze. "I doubt it. Not unless you travel in right-wing Christian circles."

"Well, why's he staring at me?"

"I don't know. But it might be worth asking him." Before I could stop him he was striding across the lobby.

"Oh, for cryin' out—" I hurried after him, Clair and Tony Jackson following. I got to George just in time to hear him ask,

"Is there some reason you're so interested in Miss Emerson?"

"It's a free country. I can watch who I want to watch." The man backed up and raised his ClueCon book bag defensively.

"Not if it's stalking," George snapped.

Tony Jackson moved up to flank him and I crowded behind the two men, peering between their shoulders. Clair peered over the top of George and glared.

"Where were you on Wednesday night?" George demanded.

"Wednesday night?" I looked at Clair. "Why do we care about Wednesday night? Oh." Suddenly it hit me. I'd been drugged on Wednesday night. In all the excitement, I'd forgotten about it.

The man's pale eyes widened. His face flushed a dark pink, the color of uncooked bacon. I felt guilty about making the pig analogy but it was so apt. He looked like a pig, from his too-tight clothing displaying layers of fat to his jiggling chins to his small eyes, darting to and fro like an animal. "What are you asking?" His voice was high and almost shrill. "What does it matter where I was on Wednesday?"

"Were you in a bar on Wednesday?"

The man straightened in outrage. "Oh, please. I wouldn't be caught dead in a place like that."

"What place?" Tony asked, moving forward slightly. "How do you know what we're talking about if you weren't there?"

I looked up at Jackson in surprise. Was he going to be another knight in shining armor?

"Most of the bars around here are trashy," the man sputtered. "I've seen their advertisements. I have higher standards than that."

"Is that why you're standing around ogling people?" Clair drawled. "I mean, there're a lot of male models here. Some people might find it quite attractive to be here."

The man's face darkened even more. Now he looked like cooked bacon. Damn. I had to get the pig analogies out of my brain.

"Perhaps we should tell Martinelli about this," George said.

"Martinelli?" The man gave a disdainful laugh. "He's no better than a whoremonger."

"I beg your pardon?" I stiffened in outrage on Pete Martinelli's behalf.

"I don't have to talk to you," the man snapped. "You people have no authorization to intimidate me. Now if you'll excuse me, I have better things to do than argue with a bunch of depraved morons." He stomped off, quivering with rage.

"You don't really think he had anything to do with the restaurant, do you?" I asked George as we both watched the man stalk through the crowds in the lobby.

"No. I just wanted to jerk his chain. So what's next on our agenda after participating in depraved photograph sessions and routing indignant

Christians?"

"Hard to top, I know, but I have the autograph signing." I looked at my Timex. "In ten minutes."

"Oh, Lord, I hate those things."

"I know, I do, too, but I promised Katherine I'd be there, so be there I will. Why don't you guys go off and do something fun? I don't need a babysitter during the autograph signing. There'll be a hundred people around me."

"I did want to talk to those authors who were brainstorming by the pool," Clair said wistfully. "We're so new to this genre, I figure I need all the tips I can get."

"Go, go." I made a shooing motion.

"I'll escort her to the autograph signing," Tony volunteered.

"Are you sure?" George asked me. "We told L.J. we'd stick with you."

"Well, now Tony will stick. Go." I led the way out of the lobby, forestalling further conversation. "I'll see you guys tonight at the award ceremony." I linked my arm through Tony's and we headed toward the ballroom where the autograph session was to take place. "Thanks," I said to him as we walked away. "I hate to think I'm ruining the conference for them."

"I think they'll be okay," Tony said with a laugh.

"This has been a pretty exciting conference for you, hasn't it?" I saw a sign in the distance. 'Authors: enter here'. I steered Tony toward the door to the left of the ballroom.

"Yeah. I'm glad I was chosen for your cover." He grimaced. "I don't think I'd make a great 'Lord of Seduction'."

"Now, now. Don't sell your talents short."

"Excuse me!"

We both turned at the sharp voice behind us. "Oh, for heaven's sake," I muttered. It was the Magic

Christian. "What the hell do you want?"

"No need to swear at me. I just want to talk to you."

"We have nothing to talk about." I continued walking forward, tugging Tony with me.

"It's about your books."

"What about my books?" I threw back over my shoulder.

The man huffed and puffed to keep up with us. "You don't need all that sex."

"What sex?" I sped up the pace, anxious to get away from my own personal rain cloud.

"Your books are cleverly crafted. You don't need all the sex to sell them."

"You've read my books?" I asked incredulously.

"Of course I've read your books. When I saw the titles, I thought you were saved. But then I realized it was just low-grade pornography."

"Titles? Saved?"

"For Jesus." He nodded vigorously, greasy hair flopping on his forehead.

"Your books," Tony muttered. *"Murdering Angels? Devils in the Dust?"*

"Holy crap," I breathed. The guy thought I was a Christian author. Boy, I'll bet he got a shock when he read my books. "Look, they're just books. I mean, if they offend you, don't read them. It's really simple."

"I have to read them. I read all the books of the women I—"

I stopped and turned to stare at him. "You read all the books of what?"

He backed up a pace and held up his hands as though I was about to attack. "Nothing."

Tony looked from me to the flustered pig-man. "Is something wrong?"

The door behind me burst open and Katherine bustled out. "Oh, there you are. Thank goodness. It's a mess, an absolute mess. K.L. Lonigan is drunk, I think. Aidan Lindsey insists on rearranging the room according to Feng Shui principles. Mary Carr is A.W.O.L., and three of the other authors haven't showed up. I was so worried you wouldn't make it."

I turned back to my harasser but he was already scurrying away. I turned to Tony. "Can you please find Clair or George and tell them—" Tell them what? That I suspected the pig-man of attempted molestation? I had no proof and nothing but one man's stuttering words. "Nothing. Thanks for the escort."

"Are you sure? Is there anything else I can do?"

I looked at Katherine, who was gesturing me into the room. "No, it's fine. Thanks. I'll see you tonight."

"That's right. We sit together at the banquet, don't we? Okay, see you there." Tony gave a little wave and started off.

"Hey, wait!"

He turned and looked expectantly at me.

"Tell Clair and George I'm meeting Detective Ramone at four o'clock in my room. I forgot to tell them earlier."

"Ramone at your room," he repeated. "Got it!"

I figured it wouldn't hurt to let them know where I'd be after the autograph session. Lucas would hopefully be back by then, so it was probably a moot point but Mavis Emerson didn't raise no fools. I had discovered it paid to be careful.

I followed Katherine into the room. She was right. It was a mess. Several tables had been set up, placards indicating where the authors were to sit. Volunteers were scurrying around, putting books next to the name placards. Aidan Langley was arguing with someone, trying to physically move the tables into a different position. K. L. Lonigan was slumped in a chair behind one of the tables, peering stupidly at the books in front of him. Other authors were wandering around the room, looking bemused, offended, or confused. "Holy crap," I muttered.

"I know," Katherine said. "I swear to God this conference is cursed."

I strode across the open space and leaned over the table to stare down at Lonigan. "Get up," I snapped.

He peered owlishly at me. "What?"

"Get up. Help me."

"You don't understand. I'm going to be arrested."

"Bullshit. If you were going to be arrested, they would have done it by now. Grow a spine and get up." I didn't listen to his reply but went to Aidan Langley, grabbing her by the arm as she tried to move a table to a 90-degree angle with another one. "Don't."

"You don't understand." She seemed panicked, her thin body vibrating with energy. "If we don't move the tables, the energy levels in the room will be all off."

"We'll move the people, not the tables." I grabbed the nearest placard and plunked it down on the table. "Move everybody toward the center. That should help the energy flow pulse into the middle and expand outward as it goes. It will have a fountain effect." I had no idea what I was saying, but it must have made sense because she blinked at me then smiled.

"Excellent!" She scurried off to gather the different author name placards.

I gestured urgently to the volunteers. "Follow her," I said. "Wherever authors sit, put some books. We'll refill as we go."

Within ten minutes the room had attained a semblance of order. I waved to the group of volunteers manning the main door. "Open 'em up."

They did as I said and a flood of people rushed

into the room. I was surprised by the volume then I remembered: we were giving away free books. That was always an inducement to people to form a line and wait. It looked as though everyone at the conference was there. K.L. and I took our seats at a table and prepared to face the hordes. He held up manfully, gulping down coffee and mumbling answers to people who gushed about his books. I caught a glimpse of Aidan Langley who was giggling and laughing with anyone within talking distance. Other authors also were fanned out across the tables, but I saw several conspicuous absences, books stacked waiting for authors who never appeared.

We were almost through the entire hour before Gwendolyn loomed in front of me, clutching my latest two books to her ample bosom. "Hey there, Gwen." I held out a hand for the books. "Shall I sign those for you?"

"Please, would you? Something personal." She beamed at me as I opened *Murdering Angels*, my first book. "I love your books so much. I've worn them out from reading and re-reading. I'm glad to pick up new copies."

"Who's your favorite character?" I asked, stalling for time as I struggled to come up with something personal to jot in the book. "Besides Cal, of course." I waited, pen poised over the page. When no answer was forthcoming, I looked up. She was staring at David Richardson, who had slipped into the room and was watching our activities with an anxious air. "I suppose he's worried something else will go wrong," I said.

"It would serve him right if it did."

The venom in her voice startled me. "Gwen?"

She jerked as though I'd prodded her. "Oh. I'm sorry. I guess I just zoned out a bit. I loved Cal's girlfriend, Mona."

I almost botched the florid "Raphael Emerson" I was signing in the front cover. Cal didn't have a girlfriend. Mona was the murderer in the story. I glanced up at Gwen. She was staring so intently at David Richardson I was surprised he didn't flinch from the effect. Of course, she wasn't the first fan to lie about how much she loved my books, but it was odd she'd screwed up such a fundamental fact.

I stared down at the blank facing page, searching for some appropriate saying then I had a flash of inspiration. I penned "From one ClueCon Survivor to another" in *Angels* then picked up *Devils* and wrote "Watch out for Mrs. White, I think she did it". I handed the books back to her with a grin.

She read the inscriptions, giving me a conspiratorial smile when she read the first one. When she read the second one, though, her entire body froze then she began to shake, her hands trembling so much the book seemed to jump like a Mexican bean.

"Thanks so much, I appreciate it," Gwen said in a rush. "I have to go."

I looked after her, perplexed, as she pushed her way through the crowd and out the door, brushing by David Richardson with barely a glance. He stared after her, his expression one I would expect if he'd seen a cockroach in the dining room—stunned, angry, and horrified.

"Whatever you wrote, I want it," Lonigan muttered next to me. "Way to get rid of the fans, B.R." He peered after Gwen. "She looks familiar. Is she...?"

"I wonder what the deal is," I muttered back. "Gwen keeps alluding to the Richardson family and how horrible they are. How bad could they be? They run a hotel."

"Richardson? Saul Richardson? The Richardsons run this hotel?" Lonigan peered around myopically

235

then winced, his incipient hangover obviously paining him.

I nodded toward David, deep in conversation with Katherine near the doorway. "That's David Richardson."

"Man oh man. And that was Gwen Bandorf you were talking to? I'm surprised she didn't kill him where he stood."

"What?" I stared from the doorway where Gwen had vanished to David Richardson, who was slipping out the side door the authors had used earlier.

"It's an old Florida murder case," Lonigan said, taking a book from a fan and signing it with a brief 'thanks' to the fan. "Bandorf's father was a bookkeeper for the mob. He was tossed in prison and died there."

"That was her husband," I corrected, taking a book from a reader. She and I chatted for a minute and I missed what Lonigan said. "What?"

"Her husband died in prison, too. Saul Richardson testified against her father at his trial. I don't remember the details but it was something like Richardson overheard Bandorf's father or found something the father left. I can't remember."

I signed another book then sat back and took a long swallow from my water bottle. "So what does that have to do with the husband?"

"He tried to kill Saul and David stopped him. The husband got prison for attempted murder and was killed there. Some kind of gang thing."

Lonigan took another book from a fan and I didn't hear what he said. When he finished singing it, he said, "She lost her father and husband within a year of each other."

"When was this?" I asked.

"A couple of years ago. I thought she'd moved away but I saw her in one of the workshops. She's sort of hard to miss."

"Thank you, authors, for your time," Katherine called out.

I looked up at the clock. It was four.

Time to meet Ms. Ramone and have my revenge.

Chapter 18

"Are you sure about Gwen Bandorf and the Richardson family?" I asked Lonigan as we stood and pushed our chairs in. "That poor woman. To have all that happen to her, to lose her father and husband so close together. What a terrible thing." I smiled automatically at a reader who thrust a book at me then took it and autographed it.

"Yep. I've lived in these parts for years. It was in all the newspapers a few years ago. She dropped out of sight. You know how it is, people have their fifteen minutes of fame and then they vanish. I thought she looked familiar, but I didn't remember until you mentioned the Richardsons. That's what made it all fall into place." He rubbed a hand across his hair and smiled ruefully. "Thanks for the slap up the side of the head earlier."

I picked up my book bag from under the table where I'd stashed it. "I'm good at it. I remember what it's like to be worried you might be arrested. I think you're in the clear, though."

"Really? Why do you say that?"

I hesitated. Lucas had told me to keep a zipped lip, but the urge to drop a little hint was strong. I succumbed, partially. "I think the police have been looking at other candidates," I said, leaning over to speak softly.

My effort was wasted. He didn't hear me amongst the chattering voices swirling around us. "Say what? Oh, hello."

I looked behind me. Gwen stood there, clutching an enormous book bag jammed full of novels. "I wanted to apologize," she said, falling into step with me as I headed for the door. "I was so rude."

"I'll see you later, B.R.," Lonigan said. "Tonight at the ceremony."

I nodded and turned back to Gwen. "No problem." I hesitated, unsure how to bring up the subject, then plunged ahead. "I can imagine how surprising it was to come here and have to face the Richardsons. It must be very difficult. I suppose you didn't realize they'd still be here."

Her face darkened, the layers of flesh tightening. She flushed a deep, painful red and for a second I was afraid she might be having a stroke then she seemed to relax. "I have to learn to face the past sometime," she muttered. "Besides, it's irrelevant how I feel. Their business has suffered so much it's only a matter of time until Saul Richardson loses the resort he loves."

The savage vindictiveness in her voice made me miss a step as we got on the escalator leading up to the lobby. "Well, I'm sure you'll be glad when the conference wraps up," I said. "It must awaken painful memories to see them."

She looked around the open atrium. "My husband and I stayed here on our honeymoon," she said, her voice soft. "I guess many memories are painful." She hesitated at the top of the escalator and I had to nudge her to get her to move. With a surprised jerk she shifted to one side. I was two steps away before I realized she wasn't keeping pace.

"Gwen?" I looked back at her and saw the grief in her eyes as she stared around the lobby beyond the open atrium. "Are you okay?"

"It's just..." She juggled the book bag in her arms and I caught a couple of books as they spilled out. "Mark and I spent such happy times here." Her eyes were bright in the light streaming in from the skylights. She ducked her head when she saw me staring at her.

"I'm sorry, Gwen. Is there anything I can do to help?"

Gwen shook her head miserably. "I'll go to my room. Maybe if I relax for a while..."

She looked like a bedraggled, lost soul. Visions of Ramone revenge vanished. "Do you want to come to my room? We can fix a drink and hang out for a while until I have to get ready for the award ceremony. I'm supposed to meet someone but it probably won't last long." In fact, the more I thought about it, the more I enjoyed the thought of the look on Ramone's face when I showed up with Gwen in tow.

"I'd like that. Would you mind?"

I was amazed at the change. Gwen straightened and she smiled, looking so relieved at the idea of not being alone I felt guilty for any uncharitable thoughts I'd had about her previously. "No, it's fine. I've got a bit of time until I need to get ready and I'm not sure if Lucas will be back yet. So come on up and we'll have a drink. Maybe I can scare up George and Clair and we'll have a little party."

"Oh, I'd hate to impose on them," she said, hanging back.

"They're probably busy anyway." I started walking to the elevator without letting her reconsider. "Come on."

Gwen trailed after me, stuffing books back into the bag in her arms. "Are you sure it's not an imposition? It's okay, I can find something else to do, you don't have to—"

"No problem." I punched the elevator button.

We talked about the books in her bag as we rode the elevator up to my room. I was relieved she seemed a bit more upbeat. I wasn't much good at cheering up people, at least not deliberately. Words always seemed to stick in my throat and I inevitably put my foot in my mouth, making some kind of comment that usually was a total faux pas.

I didn't see Ramone lurking outside my room door as we neared it. I breathed a sigh of relief. Despite my earlier cavalier thoughts, I wasn't sure how I was going to handle the inquisitive detective. Maybe Lucas was inside, waiting for me. The thought of me kissing him while Ramone watched made me hurry down the hall, Gwen struggling to keep pace.

I flung open the door. "Lucas?"

No answer. Damn.

"Oh, I'm sorry. Were you expecting him to be here? I don't want to intrude, if—"

"No, no. That's fine. Drop your stuff anywhere." I gestured vaguely to the coffee table and couch. "Can I fix you a drink? I've got bourbon and some wine, nothing fancy."

"Oh, a glass of wine would be nice." She dropped her book bag on the couch and followed it with her enormous handbag, which made a clunking sound as it hit the wooden couch arm. Gwen sank onto the sofa with a relieved sigh.

I went into the bathroom to retrieve the ice bucket. As I did, I saw my seashell in the bottom, gritty sand around it. I fished it out, relieved there were no strangled snail-creatures drifting in the bottom. I set the shell on a hand towel to dry but as I held it up, a small *something* dropped out of the shell and plunked into the water with a tiny splash.

"What the hell?" I peered into the bottom of the faux leather bucket. A small sparkly object was drifting to the bottom. I considered draining out the water but didn't want to lose the little thingie, so I ducked my hand in and plucked it up, setting it on the towel next to the seashell. It was a circlet of glittering stones, like little rhinestones. I poked it with my finger then picked it up, looping it easily around the top of my pinky.

"Damn. I wondered where that went to."

I turned at the sound of Gwen's voice.

She stood in the doorway to the bathroom, pointing a gun at me.

It didn't make sense at first. Why would Gwen be in the doorway to my hotel bathroom with a gun? "Well, shit." I was frozen in place, my hand raised and the little rhinestone pinky necklace glittering in the lights. "Is this a joke? Tell me this is a joke. It's the Colonel Mustard, right? Wasn't his award a gun?"

Her hand was steady as she pointed the small caliber gun at me. I knew it was small caliber because I'd done research on guns for my books. Of course, it still looked enormous because it was pointed at me.

"No joke, Bea."

"B.R. to you," I snapped. "What's this about?"

"It's the only one left. I had to use the gun."

"Hunh?" My brain was fogged with fear. "Do you mean the Clue game?"

"Of course." She wiggled the gun at me.

"Whoa. Calm down there, Gwen."

Her lips compressed into a small, mean line. "Don't use that tone of voice with me."

I lowered my hand and the little circlet slipped off my finger and went caroming to the floor. "What tone of voice?" I asked with as much reasonableness as I could muster.

"Thin people always treat fat people that way. They act like we're stupid because we're fat. People equate being overweight with stupidity."

I stared at her in disbelief. "You think I'm thin?" I almost laughed out loud. Granted, I wasn't obese but I certainly wasn't svelte. I could stand to lose twenty pounds.

She swept her left hand across her ample front, the right hand remaining rock steady with the gun aimed at my gut. "Compared to me you are."

"Okay, okay." I swallowed hard, trying to find some sense in this surreal conversation. "Gwen, if you want to shoot me because you think I'm thin, you're picking on the wrong person. There are a lot of other people who should move to the top of your list." Something she said suddenly intruded on my babbling. "What do you mean, it's the only one left?" I looked at the gun then looked away, not anxious to see its huge-appearing barrel pointed at me.

"We killed Mary Carr with the candlestick. The only weapon left is the gun."

I opened and closed my mouth like a beached fish, struggling to make sense of her words. "We? Who's we? Mary? When did you kill her? Why?"

She gestured impatiently with the gun and stepped back from the doorway. "Out here."

I hesitated. Was it better to stay in the bathroom or move? She wiggled the gun again. Okay. It was better to move. I took a step but heard a crunching noise under my sandal. I looked down. "It's the thing."

"Get it."

I scooped up the glittery circlet. "What is it? Why do you care about it?"

She held out a hand and I dropped the rhinestones in it. "I left it as a clue but nobody found it. I couldn't figure out why." Her eyes flickered beyond me to the ice bucket. "Now I know. You had

243

the seashell."

"What?" I edged past her and stood in the little hallway between the bedroom area of the suite and the kitchenette/living area.

"It's from Patrice Samuel's necklace. I put it next to John Brody's body."

My mouth sagged open. "Patrice?" I squeaked.

"I heard them arguing. He was trying to blackmail her about some writing contracts or something. He wanted the cover model spot with her company." Gwen gestured again with the gun and I obediently moved ahead of her, into the living room portion of the suite.

"Why would he want the contract so bad?"

Gwen laughed harshly. "He said it was worth a fortune to get the cover slot. He made it sound like his whole life was riding on it. He said something about that other model, the one who made the butter commercials."

"Butter commer—" *Fabio*? Brody thought a book cover could make him into Fabio? I considered the thought and decided it might have merit. Then I saw the gun again and all thoughts of cover models vanished. "But Patrice—she strangled him?"

Gwen gave me a scornful look. "I strangled him. She just left him for dead."

"You—She left him—"

My stupidity must have been annoying because Gwen gave a huge sigh. "Patrice and he were arguing and he was stung by a wasp or a bee. Rather than help him, she ran away. I just finished what an allergy started. It was easy. This—" and she held up the circlet, "—is from her necklace. It hung around the little cat. I left it on the beach, assuming the police would find it."

"But I fell down and must have scooped it up with the shell." I tugged my braid. "But I can't believe you did that. You couldn't have strangled him."

"Everybody underestimates the fat girls." She gave a scary kind of laugh.

"Fat, hell, Gwen. That's got nothing to do with it!" I tugged on my braid again, anxious to assure myself I wasn't dreaming. The pain I felt told me this wasn't a nightmare. It was, unfortunately, reality.

"Then what is it?" she demanded.

"You're nice, Gwen." I couldn't figure out how to articulate the shock I was experiencing. I didn't even try. "You're a nice person. Why would you—"

Like slow motion, fragments of conversation all meshed in my brain. Lonigan's tale of Gwen's woe. Katherine's talk about Gwen's past. "The Richardsons?" I breathed.

"Partly." She gestured with the gun and once again I moved, a jerky puppet at the mercy of her whim. I stood to one side so she could face the door while also keeping an eye on me.

Her positioning terrified me. What if Lucas came through the door? He had a card key and he could very easily waltz in and find a gun pointed at him. "What do you mean, 'partly'?" I started toward the couch but stopped when she shook her head.

"Stay there. Where I can see you."

I stopped so fast I was in mid-step and wobbled carefully, afraid to move. "Did you kill Patrice, too?"

"Of course. That one was easy. Hiding the body was hard."

"Hiding...?"

"I just told her to meet me to discuss Brody's death. We met in the atrium outside the ballroom late at night. The doors to these rooms are never locked, so it was easy to ask her to come in and sit down and talk. But damn, she was heavy. I needed help to move the body." Gwen frowned. "I have to admit I never thought of hiding her body under the table. It was a good idea." It sounded as though the admission was torn out of her. I wondered who had come up with the thought that so annoyed Gwen?

"I don't understand. What did you have against Brody or Patrice or Holly?"

"Nothing. But I needed to prove myself, too."

"To who?"

"When Mark died, it changed everything. I had to—"

I heard the unmistakable sound of a card key in the slot. I leaned forward, prepared to yell, prepared to jump, prepared to do what I had to do in order to rescue Lucas.

Sereta Ramone stepped into the room, pausing with the card key in her hand when she saw Gwen and I.

"Arrest her!" I shouted.

Ramone's eyes flickered to the gun then to me. "I don't think so," she said slowly, coming completely into the room and holding the door open behind her. "I checked the hall. It's clear. We can go."

I looked from her to Gwen, who was nodding. "Come on," she said to me.

"No way." I put a hand on the kitchen counter as though to restrain myself. If I had to, I'd make them drag me kicking and screaming out of there. The room was spinning and I was pretty sure I wasn't in Kansas anymore so it wasn't a tornado or other external storm. "You two are in cahoots?"

Ramone shot a disgusted look at Gwen. "Not by choice, believe me." She gestured to the hallway. "Let's go."

"What does that mean, 'not by choice'? It doesn't make sense."

"We're not using my room for it." Gwen was imperturbable. "The instructions were clear. It has to be a public place."

"What instructions?" I was stalling, stalling,

stalling, praying Lucas would appear from nowhere, gun drawn and ready to kill these two witches.

"We can't stay here," Ramone snapped. "Remarchik might come back or those two nosy faggots she hangs out with. They've been with her all day."

I stiffened in outraged anger. "Now just a minute. There's no—"

"You're right." Gwen ignored my protests without batting an eye. "We'll use the back staircase. I checked it last night. If we go down three flights, we'll be on the upper mezzanine level. We can take the short hall to the service entrance." She gestured with the gun. "Come on."

"You're crazy. There's no way I'm going to go with you."

Gwen's eyes narrowed as she walked slowly toward me. "I can kill you here if you'd prefer." Her eyes swept the room quickly. "Does it have memories for you?"

I swallowed the nausea that threatened. Visions of a breadcrumb trail danced in my head, but I didn't know what kind of crumb I could find in this immaculately cleaned room. "Not particularly." I moved to pick up my book bag but she shook her head.

"Let's go." She took up her own bag, now emptied of books, which had been tossed onto the coffee table.

I glanced at Ramone. She was still in the doorway, looking impatiently at the hallway outside the room. As always, she was stylishly dressed in low-heeled, chunky red shoes, a red shell under a navy jacket and tight-fitting navy pants. Even if she hadn't been one of the Bad Guys, I've have hated her on principle.

"Where are we going?" I inched toward the door, praying for a hurricane, lightning bolt, or a Texan to come and rescue me.

"They said you had to be found in public, so I figured the bookstore. It'll be closed since the award times were changed. It'll work out perfectly with the police here, swarming all over the place."

I had so many questions I wasn't sure where to start. "Who's this 'they' you keep talking about? Is this some kind of contest or something? Did they say it had to be me? Did they say you had to kill me? Why are the police here? Besides the fact there have been three murders in the hotel in the last three days, of course."

Ramone tossed her black hair impatiently. "There was another attempted murder."

"Attempted?"

"Attempted?"

Both Gwen and I spoke at the same moment. "You first," I mumbled, trying to get as far away from her in the crowded confines of the hotel doorway.

"Carr isn't dead." Ramone strode out of the room and took a dozen steps down the hall, to the stairwell door. She quickly opened it and gestured.

"She should be dead." Gwen grabbed my right arm and dragged me forward. "Go."

"Ow. Be careful. I was wounded."

"You should be dead, too. Go."

I scurried into the hallway, peering up and down its length frantically. It was empty. Where was the cleaning staff when you needed them? Where was Lucas, George, or Clair? I thought they'd have joined me by now. Where was the cavalry when you needed them?

Maybe someone heard me. As we entered the stairwell, my phone chimed *Lyin' Eyes*. Bless you, Eagles, wherever you were. "I'd better answer," I muttered, pulling the phone out of my pocket. "I'm expecting this call."

"Put it away." Gwen gestured with the gun but before I could comply, Ramone said,

"It may be Remarchik. Let her answer. If he's trying to get in touch with her and she doesn't answer, he might cause trouble."

"Put it on speaker," Gwen snapped.

I stared at the phone in my hand. "I have no idea how to do that," I said truthfully. "I'm not very high tech." The Eagles chimed at me again. "I'd better answer." Without waiting for permission, I opened the phone. *Oh please, please, let it be Lucas*, I prayed. "Hello?"

"You get engaged and you can't call your mother?"

Damn. God wasn't listening. I got Mavis instead. I tried to marshal my scattered brain cells as I forced a smile at Gwen. How to drop a clue? If I used Lucas' name, Ramone would be on me like a duck on a June bug. I needed something else … something neither Gwen nor Ramone would recognize.

Think think think.

"I'm so sorry," I said. "Mrs. Beauchamp? Is that you? I can't hear you very well."

"It's your mother, Beatrice. Although I don't know why I bother. You can't call and tell me the most important news of your life, so why should I —"

"Ah, yes. Mrs. Beauchamp. It's so nice to talk to you. George said you might call."

"It's your mother, Beatrice. Wake up."

"Yes, I am a bit busy."

"I don't really care. Is there some reason you didn't call and tell me? I had to learn this news from Clair? You're finally engaged, and to such a fabulous man, and I hear about it from your friends? I don't know whether to be hurt or angry. You're my daughter, and you can't —"

Mavis had a full head of steam going and I would be hard pressed to stop her. I made an attempt. "I understand that, but I can't talk right now. Please call George and discuss it with him. I'd really appreciate that."

There was a long, ominous pause. "What's going on? It's not like you to be this obtuse. I realize you're in love and probably overwhelmed with excitement, but this isn't like you. Why would I call George? I'm not even sure I have George's number, although I suspect I do. You gave me a million phone numbers and one of them is probably—"

"Good. Talk to George Delacroix about it. I don't have the number handy, I'm sorry. He can help you, Mrs. Beauchamp. Either George or Clair Johnson can help. It was nice to chat with you." I closed the phone with trembling fingers and stuffed it back into my back pocket, making sure to leave it on. If I was lucky, Lucas might indeed call. I had no doubt Mavis would call him and tell him I was acting like an idiot.

I looked around me. It was a typical stairwell in a typical hotel. Grey cinderblock walls framed concrete steps and a metal hand railing. As I started slowly down the steps, Ramone in front of me, I realized it looked eerily like the one in Abilene last year where I'd almost been killed.

Where Lucas was almost killed.

I took a deep breath and gripped the railing tighter.

Chapter 19

"It has to be before the award ceremony," Gwen said from the step above and behind me. Her voice was soft in the echoing, empty stairwell, and I cursed my luck. Why weren't there a bunch of health-conscious people using the steps? Where were the joggers and the eco-friendly people trying to conserve energy by using the stairs?

I was acutely aware of the gun, not too far from my back. "Says who?" I demanded. "You keep acting like somebody is keeping score."

Ramone barked out a harsh laugh. "Good way to phrase it."

"I wasn't talking to you." I glared at her dark hair as she danced down the steps in front of me. Damn stylish woman. Why couldn't she trip on her expensive shoes and take a tumble?

"I'll go ahead," she called back over one shoulder. "Make sure it's clear."

Behind me I heard Gwen puffing as she negotiated the steep stairs. I remembered her earlier comments about 'bad knees' and wondered if her comment was real or fake, like everything else about her. "Why, Gwen? None of this makes sense to me."

251

"I was the perfect choice. It took me a while to convince them, but—"

"Okay, that does it." I stopped so fast she almost ran into me. "Who the hell is 'they'?" I started moving again before she could get pissed off and shoot me where I stood.

"Mark's employers. When he died, they didn't think I could take over his job. I had to prove myself. They chose when and what weapon. I just had to decide who and how."

Either the stairs or the conversation was making me dizzy. I shook my head and almost pitched headlong down the next flight. "Job? He killed people?"

"He was one of the best." Her voice reflected a spouse's pride in her husband's work.

Good God. Had I fallen down a rabbit hole? Gwen, married to a hit man, an assassin? "That's hard to believe."

"That's why we were the perfect team. I was his cover."

She had a point. Who would believe overweight, plain, sweet-as-pie Gwen could be a hit man-or woman?

"I'll check the hall." Ramone disappeared through a door in front of us at the next turn of the stairs.

"Wait here."

I glanced over my shoulder. Gwen was pointing with the gun to the landing above the door where Ramone had gone. I very briefly considered jumping her for the gun but quickly realized (1) she was above and behind me and jumping would be a tricky proposition; (2) Gwen weighed about two hundred pounds more than me and was six inches taller; and (3) I was a coward and wouldn't know what to do with a gun if I did manage to wrestle it away from her grip.

I compromised and moved into the corner of the landing, which barely had enough room for me, much less my captor and the gun. "Gwen, explain this to me." I strove to keep my voice reasonable. I vaguely remembered some research I'd done on hostage negotiations and if ever I needed that info, it was now. Fragments of facts flickered into my brain. 'Try to make friends with your captor. Stay calm, be reasonable. Keep the captor talking. Don't make extreme demands.'

Would "don't shoot me" be considered extreme?

"It's simple, really. When the Richardsons ruined my life, I decided to ruin theirs."

She sounded so matter-of-fact I almost fell for it. "Um, Gwen. They didn't mean to ruin your life. It wasn't..." I almost said, 'it wasn't personal'. Well, duh. Of course it was personal, to her.

"It doesn't matter. Mark's employers were trying to get rid of the Richardsons for years, so my interests coincided with theirs. They gave me all their support." She scowled at the door where Ramone had disappeared. "They didn't trust me to do it alone, though."

I noted her disgusted expression. Maybe I could play off the antagonism each woman felt for the other. I had to do something. I couldn't count on Lucas to come to the rescue. I hadn't been able to contact him and he had no idea I was in trouble.

Before I could implement my non-existent plan, the door below me opened. "Let's go." Ramone held the door open, looking up to the stairs to me and then glancing out into the unseen hallway.

I hurried down the steps and brushed by Ramone before Gwen could lumber down after me. I had an idea I might be able to scuttle ahead of them and out into safety. But Ramone grabbed my left arm and jerked hard. The pain was agonizing, grinding me to a halt. "You bitch." I could barely get the words out because nausea threatened.

"Live with it." She dragged me to one side as Gwen burst out of the doorway.

"This way." Gwen was panting but it didn't slow her down. She gestured with the gun and I stepped into place ahead of her, Ramone leading the way. "Straight down the hall then go right. That will lead us to the main conference area. The service hall is off of that."

I was trapped in a hotel maze with two crazy women. The halls were narrow with small meeting rooms opening off to the left and right at various intervals. The rooms were dark now, the conference coming to a close as everyone presumably was in their room, prepping for the award ceremony taking place in an hour or so.

The deep carpet deadened all sound around us. It felt like I was in a deadly cocoon and realized my analogy was truer than I cared to admit. We were in a deserted place, no one knew I was there, and no one would come into these rooms until tomorrow at the earliest. I was up the proverbial creek without a paddle.

We went right at the next turn and I recognized the workshop corridor from earlier in the day. We'd come into the area from a different direction I'd used, but now I saw the familiar landmark of conference signs ahead of me.

Just as we rounded the corner, I saw a figure enter the hallway from the other direction. "Hey, B.R.!" Aidan Lindsey hurried forward.

Gwen shifted as though to give Aidan room to move in the narrow hall, dropping her gun hand out of sight but still aimed at me. Ramone shoved me and I stumbled into the wall, almost passing out from the pain.

"Get rid of her," Ramone hissed near my ear.

I had a hard time thinking much less

attempting to be creative about making up excuses. "Hi, Aidan. What are you doing here?" I shifted position so I could use the wall to hold me up.

She looked around, bewildered. "I don't know. I was looking for the Pensacola Room. My publisher is having a party there. Boy, when ClueCon changed the time for the awards they really goofed up the party schedule. Where's Pittman's party? Is it around here?"

"The parties are in the other hallway, over there." Gwen bustled past me. The gun had disappeared into the voluminous book bag slung over her shoulder.

The gun was gone. That little fact penetrated the fog of my pain. I pushed away from the wall and tried to follow Gwen and Aidan.

"Don't." Ramone stepped in front of me, her back to Gwen and Aidan. Only I saw the small gun pointed at my heart.

"Oh, I forgot to tell you. George Delacroix is looking for you." Aidan called this little tidbit back over her shoulder as Gwen hustled her away. "If I see him, I'll tell him I saw you."

"Tell him I'm looking for him, too." My voice was so weak I wasn't sure she'd heard me, but she waved a hand as they sped out of sight.

"Let's go. We'll wait for Dummy in the room."

"Dummy?" I staggered forward, moving in the direction Ramone indicated. It was in the opposite direction from the disappearing Gwen and Aidan.

"Bandorf." Ramone spat out Gwen's name like a bad taste. "Go left, through that door."

I pushed through the white door marked Employees Only. We were in another short hallway, again with doors at set intervals. This hall wasn't as attractive as the others on the more well-traveled routes in the hotel. It was probably used by service personnel. I kept walking until we got to the end of the hall. "Open it."

I stared blankly at the door in front of me. "Where's it go?"

"To the back door of the bookstore room. It should be unlocked."

"Who unlocked it?"

"You don't need to know."

I tried the door. Damn. She was right. It wasn't locked. "Did you bribe someone?"

"I think 'bribe' might be a bit glorified. It didn't take too much." Ramone shoved me, pushing against my injured shoulder. Maybe my previous pain had inured me to shock, but all I felt this time was another wave of nausea.

I stepped warily into the darkened room. We came in at the back and center of the space. During my previous forays into the room, I'd been more interested in the book covers and the Clue board game than the layout so I hadn't examined the room itself very closely. The place was in darkness now, the only light coming from the glass panels on either side of the double doors opposite us at the far end of the room and a weak glow from security lights inset into the ceiling. It was a rectangular room with six tables in the middle and an aisle between them, each about six-foot square, with books stacked on each. The tables were draped with white linen cloths reaching to the floor. In the center of each table, on a pedestal silhouetted in the dim light, the Clue weapons were poised: gun, rope, knife, pipe, wrench, and candlestick. I wished they were real. I'd lunge for any of them.

But I was trapped. I was in a locked room with a crazy woman with a real, honest-to-God gun. This wasn't some damn mystery plot. This was real, not a nightmare. I wracked my brain for a creative solution but nothing happened except I made myself dizzy again.

"Why did you call her Dummy earlier?" It was a lame attempt at conversation, but I was desperate for anything.

Ramone jerked the gun and I followed the movement, taking a spot in the center aisle near the table holding Red Nail books on one side, Aidan's books on the other. The wrench Clue weapon, about a foot long, was poised on a three-foot pedestal in the center of the table. I glanced hopefully at it but it was obviously made of rubber. How I longed for a real, heavy-duty, iron wrench. Then I remembered the one I'd seen next to Holly's body and my stomach lurched. I doubted I'd have the nerve to use such a weapon.

Ramone stayed near the back of the room where she could watch the door we'd just used and keep an eye on the front door, behind me. "Isn't it obvious? My..." She hesitated. What word was she considering and discarding? "My bosses weren't sure Gwen could pull it off so they told me to watch out for her."

"Bosses?"

Ramone's face looked sculpted in the play of shadows from the pale security lights overhead. "The mob."

I almost laughed out loud. "The mob? That's so cliché. You must be kidding."

"The Cuban mob."

"Oh." Stupid me. I didn't know Cuba had mobs. I was from Minnesota, and while we had a lot of water, we didn't have a lot of water sharing a border with another country. The area around the lakes sharing turf with Canada was sparsely populated and probably not a hotbed of suspicious activity. On the other hand, the southern coast of the U.S. was within spitting distance of Cuba, and presumably boats could come and go at will. I had no idea what kind of water patrol would be needed to keep illegal foreigners at bay.

Then I remembered Donna Del Marco's comment about 'Hispanic mobs' and it suddenly made sense. If the mob was trying to get a foothold in the area, what better person to have in your pocket than a Hispanic detective on a police force?

"Does that mean you've never worked with Gwen before?" I asked, trying to keep the conversational ball rolling.

"Be quiet." Her bored, patient voice was like a parent, tired of repeating the same lesson over and over again. 'We'll get there when we get there.' 'Don't touch your sister.' 'Be quiet.'

I tried to remember what Lucas had said about their investigation. He'd said something about tonight—Ramone was leading the police to something happening tonight. "Is it all a diversion? Is that what this is about?"

Her attention snapped to me. "Why do you say that?"

I tried to shrug nonchalantly, using the action to pick up and put down a book on the table. I had the inkling of a plan and I wanted to start implementing it. "Seems to me a lot of police attention has been on this hotel in the past few days. Maybe it's a smokescreen. Maybe something more important is going on."

Light glinted on the gun as she shifted position. "Don't count on it."

"Maybe it's why people have been killed. I'll bet it wasn't about Gwen at all. I'll bet your bosses were hoping to shift attention from them to the conference." I nodded as though this all made perfect sense. The scary thing was, it *did* make sense. "The conference was the red herring."

"What? What are you talking about?"

"There's always a red herring. The conference was the red herring." I moved slowly around the table, picking up another book and setting it back down, trying to look nervous. Hell, I was nervous. It shouldn't be hard to look the part. "Maybe that explains why you're paired with Gwen. Maybe they're worried. Maybe they're afraid she can't pull it off. Or..." I glanced at Ramone then at the book in my hand, setting it down. It knocked over a stack of books, sending them tumbling into the center of the table. The pedestal holding the rubber wrench teetered but didn't fall although a small pyramid of stiletto shoes did cascade to the floor.

"Get away from there." She gestured with the gun and I moved from the table, positioning myself between it and the next table on my right.

"Maybe your bosses weren't so much worried about Gwen as they were worried about you." I edged toward the table near my right hand, this one covered with Lonigan's books. I had my eye on a coil of rope on top of the three-foot pedestal in the middle of the table. "Maybe Gwen is keeping an eye on you, too." The sharp look Ramone shot me told me my guess had hit home. "After all, if Martinelli suspects you then—" I shut my mouth too late.

"What?"

I picked up a book and set it down, hoping for another tumble of books. These were hard cover books, though, and it would take more than one misplaced volume to cause a fall. "It just makes sense you're paired with her for a dual reason."

"Not that. What about Pete?"

"What about him?"

Her eyes narrowed and she moved closer to me, the gun aimed steadily at my chest. "You said he suspects me. Suspects me of what?"

I blurted the first thing that came to mind, probably because it had been in the forefront of my mind for the last three days. "Infidelity."

The back door opened and Gwen came in. "I got

259

rid of her. There are some publishing parties going on, but they're in the next hallway over. No one will hear anything. They've got music playing and people are talking. There must be a couple of dozen people in each of the rooms. I checked before coming here."

I looked away from Ramone, who was frozen in place, staring at me in disbelief. Gwen had retrieved her gun and had it trained on me, aiming in my general direction. She was at about two o'clock and Ramone was at ten o'clock from me. The table display with the wrench—Aidan's table—was between Ramone and I so she didn't have a clear shot. If I could take one step back, the display table with the rope would then be between Gwen and I.

It was the only chance I had. The rope table was covered with hard-backed books, not paperbacks. I prayed Lonigan's books would be dense enough to stop a bullet. I was just taking a deep breath and getting ready to duck when several things happened.

My phone thumped my butt and chimed *Victim of Love*.

The back door slammed open, hitting Gwen in the shoulder.

Someone pounded on the main doors, behind me.

Ramone's hand tightened on her gun.

I dove for cover under the display table as all hell broke loose. Light spilled in from the open door and the service hall, illuminating a man who'd barreled into the room and was now wrestling with Gwen for her gun. I tucked myself under the linen folds of the table holding Lonigan's books, cursing when I found a bunch of low, squat boxes under there and not the clear space I'd been hoping for. I ignored the stunning pain in my shoulder and clambered on top of the boxes then cautiously lifted the edge of the tablecloth to peer out.

I saw a pair of red shoes heading toward me. I

looked to the right and for an instant the man's face was illuminated by light spilling in from the hallway where the door had been left open.

It was George.

Good God, what was he doing here? He was struggling with Gwen for the gun, the weapon still in Gwen's hand. George had a grip on her wrist and was attempting to pin her to the ground, but she fought him like a crazy woman, kicking at him and punching him with her free hand. George was solidly built but Gwen outweighed him by about a hundred pounds and was younger by at least a decade.

The red shoes were very close and I felt the table over me wobble. "Get out of there," Ramone hissed, her voice low.

I knew the table was heavy with all the books on it. I was banking on her having to put down her gun, holster it, or abandon the idea of tipping the table.

I didn't count on her sweeping off the books and upending the table with one hand. Books, fiberglass pedestal with rope, and faux knives/letter openers used for Lonigan's promo all went scattering as the table flipped. Some of the books landed on George and Gwen, who still fought for the gun. The rest landed on me, or so it felt.

I rolled off the boxes I'd been resting on and sprang to my feet, diving for the table covered with Aidan's books and the Red Nail books. I caught a glimpse of the rubber wrench tipping over as Ramone kicked toward me and missed, hitting the table instead. The space under this table was clear, thank God, and I was able to dive out the other side and head for the front door and the person still out there, pounding.

The gunshot was muffled but still loud in the small space. I froze in place and looked back over my shoulder. Gwen was getting clumsily to her feet, the gun still in her hand. I saw George lying limp on the floor, his body sprawled and broken-looking.

I don't know what possessed me but I changed direction in mid-step and whirled, lurching to the right. That probably saved my life. Ramone's shot missed me by inches, thudding into the display of books behind me, toppling the pedestal with the Clue gun, appropriately enough. I dodged around the fallen table and Lonigan's scattered books as I scooped up the rope. Gwen stared at me as though I was insane, and maybe I was. She was just raising the gun when I dodged to one side and looped the rope around her neck, twisting it and turning so she was in front of me. I peered around her corpulent body at Ramone.

"Stalemate," I gasped, my heart thudding so hard I was sure I was having a heart attack.

Ramone shifted her gun and it felt as though a laser was targeting the small bit of my head peeking from under Gwen's arm. The big woman was gasping and struggling in front of me, but I had a firm grip on the rope. I knew I couldn't hold her long. She was too big and too strong. I just needed a few minutes, though. "Get help!" I screamed. "I need help!"

The unknown person outside the front door stopped pounding.

"Checkmate," Ramone said softly.

She fired.

Gwen's dead weight dragged the rope out of my hands as her body hit the floor.

I dove for the cover of the upturned table as another shot missed me by inches. My hand closed around one of the stiletto shoes that had tumbled to the floor from Aidan's promo. I saw Ramone moving toward me and I rolled over onto my stomach, bringing my right arm up and swinging down with all my might, putting the full force of my body into the blow.

The four-inch heel of the shoe bit into the arch of

Ramone's foot, stopped by cartilage and bone. She screamed and jerked back, the gun in her hand waving crazily. I got to my hands and knees and scuttled across the floor to George, who was lying so still and quiet. I looked back over my shoulder and saw Ramone taking aim at me again.

"Sereta."

Pete Martinelli's voice was eerily calm.

"Drop it."

Ramone's head moved slowly to look at the front door and I followed her gaze. Martinelli was framed in the light from the hall, Lucas behind him. Then Ramone's eyes turned back to me and she raised the gun.

I moved so I was blocking George's body with my own, staring into the barrel.

This was death. I couldn't believe it. That bitch was going to shoot me. I was seconds away from dying.

"Drop it." Martinelli's voice was still calm but there was an edge to it now. I heard desperation in his tone and I wondered if Ramone could hear it, too.

Ramone's eyes got colder as she started to squeeze the trigger.

The gunshot was deafening in the room. I jerked, expecting pain. I took a deep, experimental breath but everything seemed intact. There was no agony, no shock, no weakening from a bullet wound.

Ramone dropped the gun, falling back and clutching at her leg.

Lucas came into view, his gun still up and in firing position. "You don't get three warnings, Sereta." He lowered his gun and handed it to Pete. "I'm sorry. She was threatening the woman I love."

I did the womanly thing and fainted.

Chapter 20

"How the hell did you know to come to the rescue?" I asked George.

We were once again at the Sacred Heart of the Emerald Coast hospital, where George and I had both been taken. It was now evening. I was ambulatory, with only more bruises to my score, but he had a broken collarbone from his struggles with Gwen and would be staying overnight for observation. Clair had overcome his overwhelming fear of hospitals and was sitting next to George, jumping anxiously at every hospital machine beep, whir, or burp.

"Mavis called me," George explained. "When she told me about Mrs. Beauchamp, I remembered talking to you about her and how I said Gwen reminded me of Mrs. Beauchamp."

"So? That still doesn't explain—"

"I saw Aidan Langley. She said you were with Gwen and looking for me. Aidan pointed me in the right direction. I caught a glimpse of Gwen going into a doorway, so I followed." He glanced at Lucas, who stood next to me. "After I called in the cavalry, who, as it turns out, was on the way all the time."

Lucas put his hand on the back of my neck and gently massaged my tight muscles. I started to relax against him then remembered I was mad. "Why the hell didn't you tell me Ramone was bugged? It sounds like something out of *Get Smart*. You put the bug in her shoe?"

"Yep. Clair gave me the idea."

"I did?" Clair looked so startled I knew he hadn't been paying attention to our talk.

Lucas nodded. "All that talk about shoes you and Bea had earlier. Ramone always went to the gym to work out before her shift started. It was a simple matter to get into her locker and put in the bug."

"But what if you couldn't put it in the shoe? What if she wore flats?"

"Then it would have gone into the jacket or her blouse or somewhere else. We had to get that information." Lucas smiled down at me, his brown eyes so tender my heart almost broke. Then his next words dispelled any romantic feeling. "You can't lie to save your life, honey. I knew if you knew about it, you wouldn't be able to stop yourself from tipping our hand."

I guiltily remembered my blurt about Martinelli to Ramone a few hours earlier. Maybe Lucas was right, but still... "Tip your hand?" I tried to turn a glare on Martinelli, but Lucas' hand on my neck made the movement far more polite than I meant it to be. "You almost tipped us into getting dead, damn it. Why didn't you move sooner? Why didn't you—"

"We needed her confession on tape. We got part of it while you were in the stairwell, but we wanted more."

"Yeah, well, your 'more' almost got us 'less'." I was starting to build up a Mavis head of steam. "Because of you, George got wounded."

"We screwed up on that. I'm sorry."

His simple statement of culpability deflated me as effectively as beach sand on an ice cube. "Yeah, well, sorry doesn't cut it." That sounded lame, even to me.

"Bea." Lucas' voice was cautionary and amused.

"Hey, Ralph. It's okay. All's well that ends well." George exchanged a wry look with Lucas.

"And you?" I turned to Clair. "What was that with the pounding on the bookstore door?"

He shrugged, bony shoulders rising and falling in his Polo shirt. "George told me to call you when he took off after Gwen. So I did and I heard your cell phone. It sounded like it was coming from the bookstore, so I knocked on the door."

"That surprised Ramone, and George surprised Gwen and —" I tugged on my braid, recreating the scene in my head. "How bad is she hurt?"

"Gwen?" Lucas gently massaged my shoulder. "She didn't make it."

It felt as though someone had punched me. I wasn't sure whether to be happy or sad. I mean, yes, she'd held me at gunpoint, but... "So does Ramone get arrested for murder?" I stared defiantly at Pete Martinelli, who nodded.

"Among other things."

"Hey there—glad to see you're doing okay."

We all turned to see Donna Del Marco in the doorway. She came into the room, glancing once at Pete then going to George's bedside.

"Your first aid did the trick," George said. "Thanks. I'm glad you were on the scene."

"Your mystery conference has given the Emergency Services department more action than we normally see in a month." Donna smiled at me. "Plus two assault runs today—that's some kind of record, I think."

"Two runs?" I'd missed the action when being involved in action of my own.

She nodded. "Mary Carr was found in the what-you-call-it, the crime scene display. She'd been struck with a big metal candlestick. It didn't kill her, but she's got a bad concussion. She's lucky to be alive. How are you doing? I'm sorry you missed your big night."

"Hunh? My big night? Oh, shit. That's right. The award ceremony. Tony and I were supposed to sit together and—" I sighed. "I wonder if I won anything."

"I'm sure we'll find out when we get back," Lucas said. "Speaking of which…it's time for us to get out of here and let George get some rest." He went to George's side, Donna moving away so Lucas could bend over and talk to George. "I owe you. You shouldn't have been hurt. We screwed up."

George smiled faintly. "Believe me, if I'd known, I would never have done it." Then he looked at me and winked.

I wiggled in between them and kissed George on the cheek. "Sleep well, knight in shining armor." I looked at Clair, who sat on the edge of his chair. "Will you be okay tonight? Can you stay here?"

"The nurse said I could stay in the lounge. It'll be okay."

I recognized bravado when I saw it so I didn't question him further. As Lucas and I left, I saw Pete Martinelli and Donna in a conversation down the hall. "I wonder if they'll …"

Lucas firmly steered me away. "None of our business."

"I still have a lot of questions," I said as we waited for the elevator.

"I know you do. I can't answer them." When I started to protest, he put a gentle finger on my lips. "But I know a man who can. Will you be willing to wait until tomorrow to talk to him?"

I considered it as we rode down the three flights

of stairs and walked out to the rental car Lucas was using. "I suppose," I said as I settled against the seat. "But I'll need something to distract me tonight so I don't stay awake thinking about it."

He turned to smile at me. "I think I know just the thing."

****

I awoke to sunlight shining in our hotel room. Lucas was already dressed in black jeans and a white shirt and sat in the chair near the window, staring out at the ocean. He looked over his shoulder at me as I stirred. "Time to get up, Princess."

"Queen," I mumbled into my pillow. "Why do I have to get up so early?"

"Company is coming."

"Hunh?" I raised my head to look at him blearily.

"Remember I said a man can answer your questions?" Lucas looked at his wristwatch. "He'll be here in thirty minutes."

"Say what?"

"A person in a position of authority in the FBI is coming here to chat with you. Of course, that assumes you can get out of bed and get dressed in time to chat."

I sat upright and looked at the clock. "It's only seven a.m."

"Crime never rests and neither do the Feds. Consider this a debriefing. I'd suggest you be up and ready for him."

I flung back the covers and winced. Sore muscles protested, but this time it was from a happy activity, not from being wounded. Lucas watched as I walked naked into the bathroom. "Nice try at distracting me."

I wiggled my butt. "I must be losing my touch."

He laughed. "I'll get the coffee made."

"Make it a double," I called back.

I prepped in record time and was taking my first sip of coffee when a knock sounded on our hotel suite. Lucas opened the door to a tall man with graying hair and a craggy face dressed in lightweight summer slacks and a khaki shirt. He didn't look like any Fed I'd ever met, but then again, I hadn't met many. I suppose he was traveling incognito.

"L.J. said you have some questions," he said without preamble.

I blinked at his abrupt manner but a glance from Lucas made me swallow the sharp comment I was going to make. "Oh, a few dozen." I held up my mug. "Coffee, Mr. —?"

"No, thanks." He sat down on the couch. "Ask away. I'll answer what I can."

Lucas took the chair opposite me and picked up his coffee mug. His face was impassive but I saw humor in his brown eyes.

I took a swallow of coffee, using the moment to order my thoughts. "Who drugged me? Who knocked me out with the pipe? Who put the note in my book bag? Who threw the bottle over the balcony? Who killed Brody, Patrice, and Holly? Why were they killed? What do the Richardsons have to do with all this? How come—"

"You weren't drugged."

I straightened indignantly. "I certainly was. I didn't pass out from two drinks."

"Let me rephrase that. You weren't drugged intentionally. Gwen Bandorf drugged two of the drinks sent to your table. She didn't care which ones. You got one."

"What about the other one?"

He shrugged. "No one else passed out, so no one drank it. That was the start of it all."

"Someone said writers were being doped so..." I stopped as he shook his head.

"Rumor, that's all. Probably started by Gwen."

"But the Christian—there was the stalker guy and he said he collected books from authors he—"

"He what?"

I struggled to remember the exact phrasing but couldn't. All I could remember was it had sounded ominous at the time. "I thought he meant..."

"There is a person here who's a member of a fringe Christian group, gathering so-called data about erotica publishers." The man's face didn't waver a bit as he said the word 'erotica'. I wondered what he really thought. "But he has an airtight alibi for Wednesday night."

"Airtight?"

"He was with a prostitute." A small smile quirked the corner of the man's mouth so fast I wasn't sure I'd really seen it. "With a woman who looks something like you."

I opened and closed my mouth in stunned surprise. Even Lucas looked startled.

"Apparently he has something of a crush on you."

I tried to banish the thought of the pig-man mooning over me. The image made me nauseous. I decided to consider the idea at a later time, like never. I forced my brain back to the quandary of Gwen and the nightclub. "She wasn't there. How could she have drugged my drink?"

He slid a picture across the coffee table to me. "Recognize her?"

I took it and examined the photo of a couple, probably in their forties, standing in front of a statue. They were plump, well-dressed and obviously happy, grinning at the camera like school kids. "Nope."

"That's Gwen."

"Not." I snatched the picture back and stared closer. The woman was overweight but dressed in the height of fashion in a pretty navy-and-white knit top with matching navy capris. The outfit was slimming and very chic looking. Her hair was curly but styled, cut in such a way it made gentle wisps around her face. Her makeup—or her tan—was impeccable. Only the eyes gave her away. They were direct, unflinching, and shrewd even though the woman was relaxed and happy. "Gwen?"

"Yep."

So if that was Gwen ... she might have been in the restaurant and I wouldn't have seen her. His next words made me blink in surprise.

"She and her husband were a hit team for the mob."

"No way." I didn't care Gwen had admitted as much. It didn't make sense.

Again that little twitch of the man's mouth. "Way. They traveled everywhere for the mob and were very successful."

I slid the picture back to him. "Why didn't you arrest them?"

"No definitive proof. We were close to getting them when her father was fingered by Saul Richardson and went to prison. Mark Bandorf, Gwen's husband, tried to get revenge but we were looking for that. We intercepted him and he was put in prison, where he died."

"So Gwen was left alone..." Hit woman for the mob? I started to voice my objection but the words died in my throat. I remembered Gwen's words: 'Nobody sees the fat girl. People equate weight with stupidity.' It might have worked. "Was this conference her try-out?"

The man considered my words. "We're not sure. Maybe. The mob has been trying to get their hands on the Richardson resort for years. The gangs have hotels all up and down this coast, but they haven't been able to get a foothold in Ft. Walton Beach. The

271

Richardsons have refused to sell. Apparently someone high up in the organization thought the time was ripe for a takeover since Saul will be retiring soon and David has made some unfortunate financial decisions. Gwen wanted a shot at them, given her family history with their family. It was a chance for her to prove herself, to prove she could operate alone."

"But Martinelli said..." I tried to remember. "Something about Saul Richardson getting money from some gangster years ago."

Lucas shifted position and my eyes went to him. "Richardson's wife, David Richardson's mother, was the daughter of a well-known mobster. As far as we know, he was never directly involved, but her family did help him out from time to time."

I returned to the fantastic notion of Gwen as hit woman. "That's insane. Wouldn't that be a red flag? I mean, didn't the local police see Gwen Bandorf at the Richardson resort and think, 'oops, murder in the offing'?" I glared at him.

"Yes and no. There's no restraining order on her, so she can go where she pleases. She's been lying low since her husband died and we weren't sure if she was still connected. We kept her on a watch list so when this conference came up and she registered, it tripped alarms. It gave us an excellent excuse to put someone else in place here to check on another suspicion of ours, one we needed to have verified."

Pieces of the puzzle thunked into place. "You could have Lucas here, pretending to check on Gwen when in actual fact he was looking at Sereta Ramone. So Ramone would think Lucas' primary purpose was to investigate Gwen. Two birds with one stone."

"Bingo. L.J. said you were smart. He wasn't kidding."

I glared at Lucas. "Thanks for that vote of

confidence. But when people started turning up dead, why didn't you move in? You were putting us all in jeopardy, you jerks. You should have moved in with everything you had and—"

"Whoa. We had no proof."

I was so angry I sputtered. "No proof? Since when has that stopped the government? I don't believe you! What the hell were you doing, sitting there waiting to see who came out of it all alive? One of my dearest friends was injured. I was put into danger. And that's just people I know! What about Patrice and Holly and—"

"I told him not to get you started, Princess."

"Queen," I snapped.

"Sorry." Lucas' mustache twitched and he ducked his head, probably to hide his smirk.

"You know the rest," the man said. "Gwen killed Brody and left the clue in the seashell, but you found the shell. Gwen threw the wine bottle over the balcony. She didn't care if it hurt anyone, she just wanted to make it look like negligence on the part of the hotel. Holly Newcastle knew Patrice and Brody were talking, so she left the note and the bit of rope in your bag." The man's gaze flicked to Lucas. "Everyone knew you were involved with an ex-cop. I suppose she thought you could do something."

"But what about the big deal last night? There was some sort of special thing happening, right? Did that go on as planned? Was this all a diversion?"

Lucas and the man exchanged a look. "Can't discuss that," Lucas said.

"Now just a minute. Does that mean you have to stay here? What about the undercover work you're doing?"

The man stood up. "I don't believe this part of the conversation involves me."

"Whoa. There are still some questions."

He waited, looking down at me, his

273

unremarkable face impassive. "Yes?"

I opened and closed my mouth. "Patrice," I blurted. "Why did Gwen kill her?" Then I remembered her words. 'They choose when and what weapon'. "Was it just convenient?"

"Maybe. We're not sure. Remember, we have no proof on any of this. She was good, very good. Almost as good as her husband." He said it with grudging respect, and I realized I was hearing Gwen's eulogy.

Knowing her, she'd have been pleased. I peered up at him. "Thanks, Maxwell, for answering my questions. Even though some of the answers were a bit cryptic."

He frowned, perplexed. "Maxwell?"

Lucas got up, too. "Nothing. Private joke." He walked the man to the door and they spoke for a minute then he came back.

"This was all about revenge? Revenge and some people trying to get this resort?" I sagged back in the chair, my mind whirling with facts and conjectures.

"I suppose you could say that." Lucas held out a hand. "Care to go for a walk? We can talk some more."

I let him haul me to my feet. "So will you still be working?" I asked as we went down the hall to the elevator.

"If I do, it'll be out of the line of fire. I'm really retiring this time." He grinned at me as we got onto the elevator. "I'll have better things to do, like drive around the country in an RV."

"Good. I'd rather not have to look over my shoulder at every stop we make." I reviewed what I'd been told. "There're still some unanswered questions," I said as we stepped out of the elevator into the lower lobby.

"Just some?" Lucas' boots echoed on the marble floors as we headed for the outside doors. "I can think of a lot you must have."

"Here's one to start with. Who sent the letter to Karen, warning you away from me?"

He paused with his hand on the door leading to the pool and, beyond it, the ocean. "I don't know." We stared at each other for a long minute. "That's something to find out, I guess."

"No kidding. Here's another question: what happened to Ramone? If you'll recall, I passed out and when I came to, I was in the ambulance." We walked outside onto the patio surrounding the pool. It was a windy morning and dark clouds scuttled on the horizon. I sniffed, smelling rain on the air.

"I just winged her. She's got a broken leg and a prison term ahead of her."

I linked my arm through his as we skirted the pool and headed toward the exit to the beach. "So all the flirting was just part of the job?"

"Hmm." Lucas pulled his sunglasses out of his shirt pocket and put them on. "I believe we're being paged."

I followed his gaze and saw Saul Richardson hurrying toward us from the open-air restaurant next to the beach. Even from a distance I could see he wasn't the same worried man I'd encountered four days before. He looked as though a huge weight had been lifted. "I'm glad to see you're recovered, Miss Emerson." He took my hand in his and made a courtly bow over it, kissing it quickly.

The gesture flustered me so much I didn't know what to say, so I settled for, "I'm fine. It's just a flesh wound." Then I wanted to slap myself upside the head for sounding like such an idiot. "I hope things will work out okay for you and the hotel."

He looked back at the building behind us. "My family has had a place here for four generations. But no piece of real estate is worth a life. I need to reassess my options."

"Well, don't do it because of what happened

here. From what I can tell, we were all just in the wrong place at the wrong time. It seems to me it's not your fault."

He smiled but it was tinged with sadness. "Thank you. You're very gracious." He looked at the ocean and the waves lapping at the shore. "Going for a last walk on the beach before heading back to cold and snowy Minnesota?"

"Snowy?" Lucas started to walk to the beach and I fell into step with him.

"The last I heard they were having a snowstorm." Richardson raised his face and I know what he was feeling—a warm, ocean-kissed breeze.

I laughed. "You're making me homesick."

Richardson smiled, too. "Enjoy the remainder of your stay. If I can ever be of assistance to you, now or in the future, please don't hesitate to call." He strode off in the direction of the hotel, shoulders squared, a businessman ready to face yet another business day.

"That was nice of him," I commented as Lucas and I strolled toward the beach.

"Smart, too. He needs to keep his guests happy."

"Cynic."

"Realist." We paused and looked to the left down the beach. "Want to go visit the cats?"

I shook my head. "It's probably past their feeding time. Besides, I hate seeing them out there. I want to adopt them all."

"We'll come back when we have the RV and adopt one or two." Lucas tucked my hand under his arm again and we turned right, toward the boardwalk. "We'll have Texas cats, Minnesota cats, and traveling cats."

I smiled at the thought of Lucas and I, surrounded by animals, bouncing our way around the United States. It sounded like fun.

I saw a familiar figure in the distance, moving

slowly toward us. For one fractured moment I remembered the morning four days previously when I met Gwen. My throat tightened. She was dead— poor fumbling, overweight, anxious Gwen. Was that the real Gwen? Had she been acting all along? I wasn't sure any more. Was I that gullible? Was she right? Had I dismissed her as just one of those poor, overweight women who haunt conferences and lived their lives vicariously through my fiction? Had I underestimated her all along?

Katherine held open her arms as we neared her and I gave her an enthusiastic hug. "I'm so glad you're okay," she said, pulling back and looking at me. "I swear, you've had one hell of a conference. Good thing you won the Plum and the Black. That's a good consolation prize."

"I did? I won both of them? You're kidding. Did Tony stand in for me? I'm sorry, I forgot all about it." I turned to look at Lucas and was gratified to surprise a hint of jealousy in his eyes before he smiled at me.

"Yes, he gathered your prizes and gave a nice acceptance speech." Katherine's soft white hair blew in the breeze and she ran a hand through it, tangling it even further. "I think he'll be fun to work with."

"Work with?" Lucas asked, putting an arm around my shoulder.

"Well, sure," I said, sharing a conspiratorial look with Katherine. "He's the cover model for my hero. I'll need to coach him on how Cal would act and look."

"Coach?"

"Sure." I winked at Katherine who smiled sweetly at me. "So what's the prize for the Dr. Black award? That's the overall award, right?"

"Yep. You get the Black Plaque." Our blank looks must have been eloquent because she laughed and explained. "The overall winner gets a shadow box with each of the Clue weapons in it. Sort of like a charm bracelet."

"Oh." I hope my disappointment didn't show. I was expecting something a bit fancier.

"Of course, the charms are all gold and inset with diamonds, so it's sort of neat."

"Wow." I looked up at Lucas. "We can put it in the RV to remind us of our trip."

"RV?"

"We're going to buy an RV and do some traveling." I linked arms again with Lucas and we started to inch our way forward, down the boardwalk. "I need to recover from my vacation."

Katherine laughed again. "It has been busy. It was good to meet you...and you, Detective." She inclined her head to Lucas.

"Ex-detective," Lucas corrected.

"You can't get away from it that easy. My husband was a policeman until the day he died, even though he was retired for almost twenty years." She started to meander down the boardwalk, back to the hotel. "You kids take it easy."

"We'll do that." As I walked away, I had a sudden thought and called back over my shoulder, "Tell K.L. Lonigan his book saved my life. If he weren't so damn wordy, his books wouldn't have been so thick. They stopped a bullet."

Katherine's booming laugh startled some sea gulls nearby. "I'll be sure to tell him. It'll make his day."

Lucas and I continued down the boardwalk, which followed the curve of the bay. We finally paused at an observation deck jutting out on a promontory, giving us an uninterrupted view of the sea. Clouds were tumbling on the far horizon, dark and threatening, reminding me of the snowstorm awaiting me back home.

"What are you thinking?" Lucas asked softly, pulling me to him so my back rested against his chest. "Planning our wedding?" He gently kissed the side of my face and whispered in my ear, "Planning our honeymoon?"

I leaned against him, feeling his solid warmth and the reassuring thump-thump of his heart. His breath was warm on my neck and I shivered in his arms, which tightened slightly around me. This whole chaotic week had done what months of visits and vacations hadn't done. It had forced us to evaluate our relationship and decide where we wanted to go. I had no idea if marriage was a good idea or not, but I was sure willing to give it a try. I snuggled harder against him and as always, I said the first thing that popped into my head. "This would make a great book. I mean, it's got a great plot."

His arms tightened around me. "Don't you dare. I haven't lived down my reputation from the first book."

I just laughed.

A word about the author...

I was born in a small town in Iowa, and have traveled extensively in the U.S. and overseas, finally ending up back in the Midwest where I'm married to a glass artist who spends a lot of time in the studio, making amazingly beautiful things. We have assorted animals who live with us and who make regular appearances in my books under various pseudonyms (they know who they are). In 2003, I read my first romance novel and immediately decided this was the genre for me. But there was a problem: the books I read all featured young heroines, interested in starting a family and having babies. So I started writing romantic suspense (with an occasional side trip into paranormal fantasy) about older women, with some age on' em, who are interested in men and sex and having a good relationship (which may or may not include a marriage). I hope you enjoy reading about them as much as I enjoy writing about them.

Contact JL at jaye@jayellwilson.com

Visit JL at www.jayellwilson.com

Thank you for purchasing
this Wild Rose Press publication.
For other wonderful stories of romance,
please visit our on-line bookstore at
www.thewildrosepress.com.

For questions or more information,
contact us at info@thewildrosepress.com.

The Wild Rose Press
www.TheWildRosePress.com

Printed in the United States
135942LV00003B/2/P